Daniel Garrison Brinton

The Lenâpé and their Legends

With the Complete Text and Symbols of the Walam Olum

Daniel Garrison Brinton

The Lenâpé and their Legends
With the Complete Text and Symbols of the Walam Olum

ISBN/EAN: 9783337154486

Printed in Europe, USA, Canada, Australia, Japan

Cover: Foto ©Andreas Hilbeck / pixelio.de

More available books at **www.hansebooks.com**

LIBRARY

OF

ABORIGINAL AMERICAN

LITERATURE.

No. V.

EDITED BY

D. G. BRINTON, M. D.

———————

PHILADELPHIA:

1885.

BRINTON'S LIBRARY OF
ABORIGINAL AMERICAN LITERATURE.
NUMBER V.

———

THE LENÂPÉ

AND THEIR

LEGENDS;

WITH THE COMPLETE TEXT AND SYMBOLS

OF THE

WALAM OLUM,

A NEW TRANSLATION, AND AN INQUIRY INTO ITS AUTHENTICITY.

BY

DANIEL G. BRINTON, A.M., M.D.,

PROFESSOR OF ETHNOLOGY AND ARCHÆOLOGY AT THE ACADEMY OF NATURAL
SCIENCES, PHILADELPHIA.

President of the Numismatic and Antiquarian Society of Philadelphia; Member of the
American Philosophical Society, the American Antiquarian Society, the Pennsyl-
vania Historical Society, etc.; Membre de la Société Royale des Antiquaires du
Nord; Délégué Général de l'Institution Ethnographique; Vice-Président du
Congrès International des Américanistes; Corresponding Member of the Anthro-
pological Society of Washington, etc.

D. G. BRINTON.

PHILADELPHIA.

1885.

PREFACE.

In the present volume I have grouped a series of ethnological studies of the Indians of Eastern Pennsylvania, New Jersey and Maryland, around what is asserted to be one of the most curious records of ancient American history.

For a long time this record—the WALAM OLUM, or Red Score—was supposed to have been lost. Having obtained the original text complete about a year ago, I printed a few copies and sent them to several educated native Delawares with a request for aid in its translation and opinions on its authenticity. The results will be found in the following pages.

The interest in the subject thus excited prompted me to a general review of our knowledge of the Lenape or Delawares, their history and traditions, their language and customs. This disclosed the existence of a number of MSS. not mentioned in bibliographies, some in the first rank of importance, especially in the field of linguistics. Of these I have made free use.

In the course of these studies I have received suggestions and assistance from a number of obliging friends, among whom I would mention the native Delawares, the Rev. Albert Anthony, and the Rev. John Kilbuck; Mr. Horatio Hale and the Right Rev. E. de Schweinitz; Dr. J. Hammond Trumbull, Prof. A. M. Elliott and Gen. John Mason Brown.

Not without hesitation do I send forth this volume to the

learned world.   Regarded as an authentic memorial, the
original text of the WALAM OLUM will require a more accurate rendering than I have been able to give it ; while the
possibility that a more searching criticism will demonstrate
it to have been a fabrication may condemn as labor lost the
pains that I have bestowed upon it.   Yet even in the latter
case my work will not have been in vain.   There is, I trust,
sufficient in the volume to justify its appearance, apart from
the Red Score; and the latter, by means of this complete
presentation, can now be assigned its true position in American archæology, whatever that may be.

CONTENTS.

PAGE

CHAPTER I.—§ 1. THE ALGONKIN STOCK.............. ...., 9

Scheme of its Dialects.—Probable Primitive Location.

§ 2. THE IROQUOIS STOCK 13

The Susquehannocks.—The Hurons.—The Cherokees.

CHAPTER II.—THE WAPANACHKI OR EASTERN ALGONKIN CON-
FEDERACY.. 19

The Confederated Tribes.—The Mohegans.—The Nanticokes.—The Conoys.—The Shawnees.—The Saponies.—The Assiwikalees.

CHAPTER III.—THE LENAPE OR DELAWARES........................ 33

Derivation of the Name Lenape.—The Three Sub-Tribes : the Minsi or
Wolf, the Unami or Turtle, and the Unalachtgo or Turkey Tribes.—
Their Totems.—The New Jersey Tribes : the Wapings, Sanhicans and
Mantas.—Political Constitution of the Lenape.—Vegetable Food Re-
sources.—Domestic Architecture.—Manufactures.—Paints and Dyes.—
Dogs.—Interments.—Computation of Time.—Picture Writing.—Record
Sticks.—Moral and Mental Character.—Religious Belief.—Doctrine of
the Soul.—The Native Priests.—Religious Ceremonies.

CHAPTER IV.—THE LITERATURE AND LANGUAGE OF THE
LENAPE.. 74

§ 1. Literature of the Lenape Tongue.—Campanius ; Penn ; Thomas ;
Zeisberger ; Heckewelder ; Roth ; Ettwein ; Grube ; Dencke ;
Luckenbach ; Henry ; Vocabularies ; a Native Letter.
§ 2. General Remarks on the Lenape.
§ 3. Dialects of the Lenape.
§ 4. Special Structure of the Lenape.—The Root and the Theme ;
Prefixes ; Suffixes ; Derivatives ; Grammatical Notes.

CHAPTER V.—HISTORICAL SKETCHES OF THE LENAPE....... 109

§ 1. The Lenape as " Women."
§ 2. Recent Migrations of the Lenape.
§ 3. Missionary Efforts in the Provinces of Pennsylvania and New
Jersey.

PAGE

CHAPTER VI.—MYTHS AND TRADITIONS OF THE LENAPE....... 130

Cosmogonical and Culture Myths.—The Culture-hero, Michabo.—Myths from Lindstrom, Ettwein, Jasper Donkers, Zeisberger.—Native Symbolism.—The Saturnian Age.—Mohegan Cosmogony and Migration Myth.

National Traditions.—Beatty's Account.—The Number Seven.—Heckewelder's Account.—Prehistoric Migrations.—Shawnee Legend.—Lenape Legend of the Naked Bear.

CHAPTER VII.—THE WALAM OLUM : ITS ORIGIN, AUTHENTICITY AND CONTENTS.. 148

Biographical Sketch of Rafinesque.—Value of his Writings.—His account of the WALUM OLUM.—Was it a Forgery?—Rafinesque's Character.—The Text Pronounced Genuine by Native Delawares.—Conclusion Reached.

Phonetic System of the WALUM OLUM.—Metrical Form.—Pictographic System.—Derivation and Precise Meaning of WALUM OLUM.—The MS. of the WALAM OLUM.—General Synopsis of the WALAM OLUM.—Synopsis of its Parts.

THE WALUM OLUM.—ORIGINAL TEXT AND TRANSLATION....... 169

NOTES.. 219

VOCABULARY 233

APPENDIX................... 255

INDEX... 257

THE LENAPE

AND THEIR LEGENDS.

CHAPTER I.

§ 1. THE ALGONKIN STOCK.
Scheme of its Dialects.—Probable Primitive Location.

§ 2. THE IROQUOIS STOCK.
The Susquehannocks.—The Hurons.—The Cherokees.

§ 1. *The Algonkin Stock.*

About the period 1500–1600, those related tribes whom we now know by the name of Algonkins were at the height of their prosperity. They occupied the Atlantic coast from the Savannah river on the south to the strait of Belle Isle on the north. The whole of Newfoundland was in their possession; in Labrador they were neighbors to the Eskimos; their northernmost branch, the Crees, dwelt along the southern shores of Hudson Bay, and followed the streams which flow into it from the west, until they met the Chipeways, closely akin to themselves, who roamed over the water shed of Lake Superior. The Blackfeet carried a remote dialect of their tongue quite to the Rocky Mountains; while the fertile prairies of Illinois and Indiana were the homes of the Miamis. The area of Ohio and Kentucky was very thinly peopled by a few of their roving bands; but east of the Alleghanies, in the valleys of the Delaware, the Potomac and the Hudson, over the barren hills of New England and Nova Scotia, and throughout the swamps and forests of Virginia and the Carolinas, their osier cabins and palisadoed strongholds, their maize fields and workshops of stone implements, were numerously located.

It is needless for my purpose to enumerate the many small tribes which made up this great group. The more prominent were the Micmacs of Nova Scotia, the Abnakis of Maine, the Pequots and Narragansets, in New England, the Mohegans of the Hudson, the Lenape on the Delaware, the Nanticokes around Chesapeake Bay, the Pascataway on the Potomac, and the Powhatans and Shawnees further south; while between the Great Lakes and the Ohio river were the Ottawas, the Illinois, the Pottawatomies, the Kikapoos, Piankishaws, etc.

The dialects of all these were related, and evidently at some distant day had been derived from the same primitive tongue. Which of them had preserved the ancient forms most closely, it may be premature to decide positively, but the tendency of modern studies has been to assign that place to the Cree—the northernmost of all.

We cannot erect a genealogical tree of these dialects. It is not probable that they branched off, one after another, from a common stock. The ancient tribes each took their several ways from a common centre, and formed nuclei for subsequent development. We may, however, group them in such a manner as roughly to indicate their relationship. This I do on the following page :—

Cree,
Old Algonkin,
Montagnais.

^x Chipeway,
Ottawa,
Pottawattomie,
Miami,
Peoria,
Pea,
Piankishaw,
Kaskaskia,
Menominee,
Sac,
Fox,
Kikapoo.

Sheshatapoosh,
Secoffee,
Micmac,
Melisceet,
Etchemin,
Abnaki.

Mohegan,
Massachusetts,
Shawnee,
Minsi,
Unami,
Unalachtigo,
Nanticoke,
Powhatan,
Pampticoke.

Blackfoot,
Gros Ventre,
Sheyenne.

Granting, as we must, some common geographical centre for these many dialects, the question where this was located becomes an interesting one.

More than one attempt to answer it has been made. Mr. Lewis H. Morgan thought there was evidence to show that the valley of the Columbia river, Oregon, "was the initial point from which the Algonkin stock emigrated to the great lake region and thence to the Atlantic coast."[1] This is in direct conflict with the evidence of language, as the Blackfoot or Satsika is the most corrupt and altered of the Algonkin dialects. Basing his argument on this evidence, Mr. Horatio Hale reaches a conclusion precisely the reverse of that of Morgan. "The course of migration of the Indian tribes," writes Mr. Hale, "has been from the Atlantic coast westward and southward. The traditions of the Algonkins seem to point to Hudson's Bay and the coast of Labrador."[2] This latter view is certainly that which accords best with the testimony of language and of history.

We know that both Chipeways and Crees have been steadily pressing westward since their country was first explored, driving before them the Blackfeet and Dakotas.[3]

The Cree language is built up on a few simple, unchangeable radicals and elementary words, denoting being, relation, energy, etc.; it has extreme regularity of construction, a

---

[1] Lewis H. Morgan, *Indian Migrations*, in Beach's *Indian Miscellany*, p. 218.

[2] H. Hale, *Indian Migrations as Evidenced by Language*, p. 24. (Chicago, 1883.)

[3] See the R. P. A. Lacombe *Dictionnaire de la Langue des Cris*. Introd., p. xi. (Montreal, 1874.)

single negative, is almost wholly verbal and markedly incor-
porative, has its grammatical elements better defined than its
neighbors, and a more consistent phonetic system.[1] For
these and similar reasons we are justified in considering it the
nearest representative we possess of the pristine Algonkin
tongue, and unless strong grounds to the contrary are
advanced, it is proper to assume that the purest dialect is
found nearest the primeval home of the stock.

§ 2. *The Iroquois Stock.*

Surrounded on all sides by the Algonkins were the *Iroquois*,
once called the Five or Six Nations.   When first discovered
they were on the St. Lawrence, near Montreal, and in the
Lake Region of Central New York.   Various other tribes,
not in their confederacy, and generally at war with them,
spoke dialects of the same language.   Such were the Hurons
or Wyandots, between the Georgian Bay and Lake Erie, the
Neutral Nation on the Niagara river, the Eries on the
southern shore of the lake of that name, the Nottoways in
Virginia, and the Tuscaroras in North Carolina. The
Cherokees, found by the whites in East Tennessee, but
whose national legend, carefully preserved for generations,
located them originally on the head waters of the Ohio, were
a remote offshoot of this same stem.

The Susquehannocks.

The valley of the Susquehanna river was occupied by a
tribe of Iroquois lineage and language, known as the *Susque-*

---

[1] See Joseph Howse, *A Grammar of the Cree Language*, p. 13, et al.
(London, 1842.)

hannocks, *Conestogas* and *Andastes*. The last name is Iroquois, from *andasta*, a cabin pole. By some, "Susquehannock" has also been explained as an Iroquois word, but its
form is certainly Algonkin. The terminal *k* is the place-
sign, *hanna* denotes a flowing stream, while the adjectival
prefix has been identified by Heckewelder with *schachage*,
straight, from the direct course of the river near its mouth,
and by Mr. Guss with *woski*, new, which, he thinks, referred
to fresh or spring water.

Of these the former will appear the preferable, if we allow
for the softening of the gutturals, which was a phonetic trait
of the Unami dialect of the Lenape.

The Susquehannocks were always at deadly feud with the
Iroquois, and between wars, the smallpox and the whites,
they were finally exterminated. The particulars of their
short and sad history have been presented with his characteristic thoroughness by Dr. John G. Shea,[1] and later by Prof.
N. L. Guss.[2] They were usually called by the Delawares
Mengwe, which was the term they applied to all the Iroquois-
speaking tribes.[3] The English corrupted it to Minqua and

---

[1] In a note to Mr. Gowan's edition of George Alsop's *Province of
Maryland*, pp. 117–121 (New York, 1869); also, in 1858, in an article
"On the Identity of the Andastas, Minquas, Susquehannocks, and Con-
estogas," in the *Amer. Hist. Mag.*, Vol. II, p. 294.

[2] *Early Indian History on the Susquehanna*, p. 31. (Harrisburg,
1883.)

[3] *Mengwe* is the Onondaga *yenkwe*, males, or men, *viri*, and was
borrowed from that dialect by the Delawares, as a general term. Bishop
Ettwein states that the Iroquois called the Delawares, Mohegans, and all
the New England Indians *Agozhagauta*.

Mingo, and as the eastern trail of the Susquehannocks lay up the Conestoga Creek, and down the Christina, both those streams were called "Mingo Creek" by the early settlers.

It is important for the ethnology of Pennsylvania, to understand that at the time of the first settlement the whole of the Susquehanna Valley, from the Chesapeake to the New York lakes, was owned and controlled by Iroquois-speaking tribes. A different and erroneous opinion was expressed by Heckewelder, and has been generally received. He speaks of the Lenape Minsi as occupying the head waters of the Susquehanna. This was not so in the historic period.

The claims of the Susquehannocks extended down the Chesapeake Bay on the east shore, as far as the Choptank River, and on the west shore as far as the Patuxent. In 1654 they ceded to the government of Maryland their southern territory to these boundaries.[1] The first English explorers met them on the Potomac, about the Falls, and the Pascatoways were deserting their villages and fleeing before them, when, in 1634, Calvert founded his colony at St. Mary's.

Their subjection to the Five Nations took place about 1680, and it was through the rights obtained by this conquest that, at the treaty of Lancaster, 1744, Canassatego, the Onondaga speaker for the Nation, claimed pay from the government of Maryland for the lands on the Potomac, or, as that river was called in his tongue, the *Cohongorontas*.

[1] Bozman, *History of Maryland*, Vol. I, p. 167.

The Hurons.

The Hurons, Wyandots, or Wendats, were another Iroquois people, who seem, at some remote epoch, to have come into contact with the Lenape. The latter called them *Delamattenos*,[1] and claimed to have driven them out of a portion of their possessions. A Chipeway tradition also states that the Hurons were driven north from the lake shores by Algonkin tribes.[2] We know, from the early accounts of the Jesuits, that there was commercial intercourse between them and the tribes south of the lakes, the materials of trade being principally fish and corn.[3] The Jesuit *Relations* of 1648 contain quite a full account of a Huron convert who, in that year, visited the Lenape on the Delaware River, and had an interview with the Swedish Governor, whom he took to task for neglecting the morals of his men.

The Cherokees.

The Cherokees were called by the Delawares *Kittuwa* (*Kuttoowauw*, in the spelling of the native Aupaumut). This word I suppose to be derived from the prefix, *kit*, great, and the root *tawa* (Cree, *yette*, *tawa*), to open, whence *tawatawik*, an open, *i. e.*, uninhabited place, a wilderness (Zeisberger).

The designation is geographical. According to the tradition of the Cherokees, they once lived (probably about the

---

[1] Heckewelder, *History of the Indian Nations*, p. 80.

[2] Peter Jones, *History of the Ojibway Nation*, p. 32.

[3] *Relation des Jesuites*, 1637, p. 154. The Hurons, at that time, are stated to have had reliable traditions running back more than two hundred years. *Relation de* 1639, p. 50.

fourteenth century) in the Ohio Valley, and claimed to have been the constructors of the Grave Creek and other earthworks there.[1] Some support is given to this claim by the recent linguistic investigations of Mr. Horatio Hale,[2] and the archæological researches of Prof. Cyrus Thomas.[3] They were driven southward by their warlike neighbors, locating their council fire first near Monticello, Va., and the main body reaching East Tennessee about the close of the fifteenth century. As late as 1730 some of them continued to live east of the Alleghanies, while, on the other hand, it is evident, from the proper names preserved by the chroniclers of De Soto's expedition (1542), that at that period others held the mountains of Northern Georgia. To the Delawares they remained *kit-tawa-wi*, inhabitants of the great wilderness of Southern Ohio and Kentucky.

Delaware traditions distinctly recalled the period when portions of the Cherokees were on the Ohio, and recounted

[1] "The Cherokees had an oration, in which was contained the history of their migrations, which was lengthy." This tradition related "that they came from the upper part of the Ohio, where they erected the mounds on Grave Creek, and that they removed hither [to East Tennessee] from the country where Monticello is situated." This memory of their migrations was preserved and handed down by official orators, who repeated it annually, in public, at the national festival of the green corn dance. J. Haywood, *Natural and Aboriginal History of Tennessee*, pp. 224-237. (Nashville, 1823.) Haywood adds: "It is now nearly forgotten." I have made vain attempts to recover some fragments of i from the present residents of the Cherokee Nation.

[2] *Indian Migrations as Evidenced by Language*, p. 22.

[3] Prof. Thomas has shown beyond reasonable doubt that the Cherokees were mound builders within the historic period.

long wars with them.[1]   When the Lenape assumed the office
of peacemaker, this feud ceased, and was not renewed until
the general turmoil of the French-Indian wars, 1750–60. After
this closed, in 1768, the Cherokees sought and effected a re-
newal of their peaceful relations with the Delawares, and in
1779 they even sent a deputation of "condolence" to their
"grandfather," the Lenape, on the death of the head chief,
White Eyes.[2]

[1] Loskiel, *Geschichte der Mission*, etc., p. 160; Heckewelder, *History
of the Indian Nations*, p. 54. Bishop Ettwein states that the last Cherokees were driven from the upper Ohio river about 1700–10. His essay on
the "Traditions and Languages of the Indian Nations," written for General
Washington, in 1788, was first published in the *Bulletin of the Pa. Hist.
Soc.*, 1844.

[2] Heckewelder, *Indian Nations*, pp. 88, 327. Mr. H. Hale, in *The
Iroquois Book of Rites*, has fully explained the meaning and importance
of the custom of "condolence."   The Stockbridge Indian, Aupaumut, in
his *Journal*, writes of the Delawares, that when they lose a relative, " according to ancient custom, long as they are not comforted, they are not to
speak in public, and this ceremonie of comforting each other is highly
esteemed among these nations." *Narrative of Hendrick Aupaumut*, in
Mems. Hist. Soc. Pa., Vol. II, p. 99.

CHAPTER II.

The Confederated Tribes.—The Mohegans.—The Nanticokes.—The Conoys.—The
Shawnees.—The Saponies.—The Assiwikalees.

The Confederated Tribes.

All the Algonkin nations who dwelt north of the Potomac, on the east shore of Chesapeake Bay, and in the basins of the Delaware and Hudson rivers, claimed near kinship and an identical origin, and were at times united into a loose, defensive confederacy.

By the western and southern tribes they were collectively known as *Wapanachkik*—"those of the eastern region"—which in the form *Abnaki* is now confined to the remnant of a tribe in Maine. The Delawares in the far West retain traditionally the ancient confederate name, and still speak of themselves as "Eastlanders"—*O-puh-narke*. (Morgan.)

The members of the confederacy were the Mohegans (Mahicanni) of the Hudson, who occupied the valley of that river to the falls above the site of Albany, the various New Jersey tribes, the Delawares proper on the Delaware river and its branches, including the Minsi or Monseys, among the mountains, the Nanticokes, between Chesapeake Bay and the Atlantic, and the small tribe called Canai, Kanawhas or Ganawese, whose towns were on tributaries of the Potomac and Patuxent.

That all these were united in some sort of an alliance, with

19

the Delawares at its head, is not only proved by the traditions of this tribe itself, but by the distinct assertion of the Mohegans and others, and by events within historical times, as the reunion of the Nanticokes, New Jersey and Eastern Indians with the Delawares as with the parent stem.[1]

The Mohegans.

The Mohegans, *Mo-hé-kun-ne-uk*, dwelt on the tide-waters of the Hudson, and from this their name was derived.   Dr. Trumbull, indeed, following Schoolcraft, thinks that they "took their tribal name from *maingan*, a wolf, and *Moheganick* = Chip. *maniganikan*, 'country of wolves.'"[2]   They, themselves, however, translate it, "seaside people," or more fully, "people of the great waters which are constantly ebbing

---

[1] Heckewelder, *History of the Indian Nations*, p. 60, and *Narrative of Hendrick Aupaumut*, 1791, in *Mems. Hist. Soc. Pa.*, Vol. II.   The latter, himself a native Mohegan, repeatedly refers to "the ancient covenant of our ancestors," by which this confederacy was instituted, which included the "Wenaumeew (Unami), the Wemintheew (Minsi), the Wenuhtokowuk (Nanticokes) and Kuhnauwantheew (Kanawha)."   From old Pennsylvania documents, Proud gives the members of the confederacy or league as "the Chiholacki or Delawares, the Wanami, the Munsi, the Mohicans and Wappingers." *History of Penna.*, Vol. II, p. 297, note. Compare J. Long, *Voyages and Travels*, p. 10 (London, 1791), who gives the same list.   Mr. Ruttenber writes: "In considering the political relations of the Lenapes, they should be considered as the most formidable of the Indian confederacies at the time of the discovery of America, and as having maintained for many years the position which subsequently fell to the Iroquois."—*Indian Tribes on Hudson River*, p. 64.

[2] Trumbull, *Indian Names in Connecticut*, p. 31. Schoolcraft had already given the same derivation in his *History and Statistics of the Indian Tribes*.

or flowing."[1] The compound is *machaak*, great, *hickan*, tide ("ebbing tide," Zeis.; "tide of flood," Campanius) and *ik*, animate plural termination.

The Mohegans on the Hudson are said to have been divided into three phratries, the Bear, the Wolf and the Turtle, of whom the Bear had the primacy.[2] Mr. Morgan, however, who examined, in 1860, the representatives of the nation in Kansas,[3] discovered that they had precisely the same phratries as the Delawares, that is the Wolf, the Turtle, and the Turkey, each subdivided into three or four gentes. He justly observes that this "proves their immediate connection with the Delawares and Munsees by descent," and thus renders their myths and traditions of the more import in the present study.

Linguistically, the Mohegans were more closely allied to the tribes of New England than to those of the Delaware Valley. Evidently, most of the tribes of Massachusetts and Connecticut were comparatively recent offshoots of the parent stem on the Hudson, supposing the course of migration had been eastward.

In some of his unpublished notes Mr. Heckewelder identifies the *Wampanos*, who lived in Connecticut, along the shore of Long Island Sound, and whose council fire was where New Haven now stands, as Mohegans, while the *Wapings* or *Opings* of the Northern Jersey shore were a mixed

---

[1] Capt. Hendricks, in *Mass. Hist. Soc. Colls.*, Vol. IX, p. 101. Lewis H. Morgan, *Systems of Consanguinity and Affinity*, p. 289.

[2] Ruttenber, *History of the Indian Tribes of Hudson's River*, p. 50.

[3] Morgan, *Ancient Society*, pp. 173-4.

clan derived from intermarriages between Mohegans and Monseys.[1]

The Nanticokes.

The Nanticokes occupied the territory between Chesapeake Bay and the ocean, except its southern extremity, which appears to have been under the control of the Powhatan tribe of Virginia.

The derivation of Nanticoke is from the Delaware *Unéchtgo*, "tide-water people," and is merely another form of *Una-lachtgo*, the name of one of the Lenape sub-tribes. In both cases it is a mere geographical term, and not a national eponym.

In the records of the treaty at Fort Johnston, 1757, the Nanticokes are also named *Tiawco*. This is their Mohegan name, *Otayáchgo*, which means "bridge people," or bridge makers, the reference being to the skill with which the Nanti-cokes could fasten floating logs together to construct a bridge across a stream. In the Delaware dialect this was *Tawach-*

---

[1] These opinions are from a MS. in the library of the American Philo-sophical Society, in the handwriting of Mr. Heckewelder, entitled *Notes, Amendments and Additions to Heckewelder's History of the Indians* (Svo, pp. 38.) Unfortunately, this MS. was not placed in the hands of Mr. Reichel when he prepared the second edition of Heckewelder's work for the Historical Society of Pennsylvania.

An unpublished and hitherto unknown work on the Mohegan language is the *Miscellanea Linguæ Nationis Indicæ Mahikan dictæ, curâ suscepta à Joh. Jac. Schmick,* 2 vols., small Svo.; MS. in the possession of the American Philosophical Society. Schmick was a Moravian missionary, born in 1714, died 1778. He acquired the Mohegan dialect among the converts at Gnadenhütten. His work is without date, but may be placed at about 1765. It is grammatical rather than lexicographical, and offers numerous verbal forms and familiar phrases.

guáno, from *taiachquoan*, a bridge. The latter enables us to
identify the *Tockwhoghs*, whom Captain John Smith met on
the Chesapeake, in 1608, with the Nanticokes. The *Kuscarawocks*, whom he also visited, have been conclusively
shown by Mr. Bozman[1] to have been also Nanticokes.

By ancient traditions, they looked up to the Lenape as their
"grandfather," and considered the Mohegans their "brethren."[2] That is, they were, as occasion required, attached
to the same confederacy.

In manners and customs they differed little from their northern relatives. The only peculiarity in this respect which
is noted of them was the extravagant consideration they bestowed on the bones of the dead. The corpse was buried for
some months, then exhumed and the bones carefully cleaned
and placed in an ossuary called *man-to-kump* ($=$ *manito*, with
the locative termination, place of the mystery or spirit).

When they removed from one place to another these bones
were carried with them. Even those who migrated to northern
Pennsylvania, about the middle of the last century, piously
brought along these venerable relics, and finally interred them
near the present site of Towanda, whence its name, *Tawun-
deunk*, "where we bury our dead."[3]

---

[1] J. Bozman, *History of Maryland*, Vol. I, pp. 112, 114, 121, 177.
This laborious writer still remains the best authority on the aboriginal
inhabitants of Maryland.

[2] "The We nuh tok o wuk are our brothers according to ancient agree-
ment." *Journal of Hendrick Aupaumut, Mems. Hist. Soc. Pa.*, Vol. II,
p. 77.

[3] Charles Beatty, *Journal of a Journey*, etc., p. 87. Heckewelder,
Indian Nations, pp. 90, et seq. Ibid. *Trans. Am. Phil. Soc.*, Vol. IV, p. 362.

Their dialect varied considerably from the Delaware, of which it is clearly a deteriorated form. It is characterized by abbreviated words and strongly expirated accents, as *tah! quah! quah! su*, short; *quah! nah! qut*, long.

Our knowledge of it is limited to a few vocabularies. The earliest was taken down by Captain John Smith, during his exploration of the Chesapeake. The most valuable is one obtained by Mr. William Vans Murray, in 1792, from the remnant in Maryland. It is in the library of the American Philosophical Society, and has never been correctly or completely printed.

The Nanticokes broke up early. Between the steady encroachments of the whites and the attacks of the Iroquois they found themselves between the upper and the nether millstones.

According to their own statement to Governor Evans, at a conference in 1707, they had at that time been tributary to the latter for twenty-seven years, *i. e.*, since 1680. Their last head chief, or "crowned king," Winicaco, died about 1720. A few years after this occurrence bands of them began to remove to Pennsylvania, and at the middle of the century were living at the mouth of the Juniata, under the immediate control of the Iroquois. Thence they removed to Wyoming, and in 1753, "in a fleet of twenty-five canoes," to the Iroquois lands in western New York. Others of their nation were brought there by the Iroquois in 1767; but by the close of the century only five families survived in that region.[1]

[1] The authorities for these facts are Bozman, *History of Maryland*, Vol. I, pp. 175–180; Heckewelder, *Indian Nations*, pp. 93, sqq.; E. de

A small band called the *Wiwash* remained on Goose creek, Dorchester county, Maryland, to the same date.

The Conoys.

The fourth member of the Wapanachki was that nation variously called in the old records *Conoys*, *Ganawese* or *Canaways*, the proper form of which Mr. Heckewelder states to be *Canai.*[1]

Considerable obscurity has rested on the early location and affiliation of this people. Mr. Heckewelder vaguely places them "at a distance on the Potomac," and supposes them to have been the Kanawhas of West Virginia.[2] This is a loose guess. They were, in fact, none other than the Piscataways of Southern Maryland, who occupied the area between Chesapeake Bay and the lower Potomac, about St. Mary's, and along the Piscataway creek and Patuxent river.

Proof of this is furnished by the speech of their venerable head chief, "Old Sack," at a conference in Philadelphia in 1743.[3] His words were: "Our forefathers came from Pis-

Schweinitz, *Life of Zeisberger*, pp. 208, 322, etc.; the Treaty Records, and MSS. in the library of the American Philosophical Society.

That the Nanticokes came from the South into Maryland has been maintained, on the ground that as late as 1770 they claimed land in North Carolina. *New York Colonial Documents*, Vol. VIII, p. 243. But the term "Carolina" was, I think, used erroneously in the document referred to, instead of Maryland, where at that date there were still many of the tribe.

[1] *History of the Indian Nations*, Introduction, p. xlii.

[2] Ibid., pp. 90–122.

[3] *Minutes of the Provincial Council of Penna.*, Vol. IV, p. 657.

C

catua to an island in Potowmeck ; and from thence down to
Philadelphia, in old Proprietor Penn's time, to show their
friendship to the Proprietor. After their return they brought
down all their brothers from Potowmeck to Conejoholo, on
the east side Sasquehannah, and built a town there."

This interesting identification shows that they were the
people whom Captain John Smith found (1608) in numerous
villages along the Patuxent and the left bank of the lower
Potomac. The local names show them to have been of
Algonkin stock and akin to the Nanticokes.

Conoy, Ganawese, Kanawha, are all various spellings of a
derivative from an Algonkin root, meaning "it is long"
(Del. *guneu*, long, Cree *kinowaw*, it is long,) and is found
applied to various streams in Algonkin territory.[1]

Piscataway, or Pascatoway, as it is spelled in the early
narratives, also recurs as a local name in various parts of the
Northern States. It is from the root *pashk*, which means to
separate, to divide. Many derivatives from it are in use in
the Delaware tongue. In the Cree we have the impersonal
form, *pakestikweyaw*, or the active animate *pasketiwa*, in the
sense of "the division or branch of a river."[2] The site of

Further proof of this in a Treaty of Peace concluded in 1682 by the New
York colonial government, between the Senecas and Maryland Indians.
In this instrument we find this tribe referred to as "the Canowes alias
Piscatowayes," and elsewhere as the "Piscatoway of Cachnawayes."
New York Colonial Documents, Vol. III, pp. 322, 323.

[1] I am aware that Mr. Johnston, deriving his information from Shawnee
interpreters, translated the name Kanawha, as "having whirlpools."
(*Trans. of the Amer. Antiq. Soc.*, Vol. I, p. 297.) But I prefer the
derivation given in the text.

[2] Lacombe, *Dictionnaire de la Langue des Cris*, s. v. In Delaware the

Kittamaquindi (*kittamaque-ink*, Great Beaver Place,) the so-called "metropolis of Pascatoe,"[1] was where Tinker's creek and Piscataway creek branch off from their common estuary, about fifteen miles south of Washington city.

The "emperor" Chitomachen, Strong Bear (*chitani*, strong, *macha*, bear), who bore the title *Tayac* (Nanticoke, *tallak*, head chief) ruled over a dominion which extended about 130 miles from east to west.

The district was thinly peopled. On the upper shores of the west side of the Chesapeake Captain John Smith and the other early explorers found scarcely any inhabitants. In 1631 Captain Henry Fleet estimated the total number of natives "in Potomack and places adjacent," at not over 5000 persons.[2] This included both sides of the river as high up as the Falls, and the shores of Chesapeake Bay.

Chitomachen, with his family, was converted to the Catholic faith in 1640, by the exertions of the Jesuit missionary, Father Andrew White, but died the year after. When the English first settled at St. Mary's, the tribe was deserting its ancient seats, through fear of the Susquehannocks, and diminished rapidly after that date.

root takes the form *pach*, from which are derived, by suffixes, the words *pach-at*, to split, *pachgeechen*, where the road branches off, *pachshican*, a knife = something that divides, etc.

[1] *Relatio Itineris in Marylandiam*, p. 63. (Edition of the Md. Hist. Soc. 1874.)

[2] See his *Journal*, published in Neill's *Founders of Maryland* (Albany, 1876). Fleet was a prisoner among the Pascatoways for five years, and served as an interpreter to Calvert's colony.

Father White was among them from 1634 to 1642, and composed a grammar, dictionary and catechism of their tongue. Of these, the catechism is yet preserved in manuscript, in the library of the Domus Professa of the Jesuits, in Rome. It would be a great benefit to students of Algonkin dialects to have his linguistic works sought out and published. How far his knowledge of the language extended is uncertain. In a letter from one of the missionaries, dated 1642, who speaks of White, the writer adds: "The difficulty of the language is so great that none of us can yet converse with the Indians without an interpreter."[1]

That it was an Algonkin dialect, closely akin to the Nanticoke, is clear from the words and proper names preserved in the early records and locally to this day. The only word which has created doubts has been the name of "a certain imaginary spirit called *Ochre*."[2] It has been supposed that this was the Huron *oki*. But it is pure Algonkin. It is the Cree *oki-sikow* (*être du ciel*, *ange*, Lacombe), the Abnaki *ooskoo* (*katini ooskoo*, Bon Esprit, *matsini ooskoo*, Mauvais Esprit, Rasles).

It was nearly allied to that spoken in Virginia among Pow-

---

[1] *Relatio Itineris in Marylandiam*, p. 84. The Rev. Mr. Kampman, at one time Moravian missionary among the Delawares, told me that even with the modern aids of grammars, dictionaries and educated native instructors, it is considered to require five years to obtain a sufficient knowledge of their language to preach in it. The slowness of the early Maryland priests to master its intricacies, therefore, need not surprise us.

[2] " Omni vero ratione placare conantur phantasticum quemdam spiritum quem *Ochre* nominant, ut ne noceat." *Relatio Itineris in Marylandiam*, p. 40.

hatan's subjects, as an English boy who had lived with that
chieftain served as an interpreter between the settlers and the
Patuxent and neighboring Indians.[1]

The Conoys were removed, before 1743, from Conejoholo to
Conoy town, further up the Susquehanna, and in 1744 they
joined several other fragmentary bands at Shamokin (where
Sunbury, Pa., now stands). Later, they became merged with
the Nanticokes.[2]

The Shawnees.

The wanderings of the unstable and migratory Shawnees
have occupied the attention of several writers, but it cannot
be said that either their history or their affiliations have been
satisfactorily worked out.[3]

Their dialect is more akin to the Mohegan than to the
Delaware, and when, in 1692, they first appeared in the area
of the Eastern Algonkin Confederacy, they came as the
friends and relatives of the former.[4]

They were divided into four bands, as follows :—

1. *Piqua*, properly *Pikoweu*, "he comes from the ashes."

2. *Mequachake*, "a fat man filled," signifying completion
or perfection. This band held the privilege of the hereditary
priesthood.

---

[1] Bozman, *History of Maryland*, Vol. I, p. 166.

[2] "The Nanticokes and Conoys are now one nation." *Minutes of the
Provincial Council of Penna.*, 1759, Vol. VIII, p. 176.

[3] On this tribe see "The Shawnees and Their Migrations," by Dr.
D. G. Brinton, in the *American Historical Magazine*, 1866; M. F. Force,
Some Early Notices of the Indians of Ohio. Cincinnati, 1879.

[4] See *Colonial History of New York*, Vol. IV. Index. Loskiel,
Geschichte der Mission, etc., p. 25.

3. Kiscapocoke.

4. Chilicothe.[1]

Of these, that which settled in Pennsylvania was the *Pikoweu*, who occupied and gave their name to the Pequa valley in Lancaster county.[2]

According to ancient Mohegan tradition, the New England *Pequods* were members of this band. These moved eastwardly from the Hudson river, and extended their conquests over the greater part of the area of Connecticut. Dr. Trumbull, however,[3] assigns a different meaning to their name, and a more appropriate one—*Pequttóog*, the Destroyers. Some countenance is given to the tradition by the similarity of the Shawnee to the Mohegan, standing, as it does, more closely related to it than to the Unami Delaware.

It has been argued that a band of the Shawnees lived in Southern New Jersey when that territory first came to the knowledge of the whites. On a Dutch map, drawn in 1614 or thereabouts, a tribe called *Saw wanew* is located on the left

---

[1] These names are as given by John Johnston, Indian agent, in 1819. *Archæologia Americana*, Vol. I, p. 275. Heckewelder says they had four divisions, but mentions only two, the *Pecuwési* and *Woketamósi*. (MSS. in Lib. Am. Philos. Soc.)

[2] "That branch of Shawanos which had settled part in Pennsylvania and part in New England were of the tribe of Shawanos then and ever since called *Pi'coweu* or *Pe'koweu*, and after emigrating to the westward settled on and near the Scioto river, where, to this day, the extensive flats go under the name of ' Pickoway Plains.' " Heckewelder MSS. in Lib. Am. Phil. Soc.

[3] In a note to Roger Williams, *Key into the Language of America*, p. 22. The tradition referred to is mentioned in the Heckewelder MSS.

bank of the Delaware river, near the Bay;[1] and DeLaet speaks of the *Sawanoos* as living there.

I am inclined to believe that, in both these cases, the term was used by the natives around New York Bay in its simple geographical sense of "south" or "southern," and not as a tribal designation. It frequently appears with this original meaning in the WALAM OLUM.

The Sapoonees.

A tribe called the Sapoonees, or Saponies, is mentioned as living in Pennsylvania, attached to the Delawares, about the middle of the last century.[2]

They are no doubt the Saponas who once dwelt on a branch of the Great Pedee river in North Carolina, and who moved north about the year 1720.[3] They were said to have joined the Tuscaroras, but the Pennsylvania records class them with the Delawares. Others, impressed by the similarity of Sa-*po-nees* to *Pa-nis*, have imagined they were the Pawnees, now of the west. There is not the slightest importance to be attached to this casual similarity of names.

They were called, by the Iroquois, *Tadirighrones*, and were distinctly identified by them with the nation known to the English as the Catawbas.[4] For a long time the two nations carried on a bitter warfare.

[1] Printed in the *Colonial History of New York*, Vol. I. Compare Force, *ubi suprà*, pp. 16, 17.

[2] Rev. J. Morse, *Report on Indian Affairs*, p. 362.

[3] See Gallatin, *Synopsis of the Indian Tribes*, pp. 85, 86.

[4] See *New York Colonial Documents*, Vol. V, pp. 660, 673, etc.

The Assiwikales.

This band of about fifty families, or one hundred men (about three hundred souls), are stated to have come from South Carolina to the Potomac late in the seventeenth century, and in 1731 were settled partly on the Susquehanna and partly on the upper Ohio or Alleghany. Their chief was named Aqueioma, or Achequeloma.

Their name appears to be a compound of *assin*, stone, and *wikwam*, house, and they were probably Algonkin neighbors of the Shawnees in their southern homes, and united with them in their northern migration.[1]

---

[1] *Pennsylvania Archives*, Vol. I, pp. 299, 300, 302. Gov. Gordon writes to the "Chiefs of ye Shawanese and Assekelaes," under date December, 1731, "I find by our Records that about 34 Years since some Numbers of your Nation came to Sasquehannah," etc. Ibid., p. 302.

CHAPTER III

The Lenape or Delawares.

Derivation of the Name Lenape.—The Three Sub-Tribes: the Minsi or Wolf, the Unami or Turtle, and the Unalachtgo or Turkey Tribes.—Their Totems.—The New Jersey Tribes: the Wapings, Sanhicans and Mantas.—Political Constitution of the Lenape.—Vegetable Food Resources.—Domestic Architecture.—Manufactures. — Paints and Dyes. — Dogs. — Interments. — Computation of Time.—Picture Writing.—Record Sticks.—Moral and Mental Character.—Religious Belief.— Doctrine of the Soul.— The Native Priests.— Religious Ceremonies.

Derivation of Lenni Lenape.

The proper name of the Delaware Indians was and is *Lenâpé* (*â* as in father, *é* as *a* in mate). Dr. J. Hammond Trumbull[1] is quite wide of the mark both in calling this a "misnomer," and in attributing its introduction to Mr. Heckewelder.

Long before that worthy missionary was born, the name was in use in the official documents of the commonwealth of Pennsylvania as the synonym in the native tongue for the Delaware Indians,[2] and it is still retained by their remnant

[1] See his remarks in the Transactions of the *American Philological Association*, 1872, p. 157.

[2] For instance, in Governor Patrick Gordon's Letter to the Friends, 1728, where he speaks of "Our Lenappys or Delaware Indians," in *Penna. Archives*, Vol. I, p. 230. At the treaty of Easton, 1756, Tedyuscung, head chief of the Delawares, is stated to have represented the "Lenopi" Indians (*Minutes of the Council*, Phila., 1757), and in the "Conference of Eleven Nations living West of Allegheny," held at Philadelphia, 1759, the Delawares are included under the tribal name

in Kansas as the proper term to designate their collective nation, embracing its sub-tribes.[1]

The derivation of *Lenape* has been discussed with no little learning, as well as the adjective *lenni*, which often precedes it (Lenni Lenape). Mr. Heckewelder stated that *lenni* means "original, pure," and that *Lenape* signifies "people."[2] Dr. Trumbull, in the course of a long examination of the words for "man" in the Algonkin dialects, reaches the conclusion that "Len-âpé" denotes "a common adult male," *i. e.*, an Indian man ; *lenno lenâpé*, an Indian of *our* tribe or nation, and, consequently, *vir*, "a man of men."[3] He derives these two words from the roots *len* (= *nen*), a pronominal possessive, and *ape*, an inseparable generic particle, "denoting an adult male."

I differ, with hesitation, from such an eminent authority ; but this explanation does not, to my mind, give the precise meaning of the term. No doubt, both *lenno*, which in Delaware means *man*, and *len*, in Lenape, are from the pronominal radicle of the first person *nê*, I, we, mine, our. As the native considered his tribe the oldest, as well as the most important of created beings, "ours" with him came to be synonymous with what was esteemed ancient, indigenous, primeval, as well as human, man-like, *par excellence.* "We"

"Leonopy." See *Minutes of the Provincial Council of Penna.*, Vol. VIII, p. 418.

[1] So Mr. Lewis H. Morgan says, and he obtained the facts on the spot. "Len-â'-pe was their former name, and is still used." *Systems of Consanguinity and Affinity*, p. 289 (Washington, 1871).

[2] *History of the Indian Nations*, p. 401.

[3] *Transactions of the American Philological Association*, 1871, p. 144.

and "men" were to him the same. The initial *l* is but a slight modification of the *n* sound, and is given by Campanius as an *r*, "*rhenus*, homo."

Lenape, therefore, does not mean "a common adult male," but rather "a male of our kind," or "our men."[1]

The termination *apé* is said by Heckewelder to convey the idea of "walking or being in an erect posture." A comparison of the various Algonkin dialects indicates that it was originally a locative, signifying staying in a place, abiding or sitting. Thus, in Cree, *apú*, he is there; in Chipeway, *abi*, he is at home; in Delaware, *n'dappin*, I am here. The transfer of this idea to the male sex is seen in the Cree, *ap*, to sit upon, to place oneself on top, *apa*, to cover (animate and active); Chipeway, *nabe*, the male of quadrupeds. Baraga says that for a Chipeway woman to call her husband *nin nabem* (lit. my coverer, comp. French, *femme couverte*), is coarse.

---

[1] Zeisberger's translation of Lenni Lenape as "people of the same nation," would be more literal if it were put "men of our nation."

President Stiles, in his *Itinerary*, makes the statement: "The Delaware tribe is called *Poh-he-gan* or *Mo-hee-gan* by themselves, and *Auquitsau-kon*." I have not been able to reach a satisfactory solution of the first and third of these names.

That the Delawares did use the term Lenape as their own designation, is shown by the refrain of one of their chants, preserved by Heckewelder. It was—

"*Husca*   *n'lenape-win*,"
Truly   I—a Lenape—am.

Or: "I am a true man of our people." *Trans. Amer. Philos. Soc.*, Vol. IV, N. Ser., p. 381.

The Lenape Sub-Tribes.

The Lenape were divided into three sub-tribes :—

1. The Minsi, Monseys, Montheys, Munsees, or Minisinks.
2. The Unami, or Wonameys.
3. The Unalachtigo.

No explanation of these designations will be found in Hecke-welder or the older writers. From investigations among living Delawares, carried out at my request by Mr. Horatio Hale, it is evident that they are wholly geographical, and refer to the locations of these sub-tribes on the Delaware river.

Minsi, properly *Minsīu*, and formerly *Minassiniu*, means "people of the stony country," or briefly, "mountaineers." It is a synthesis of *minthiu*, to be scattered, and *achsin*, stone, according to the best living native authorities.[1]

Unāmi, or *W'nāmiu*, means "people down the river," from *naheu*, down-stream.

Unalachtigo, properly *W'nalāchtko*, means "people who live near the ocean," from *wunalawat*, to go towards, and *t'kow* or *t'kòu*, wave.

Historically, such were the positions of these sub-tribes when they first came to the knowledge of Europeans.

The Minsi lived in the mountainous region at the head waters of the Delaware, above the Forks, or junction of the Lehigh river. One of their principal fires was on the Minisink plains, above the Water Gap, and another on the

---

[1] Mr. Eager, in his *History of Orange County*, quotes the old surveyor, Nicolas Scull (1730), in favor of translating *minisink* "the water is gone;" and Ruttenber, in his *History of the Native Tribes of the Hudson River*, supposes that it is derived from *menatey*, an island. Neither of these commends itself to modern Delawares.

East Branch of the Delaware, which they called *Namaes Sipu*,
Fish River.   Their hunting grounds embraced lands now in
the three colonies of Pennsylvania, New York and New
Jersey.   The last mentioned extinguished their title in 1758,
by the payment of one thousand pounds.

That, at any time, as Heckewelder asserts, their territory
extended up the Hudson as far as tide-water, and westward
"far beyond the Susquehannah," is surely incorrect.   Only
after the beginning of the eighteenth century, when they
had been long subject to the Iroquois, have we any
historic evidence that they had a settlement on the last
named river.

The Unamis' territory on the right bank of the Delaware
river extended from the Lehigh valley southward.   It was
with them and their southern neighbors, the Unalachtigos,
that Penn dealt for the land ceded him in the Indian Deed
of 1682.   The Minsis did not take part in the transaction,
and it was not until 1737 that the Colonial authorities
treated directly with the latter for the cession of their
territory.[1]

The Unalachtigo or Turkey totem had its principal seat on
the affluents of the Delaware near where Wilmington now
stands.   About this point, Captain John Smith, on his map
(1609,) locates the *Chikahokin*.   In later writers this name is
spelled *Chihohockies, Chiholacki* and *Chikolacki*, and is stated
by the historians Proud and Smith to be synonymous with
Delawares.[2]   The correct form is *Chikelaki*, from *chik'eno*,

---

[1] See *Penna. Archives*, Vol. I, pp. 540-1.

[2] Proud, *History of Penna.*, Vol. II, p. 297 ; S. Smith, *Hist. of New Jersey*, p. 456 ; Henry, *Dict. of the Delaware Lang.*, MS., p. 539.

turkey, the modern form as given by Whipple,[1] and *aki*
land.   The *n, l* and *r* were alternating letters in this
dialect.

The population was, however, very sparse, owing to the
predatory incursions of the Susquehannocks, whose trails,
leading up the Octorara and Conestoga, and down the Christina and Brandywine Creeks, were followed by war parties
annually, and desolated the west shores of the Bay and lower
river.   When, in 1634, Captain Thomas Young explored the
river, the few natives he found on the west side told him
(through the medium of his Algonkin Virginian interpreter)
that the "Minquaos" had killed their people, burnt their
villages, and destroyed their crops, so that " the Indians had
wholly left that side of the river which was next their
enemies, and had retired themselves on the other side farre
up into the woods."[2]

North of the Chikelaki, Smith's map locates the *Macocks*.
This name does not appear in later authors, but near that site
were the *Okahoki* band, who occupied the shores of Ridley
and Crum creeks and the land between them.   There they
remained until 1703, when they were removed to a small
reservation of 500 acres in what is now Willistown township,
Chester county.[3]

---

[1] Delaware Vocabulary in Whipple, Ewbank & Turner's *Report*, 1855.
The German form is *tsichenum*.

[2] *A Brief Relation of the Voyage of Captayne Thomas Yong*, in *Mass.
Hist. Soc. Colls.*, 4th series, Vol. IX, p. 119.

[3] See the original Warrant of Survey and Minutes relating thereto, in
Dr. George Smith's *History of Delaware County, Pa.*, pp. 209, 210
(Phila., 1862).   The derivation is uncertain.   Captain John Smith gives

The Totemic Animals.

These three sub-tribes had each its totemic animal, from which it claimed a mystical descent. The Minsi had the Wolf, the Unami the Turtle, and the Unalachtigo the Turkey. The Unamis claimed and were conceded the precedence of the others, because their ancestor, the Turtle, was not the common animal, so-called, but the great original tortoise which bears the world on its back, and was the first of living beings, as I shall explain on a later page.

In referring to the totemic animals the common names were not used, but metaphorical expressions. Thus the Wolf was referred to as *Ptuksit*, Round Foot (*ptuk*, round, *sit*, foot, from the shape of its paws ;) the turtle was *Pakoango*, the Crawler ; and the turkey was *Pullaeu*, he does not chew,[1] referring to the bird's manner of swallowing food.

The signs of these animals were employed in their picture writing, painted on their houses or inscribed on rocks, to designate the respective sub-tribes. But only in the case of the Unamis was the whole animal represented. The Turkey

mahcawq for pumpkin, and this appears to be the word in the native name of Chester Creek, *Macopanackhan*, which is also seen in *Marcus* Hook. (See Smith's *Hist. Del. Co.*, pp. 145, 381.) I am inclined to identify the *Macocks* with the *M'okahoki* as "the people of the pumpkin place," or where those vegetables were cultivated.

[1] The Shawnee word is the same, *pellewaa*, whence their name for the Ohio River, *Pellewaa seepee*, Turkey River. (Rev. David Jones, *Journal of Two Visits Made to Some Nations of Indians on the West Side of the River Ohio in* 1772 *and* 1773, p. 20.) From this is derived the shortened form *Plaen*, seen in *Playwickey*, or *Planwikit*, the town of those of the Turkey Tribe, in Berks county, Pa. (Heckewelder, *Indian Names*, p. 355.)

tribe painted only one foot of their totemic bird, and the Minsi the extended foot of the wolf, though they sometimes added an outline of the rest of the animal.[1]

These three divisions of the Lenape were neither "gentes" nor "phratries," though Mr. Morgan has endeavored to force them into his system by stating that they were " of the nature of phratries."[2] Each was divided into twelve families bearing female names, and hence probably referring to some unexplained matriarchal system. They were, as I have called them, sub-tribes. In their own orations they referred to each other as " playmates." (Heckewelder.)

The New Jersey Lenape.

The native name of New Jersey is given as Shä'akbee (English orthography: ä as in fate); or as the German missionaries wrote it, *Sche'jachbi.* It is a compound of *bi*, water, *aki*, land, and the adjective prefix *schey*, which means something long and narrow (*scheyek*, a string of wampum; *schaje-linquall*, the edge of the eyes, the eyelids, etc.) This would be equivalent to "long-land water," and, according to the rules of Delaware grammar, which place the noun used in the genitive sense before the noun which governs it, the term would be more suitable to some body of water, Delaware bay or the ocean, than to the main land.

The Lenape distinctly claimed the whole of the present area of New Jersey. Their great chief, Tedyuscung, stated at the Conference at Easton (1757), that their lands reached eastward to the shore of the sea. The New Jersey tribes

[1] Heckewelder, *Hist. Indian Nations*, pp. 253-4.

[2] Lewis H. Morgan, *Ancient Society*, pp. 171-2.

fully recognized their unity. As early as 1694, at an interview with Governor Markham at Philadelphia, when the famous Tamany and other Lenape chieftains were present, Mohocksey, a chief of the Jersey Indians, said: "Though we live on the other side of the water (*i. e.*, the Delaware river), yet we reckon ourselves all one, because," he added, giving a characteristically native reason, "because we drink one water."[1]

The names, number and position of the Jersey tribes have not been very clearly made out.

A pamphlet published in London, in 1648, states that there were twenty-three Indian kinglets in its area, with about 2000 warriors in all. Of these, Master Robert Evelin, a surveyor, who spent several years in the Province about 1635, names nine on the left bank of the Delaware, between Cape May and the Falls. The names are extremely corrupt, but it may be worth while giving them.[2]

1. Kechemeches, 500 men, five miles above Cape May.

2. Manteses, 100 bowmen, twelve leagues above the former.

3. Sikonesses.

4. Asomoches, 100 men.

5. Eriwoneck, 40 men.

6. Ramcock, 100 men.

---

[1] *Minutes of the Provincial Council of Pennsylvania*, July 6th, 1694.

[2] Master Evelin's Letter is printed in Smith's *History of New Jersey*, 2d ed. Some doubt has been cast on his letter, because of its connection with the mythical "New Albion," but his personality and presence on the river have been vindicated. See *The American Historical Magazine*, Vol. I, 2d series, pp. 75, 76.

D

7. Axion, 200 men.

8. Calcefar, 150 men.

9. Mosilian, 200 men, at the Falls.

Of these, the Mantes lived on Salem creek; *Ramcock* is Rancocas creek; the *Eriwoneck* are evidently the *Ermomex* of Van der Donck's map of 1656; *Axion* may be for Assiscunk creek, above Burlington, from Del. *assiscu*, mud; *assiscunk*, a muddy place. Lindstrom and Van der Donck name the most Southern tribe in New Jersey *Naraticons*. They were on and near Raccoon creek, which on Lindstrom's map is *Narraticon Sipu*, the Naraticon river. Probably the English name is simply a translation of the Del. *nachenum*, raccoon.

In 1675 the number of sachems in Jersey of sufficient importance for the then Governor Andros to treat with were four. It is noted that when he had made them the presents customary on such occasions, "They return thanks and fall a kintacoying, singing *kenon, kenon*."[1] This was the Delaware *genan (genama*, thank ye him. Zeis).

The total number in New Jersey a few years before this (1671) were estimated by the authorities at "about a thousand persons, besides women and children."[2]

The "*Wapings, Opings* or *Pomptons*," as they are named in the old records, were the tribe which dwelt on the west shore of New York harbor and southwardly, or, more exactly, "from Roeloff Jansen's Kill to the sea."[3] They were of the Minsi totem, and were the earliest of the

[1] *New Jersey Archives*, Vol. I, p. 183.

[2] Ibid, Vol. I, p. 73.

[3] Ruttenber, *Hist. of the Indian Tribes of Hudson River*. s. v.

Lenape who saw white men, when, in 1524, the keel of
Verrazano was the first to plough the waters of New York
harbor.

The name Waping or Oping is derived from *Wapan*, east,
and was applied to them as the easternmost of the Lenape
nation.[1] Their other name, Pompton, Mr. Heckewelder
identifies with *pihm-tom*, crooked-mouthed, though its appli-
cability is not obvious.[2]

In the middle of the eighteenth century the remains of the
Pompton Indians resided on the Raritan river. The bound-
aries of their territory were defined in 1756, at the Treaty of
Crosswicks.

The *Sanhicans* occupied the Delaware shore at the Falls,
near where Trenton now stands, and extended eastward along
the upper Indian path quite to New York bay. Heckewelder
says that this name, *Sankhicani*, means a gun lock, and was
applied by the Lenape to the Mohawks who were first furnished
with muskets by the Europeans. This has led some writers
to locate a band of Mohawks at the Falls.

The Sanhicans were, however, undoubtedly Lenape. Campanius, who quotes the name of the place in 1642, classes

---

[1] Heckewelder, in his unpublished MSS., asserts that both these names
mean "Opossum." It is true that the name of this animal in Lenape is
woapink, in the New Jersey dialect *opiing*, and in the Nanticoke of Smith
oposon; but all these are derived from the root *woab*, which originally
meant "white," and was applied to the East as the place of the dawn
and the light. The reference is to the light gray, or whitish, color of the
animal's hair. Compare the Cree, *wapiskowes*, cendré, il a le poil blafard.
Lacombe, *Dictionnaire de la Langue des Cris.* s. v.

[2] *On Indian Names*, p. 375, in *Trans. American Philosophical Society*,
Vol. III, n. ser.

them as such. In Van der Donck's map, of 1656, they are marked as possessing the land at the Falls and Manhattan Bay; and De Lact gives the numerals and a number of words from their dialect, which are all pure Delaware, as :—

	Sanhican.	*Delaware.*
Deer,	atto,	achtu.
Bear,	machquoyuo,	machquak.
Wolf,	metumnu,	metemmeu.
Turkey,	sickenum,	tschickenum.

Their name has lost its first syllable. It should be *assan-hican*. This means not merely and not originally a gun-flint, but any stone implement, from *achsin*, or, in the New Jersey dialect, *assun*, a stone, and *hican*, an instrument. They were distinctively " the stone-implement people."

This is plainly with reference to their manufactures near Trenton. The great deposit of post-glacial gravels at this point abound with quartzite fragments suitable for working into stone implements, and to what extent they were utilized by the natives is shown by the enormous collection, num-bering over thirty thousand specimens, which Dr. Charles C. Abbott, of Trenton, has made in that immediate vicinity. A horde of over 125 beautifully chipped lance heads of quartz and jasper, and the remains of a workshop of remarkable magnitude, were evidences of the extensive manufacture that once prevailed there.

The left bank of the Delaware, from the vicinity of Bur-lington quite to and below Salem, was held by a warlike tribe known to the settlers as the *Mantas*, or *Mantos*, or *Mandes*, otherwise named the Frog Indians. They extended eastward along the main or southern Indian path, which led from the Delaware, below the mouth of Rancocas Creek, to the extensive Indian plantations or corn fields near Sandy Hook, mentioned by Campanius and Lindström.[1]

Mr. Henry has derived their name from *mangi*, great,[2] and others have suggested *menatey*, an island; but I do not think either of these is tenable. I have no doubt that *mante* is simply a mis-spelling of *monthee*, which is the form given by the East Jersey and Stockbridge Indians to the name of the Minsi or Monsey sub-tribe of the Delawares.[3] This is further indicated by the fact that toward the beginning of the eighteenth century they incorporated themselves wholly with the two other Lenape sub-tribes.[4] We thus find that the Minsis were not confined to the North and Northwest, as Heckewelder and others wrote, but had pressed southward in New Jersey, quite to the shores of Delaware Bay.

The New Jersey Indians disappeared rapidly. As early as 1721 an official document states that they were "but few, and very innocent and friendly."[5] When, in 1745, the missionary Brainerd visited their settlement at Crosweeksung, Burlington county, he found some "who had lived with the

---

[1] Proud, *History of Pennsylvania*, Vol. I, 144, II, p. 295. Heckewelder, *Trans. Am. Philo. Soc.*, Vol. IV, p. 376.

[2] Matthew G. Henry, *Delaware Indian Dictionary*, p. 709. (MS. in the Library of the Am. Phil. Soc.)

[3] "The Monthees who we called Wemintheuw," etc. *Journal of Hendrick Aupaumut, Mems. Hist. Soc. Pa.*, Vol. II, p. 77.

[4] Heckewelder, *ubi suprâ*.

[5] *New Jersey Archives*, Vol. V, p. 22.

white people under gospel light, had learned to read, were
civil, etc."[1] Those with whom he labored at this place
subsequently removed to New Stockbridge, Mass., and united
with the Mohegans and others there.[2]

The Swedish traveler, Peter Kalm, who spent about a year
in New Jersey in 1749, observes that the disappearance of
the native population was principally due to two agencies.
Smallpox destroyed "incredible numbers," "but brandy
has killed most of the Indians."[3]

The dialect of the New Jersey Indians was soft and vocalic,
avoiding the gutturals of their northern relatives, and without the frequent unpleasant forcible expirations of the Nanticoke. A vocabulary of it, obtained for Mr. Thomas Jefferson,
in 1792, at the village of Edgpiiliik, West New Jersey, is in
MS. in the library of the American Philosophical Society.

Political Constitution.

Each totem of the Lenape recognized a chieftain, called
sachem, *sakima*, a word found in most Algonkin dialects,
with slight variations (Chip. *ogima*, Cree, *okimaw*, Pequot,
sachimma), and derived from a root *ŏki*, signifying above in
space, and by a transfer frequent in all languages, above in
power. Thus, in Cree,[4] we have *sâkamow*, "il projecte, il

---

[1] *The Rise and Progress of a Remarkable Work of Grace Among the
Indians.* By David Brainerd, in *Works*, p. 304.

[2] E. de Schweinitz, *Life of Zeisberger*, p. 660, note.

[3] *Travels into North America*, Vol. II, pp. 93–94 (London, 1771).

[4] Lacombe, *Dictionnaire de la Langue des Cris*, p. 711. Dr. Trumbull,
however, maintains that it is derived from *sohkau-au*, he prevails over
(note to Roger Williams' *Key*, p. 162). If there is a genetic connection,

montre la tête," and in Delaware, *w'ochgitschi*, the part above, the upper part (Zeisberger), etc.

It appears from Mr. Morgan's inquiries, that at present and of later years, "the office of sachem is hereditary in the gens, but elective among its members."[1] Loskiel, however, writing on the excellent authority of Zeisberger, states explicitly that the chief of each totem was selected and inaugurated by those of the remaining two.[2] By common and ancient consent, the chief selected from the Turtle totem was head chief of the whole Lenape nation.

These chieftains were the "peace chiefs." They could neither go to war themselves, nor send nor receive the war belt—the ominous string of dark wampum, which indicated that the tempest of strife was to be let loose. Their proper badge was the wampum belt, with a diamond-shaped figure in the centre, worked in white beads, which was the symbol of the peaceful council fire, and was called by that name.

War was declared by the people at the instigation of the "war captains," valorous braves of any birth or family who had distinguished themselves by personal prowess, and especially by good success in forays against the enemy.[3]

---

the latter is the derivative. The word *sakima* is not known among the Minsi. In place of it they say *k'htai*, the great one, from *kehtan*, great. From this comes the corrupted forms *tayach* or *tallach* of the Nanticokes, and the *tayac* of the Pascatoways.

[1] Lewis H. Morgan, *Ancient Society*, p. 172.

[2] Loskiel, *Geschichte der Mission*, p. 168.

[3] For these particulars see Ettwein, *Traditions and Language of the Indians*, in *Bulletin of the Pa. Hist. Soc.*, Vol. I; Charles Beatty, *Journal of a Tour*, etc., p. 51.

Nor did the authority of the chiefs extend to any infringe-
ment on the traditional rights of the gens, as, for instance,
that of blood revenge.   The ignorance of this limitation of
the central power led to various misunderstandings at the
time, on the part of the colonial authorities, and since then,
by later historians.   Thus, in 1728, "the Delaware Indians
on Brandywine" were summoned by the Governor to answer
about a murder.   Their chief, Civility, answered that it was
committed by the Minisinks, "over whom they had no
authority."[1]   This did not mean but that in some matters
authority could be exerted, but not in a question relating to
a feud of blood.

Agriculture and Food Resources.

The Lenape did not depend solely on the chase for subsistence.   They were largely agricultural, and raised a variety
of edible plants.   Indian corn was, as usual, the staple; but
in addition to that, they had extensive fields of squashes,
beans and sweet potatoes.[2]   The hardy variety of tobacco
was also freely cultivated.

The value of Indian corn, the *Zea mais*, must have been
known to the Algonkin tribes while they still formed one
nation, as the same name is applied to it by tribes geographically the widest apart.   Thus the Micmacs of Nova
Scotia call it *pe-ās'kūmŭn-ŭl* whose theme *ās'kŭ-mŭn* re-

---

[1] C. Thompson, *Inquiry into the Causes of the Alienation of the Delaware and Shawnee Indians*, p. 16.

[2] I assign them the sweet potato on the excellent authority of Dr. C.
Thompson, *Essay on Indian Affairs*, in *Colls. of the Hist. Soc. of Penna.*,
Vol. I, p. 81.

appears in the *wuskannem* (Elliott) and the *scannemeneash* (Roger Williams) of New England, in the Delaware *jesquem* (Campanius), and *chasquem* (Zeis.), and even in the Piegan Blackfoot *esko-tope*.

The first radical *ask*, Chip. *ashk*, Del. *aski*, means "green." The application is to the green waving plant, so conspicuous in the fields during the summer months. The second *mŭn* or *min* is a generic suffix applied to all sorts of small edible fruits. In the Blackfoot its place is supplied by another, and in the Unami Delaware it is abbreviated to the letter *m*.

On the other hand, in the Chipeway word for corn, *mandamin*, Ottawa *mindamin*, Cree *mattamin*, the second radical is retained in full, while for the first is substituted an abbreviation of *manito*, divine ("it is divine, supernatural, or mysterious"); if we may accept the opinion of Mr. Schoolcraft, and I know of no more plausible etymology.

Tobacco was called by the Delawares *kscha-tey*, Zeis., *seka-ta*, Camp., or in the English orthography *shuate* (Vocab. N. J. Inds.), and *koshähtahe* (Cummings). I am inclined to think that these are but dialectic variations and different orthographies of the root *'ta* or *'dam* (*a* nasal) found in the New England *wuttäm-anog*, Micmac *tŭmawa*, Abnaki *wh'dāman* (Rasle), Cree *tchistémaw*, Chip. *asséma* (= *astémaw*), Blackfoot *pi-stä-kan;* a root which Dr. J. H. Trumbull has satisfactorily identified as meaning "to drink," the smoke being swallowed and likened to water. "To drink tobacco" was the usual old English expression for "to smoke."

If this etymology is correct, it leads to the inference that tobacco also was known to the ancient Algonkins before they split up into the many nations which we now know, and furthermore that they must have lived in a region where these two semi-tropical or wholly tropical plants, Indian corn and tobacco, had been already introduced and cultivated by some more ancient race. To conclude that they themselves brought them from a tropical land, would be too hazardous.

The pipes in which the tobacco was smoked were called *appooke* (modern Delaware *o'pahokun'*, Cumings' Vocab.) They were of earthenware and of stone; sometimes, it is said, of copper. According to Kalm, the ceremonial pipes were of a red stone, possibly the western pipe stone, and were very highly prized.[1]

Of wild fruits and plants they consumed the esculent and nutritious tubers on the roots of the Wild Bean, *Apios tuberosa*, the large, oval, fleshy roots of the arrow-leaved *Sagittaria*, the former of which the Indians called *hobbenis*, and the latter *katniss*, names which they subsequently applied to the European turnip. They also roasted and ate the acrid cormus of the Indian turnip, *Arum triphyllum*, in Delaware *taw-ho*, *taw-hin* or *tuck-ah*, and collected for food the seeds of the Golden Club, *Orontium aquaticum*, common in the pools along the creeks and rivers. Its native name was *taw-kee*.[2]

House Building.

In their domestic architecture they differed noticeably from the Iroquois and even the Mohegans. Their houses were not communal, but each family had its separate residence, a wattled hut, with rounded top, thatched with mats

---

[1] Peter Kalm, *Travels in North America*, Vol. II, p. 42.

[2] See Peter Kalm, *Travels in North America*, Vol. II, pp. 110–115; William Darlington, *Flora Cestrica*. (West Chester, Pa., 1837.)

woven of the long leaves of the Indian corn or the stalks of
the sweet flag (*Acorus calamus*,) or of the bark of trees
(*anacon*, a mat, Z.) These were built in groups and surrounded with a palisade to protect the inhabitants from
sudden inroads.[1]

In the centre was sometimes erected a mound of earth,
both as a place of observation and as a location to place the
children and women. The remains of these circular ram-
parts enclosing a central mound were seen by the early
settlers at the Falls of the Delaware and up the Lehigh
valley.

Manufactures.

The art of the potter was known and extensively practiced,
but did not indicate any unusual proficiency, either in the
process of manufacture or in the methods of decoration,
although the late Mr. F. Peale thought that, in the latter
respect, the Delaware pottery had some claims to a high
rank.[2] The representation of animal forms was quite unusual,
only some few and inferior examples having been found.

[1] For these facts, see Bishop Ettwein's article on the Traditions and
Languages of the Indians, *Bulletin of the Pa. Hist. Soc.*, 1848, p. 32.
Van der Donck (1656) describes these palisaded strongholds, and Cam-
panius (1642–48) gives a picture of one. See also E. de Schweinitz,
Life of Zeisberger, p. 83. The Mohegan houses were sometimes 180
feet long, by about 20 feet wide, and occupied by numerous families.
Van der Donck, *Descrip. of the New Netherlands*, pp. 196–7. *Coll. N.
Y. Hist. Soc.*, Ser. II, Vol. I.

The native name of these wooden forts was *menachk*, derived from
manachen, to cut wood (Cree, *manikka*, to cut with a hatchet). Roger
Williams calls them *aumansk*, a form of the same word.

[2] See the communication on "Pottery on the Delaware," by him, in the

Their skill in manufacturing bead work and feather mantles, and in dressing deer skins, excited the admiration of the early voyagers. Although their weapons and utensils were mostly of stone, there was a considerable supply of native copper among them, in use as ornaments, for arrow heads and pipes. Some specimens of it have been found by Dr. Abbott near Trenton, and by other collectors in Pennsylvania,[1] and its scarcity in modern collections is to be attributed to its being bought up and melted by the whites rather than to its limited employment.

Soap stone was hollowed out with considerable skill, to form bowls, and the wood of the sassafras tree was highly esteemed for the same purpose (Kalm).

The maize was broken up in wooden or stone mortars with a stone pestle, the native name of which was *pocohaac*, a word signifying also the virile member.

Proceedings of the *Am. Phil. Soc.*, 1868. The whole subject of the archæology of the Delaware valley and New Jersey has been treated in the most satisfactory manner by the distinguished antiquary, Dr. Charles C. Abbott, in his work, *Primitive Industry* (Salem, Mass., 1881), and his *Stone Age in New Jersey* (1877).

[1] Four specimens are reported from Berks Co., Pa., by Prof. D. P. Brunner, in his volume, *The Indians of Berks Co., Pa.*, pp. 94, 95 (Reading, 1881). These were an axe, a chisel, a knife and a gouge. The metal was probably in part obtained in New Jersey, in part imported from the Lake Superior region. See further, Abbott, *Primitive Industry*, chap. xxviii. Peter Kalm, the Swedish naturalist, who visited New Jersey in 1748, says that when the copper mines "upon the second river between Elizabeth Town and New York" were discovered, old mining holes were found and tools which the Indians had made use of. *Travels in North America*, Vol. I, p. 384.

Their arms were the war club or tomahawk, *tomhickan*, the bow, *hattape*, and arrow, *alluns*, the spear, *tanganaoun*, and for defence Bishop Ettwein states they carried a round shield of thick, dried hide.

The spear was also used for spearing fish, which they, moreover, knew how to catch with "brush nets," and with fish hooks made of bone and the dried claws of birds (Kalm).[1]

Paints and Dyes.

The paints and dyes used by the Lenape and neighboring Indians were derived both from the vegetable and mineral realms. From the former they obtained red, white and blue clays, which were in such extensive demand that the vicinity of those streams in New Castle county, Delaware, which are now called White Clay Creek and Red Clay Creek, was widely known to the natives as *Walamink*, the Place of Paint.

The vegetable world supplied a variety of dyes in the colored juices of plants. These were mixed with the acid juice of the wild, sweet-scented crab apple (*Pyrus coronaria;* in Lenape, *tombic'anall*), to fix the dye.

A red was yielded by the root of the *Sanguinaria Canadensis*, still called "Indian paint root;" an orange by the root of *Phytolacca decandra*, the poke or pocoon; a yellow by the

---

[1] Some antiquaries appear to have doubted whether the spear was in use as a weapon of war among the Pennsylvania Indians (See Abbott, *Primitive Industry*, p. 248.) But the Susquehannocks are distinctly reported as employing as a weapon "a strong and light spear of locust wood." *Relatio Itineris in Marylandiam*, p. 85.

root of *Hydrastis Canadensis;* a black by a mixture of sumac and white walnut bark, etc.[1]

Dogs.

The only domestic animal they possessed was a small species of dogs with pointed ears. These were called *allum,* and were preserved less for protection or for use in hunting than for food, and especially for ceremonial purposes.[2]

Interments.

The custom of common ossuaries for each gens appears to have prevailed among the Lenape. Gabriel Thomas states that: "If a person of Note dies very far away from his place of residence, they will convey his Bones home some considerable Time after, to be buried there."[3] Bishop Ettwein speaks of mounds for common burial, though he appears to limit their use to times of war.[4]

---

[1] For further information on this subject, an article may be consulted in the *Transactions of the American Philosophical Society,* 1st Ser., Vol. III, pp. 222, et seq., by Mr. Hugh Martin, entitled "An Account of the Principal Dies employed by the American Indians."

[2] The Delawares had three words for dog. One was *allum,* which recurs in many Algonkin dialects, and is derived by Mr. Trumbull from a root signifying "to lay hold of," or "to hold fast." The second was *lennochum* or *knchum,* which means "the quadruped belonging to man;" *lenno,* man; *chum,* a four-footed beast. The third was *mockaneu,* a name derived from a general Algonkin root, in Cree, *mokku,* meaning "to tear in pieces," from which the Delaware word for bear, *machque,* has its origin, and also, significantly enough, the verb "to eat" in some dialects.

[3] *History of West New Jersey,* p. 3 (London, 1698).

[4] *Bulletin Hist. Soc. of Penna.,* 1848, p. 32.

One of these communal graveyards of the Minsis covers an area of six acres on the Neversink creek,[1] while, according to tradition, another of great antiquity and extent was located on the islands in the Delaware river, above the Water-Gap.[2]

Computation of Time.

The accuracy with which the natives computed time becomes a subject of prime consideration in a study of their annals. It would appear that the Eastern Algonkins were not deficient in astronomical knowledge. Roger Williams remarks, " they much observe the Starres, and their very children can give names to many of them ;"[3] and the same testimony is borne by Wassenaer. The latter, speaking of the tribes around New York Harbor, in 1630, says that their year began with the first moon after the February moon ; and that the time for planting was calculated by the rising of the constellation Taurus in a certain quarter. They named this constellation the horned head of some great · fictitious animal.[4]

Zeisberger observes that, in his day, the Lenape did not have a fixed beginning to their year, but reckoned from one seeding time to another, or from when the corn was ripe, etc.[5] Nevertheless, they had a word for year, *gachtin*, and counted their ages and the sequence of events by yearly periods. The

[1] E. M. Ruttenber, *History of the Indian Tribes of Hudson River,* p. 96, note.

[2] Maximilian, Prince of Wied, *Travels in America,* p. 35.

[3] *A Key into the Language of America,* p. 105.

[4] *Documentary History of New York,* Vol. III, pp. 29, 32.

[5] *Grammar of the Language of the Lenni Lenape,* pp. 108–109.

Chipeways count by winters (*pipun-agak*, in which the first word means winter, and the second is a plural form similar to the Del. *gachtin*); but the Lenape did not apparently follow them in this. They recognized only twelve moons in the year and not thirteen, as did the New England nations; at least, the names of but twelve months have been preserved.[1] The day periods were reckoned usually by nights, but it was not improper to count by "suns" or days.

Pictographic Signs.

The picture writing of the Delawares has been quite fully described by Zeisberger, Loskiel and Heckewelder. It was scratched upon stone (Loskiel), or more frequently cut in or painted upon the bark of trees or pieces of wood. The colors were chiefly black and red. The system was highly conventionalized, so that it could readily be understood by all their tribes, and also by others with whom they came in contact, the Shawnees, Wyandots, Chipeways, etc.

The subjects had reference not merely to matters of present interest, but to the former history of their nation, and were directed "to the preservation of the memory of famous men, and to the recollection of events and actions of note." Therefore, their Agamemnons felt no anxiety for the absence of a Homer, but "confidently reckoned that their noble deeds would be held in memory long after their bodies had perished."[2]

The material on which the drawings were made was

---

[1] They are given, with translations, in Zeisberger's *Grammar*, p. 109.

[2] See Loskiel, *Geschichte der Mission*, etc., pp. 32, 33; Heckewelder, *History of the Indian Nations*, chap. X.

generally so perishable that few examples have been left to us. One, a stone about seven inches long, found in central New Jersey, has been described and figured by Dr. Abbott.[1] It represents an arrow crossing certain straight lines. Several "gorgets" (smooth stone tablets pierced with holes for suspension, and probably used for ceremonial purposes), stone knives and pebbles, showing inscribed marks and lines, and rude figures, are engraved in Dr. Abbott's book ; others similar have been seen in Bucks and Berks counties, Pa.

There was a remarkable series of hieroglyphics, some eighty in number, on a rock at Safe Harbor, on the Susquehanna. They have been photographed and described by Prof. T. C. Porter, of Lancaster, but have yet to be carefully analyzed.[2] From its location, it was probably the work of the Susquehannocks, and did not belong to the general system of Algonkin pictography.

If the rude drawings appended to the early treatises as signatures of native sachems be taken as a guide, little or no uniformity prevailed in the personal signs. The same chieftain would, on various occasions, employ symbols differing so widely that they have no visible relation.[3]

---

[1] Dr. Charles C. Abbott, *Primitive Industry*, pp. 71, 207, 347, 379, 384, 390, 391. Dr. Abbott's suggestion that the bird's head seen on several specimens might represent the totem of the Turkey gens of the Lenape cannot be well founded, if Heckewelder is correct in saying that their totemic mark was only the foot of the fowl. *Ind. Nations*, p. 253.

[2] See *Proceedings Amer. Philos. Soc.*, Vol. X.

[3] The subject is discussed, and comparative drawings of the native signatures reproduced, by Prof. D. B. Brunner, in his useful work, *The Indians of Berks County, Pa.*, p. 68 (Reading, 1881).

E

An interesting incident is recorded by Friend John Richardson when on a visit to William Penn, at his manor of Pennsburg, in 1701. Penn asked the Indian interpreter to give him some idea of what the native notion of God was. The interpreter, at a loss for words, had recourse to picture writing, and describing a number of circles, one inside the other, he pointed to the centre of the innermost and smallest one, and there, "placed, as he said, by way of representation, the Great Man."[1] The explanation was striking and suggestive, and hints at the meaning of the not infrequent symbol of the concentric circles.

An alleged piece of Delaware pictography is copied by Schoolcraft[2] from the London *Archæologia*, Vol. IV. It purports to be an inscription found on the Muskingum river in 1780, and the interpretation is said to have been supplied by the celebrated Delaware chief, Captain White Eyes (Coquethagechton). As interpreted, it relates to massacres of the whites by the Delaware chief, Wingenund, in the border war of 1763.

There is a tissue of errors here. The pictograph, "drawn with charcoal and oil on a tree," must have been quite recent, and is not likely to have referred to events seventeen years antecedent. There is no evidence that Wingenund took part in Pontiac's conspiracy, and he was the consistent friend of

---

[1] John Richardson's Diary, quoted in *An Account of the Conduct of the Society of Friends toward the Indian Tribes*, pp. 61, 62 (London, 1844).

[2] *History and Statistics of the Indian Tribes*, Vol. I, plate 47, B, and pages 353, 354.

the whites.[1] Several of the characters are not like Indian pictographs. And finally, White Eyes, the alleged interpreter in 1780, had died at Tuscarawas, two years before, Nov. 10th, 1778![2]

Record Sticks.

The Algonkin nations very generally preserved their myths, their chronicles, and the memory of events, speeches, etc., by means of marked sticks. As early as 1646, the Jesuit missionaries in Canada made use of these to teach their converts the prayers of the Church and their sermons.[3]

The name applied to these record or tally sticks was, among the Crees and Chipeways, *massinahigan*, which is the common word now for book, but which originally meant "a piece of wood marked with fire," from the verb *masinákisan*, I imprint a mark upon it with fire, I burn a mark upon it,[4] thus indicating the rude beginning of a system of mnemonic aids. The Lenape words for book, *malackhickan*, Camp., *mamalekhican* Zeis., were probably from the same root.

In later days, instead of burning the marks upon the sticks, they were painted, the colors as well as the figures having certain conventional meanings.[5]

These sticks are described as about six inches in length, slender, though varying in shape, and tied up in bundles.[6]

---

[1] "Amiable and benevolent," says Heckewelder, whose life he aided in saving on one occasion. *Indian Nations*, p. 285.

[2] E. de Schweinitz, *Life of Zeisberger*, p. 469.

[3] *Relation des Jesuites*, 1646, p. 33.

[4] Baraga, *A Dictionary of the Otchipwe Language*, s. v.

[5] For an example, see de Schweinitz, *Life of Zeisberger*, p. 342.

[6] *Documentary History of New York*, Vol. IV, p. 437.

Such bundles are mentioned by the interpreter Conrad Weiser, as in use in 1748 when he was on his embassy in the Indian country.[1] The expression, "we tied up in bundles," is translated by Mr. Heckewelder, *olumapisid*, and a head chief of the Lenape, usually called *Olomipees*, was thus named, apparently as preserver of such records.[2] I shall return on a later page to the precise meaning of this term.

The word signifying to paint was *walamén*, which does not appear in western dialects, but is found precisely the same in the Abnaki, where it is given by Rasles, *8ramann*,[3] which, transliterated into Delaware (where the *l* is substituted for the *r*), would be *w'lam'an*. From this word came *Wallamünk*, the name applied by the natives to a tract in New Castle county, Delaware, since at that locality they procured supplies of colored earth, which they employed in painting. It means "the place of paint."[4]

Roger Williams, describing the New England Indians,

---

[1] *Journal of Conrad Weiser*, in *Early History of Western Penna.*, p. 16.

[2] *Trans. Am. Phil. Soc.*, Vol. IV, p. 384.

[3] *A Dictionary of the Abnaki Language*, s. v. *Peinture*.

[4] See anté p. 53. Mr. Francis Vincent, in his *History of the State of Delaware*, p. 36 (Phila., 1870), says of the colored earth of that locality, that it is "a highly argillaceous loam, interspersed with large and frequent masses of yellow, ochrey clay, some of which are remarkable for fineness of texture, not unlike lithomarge, and consists of white, yellow, red and dark blue clay in detached spots."

The Shawnees applied the same word to Paint Creek, which falls into the Scioto, close to Chilicothe. They named it *Alamonce sepee*, of which Paint Creek is a literal rendering. Rev. David Jones, *A Journal of Two Visits to the West Side of the Ohio in 1772 and 1773*, p. 50.

speaks of " *Wunnam*, their red painting, which they most delight in, and is both the Barke of the Pine, as also a red Earth."[1]

The word is derived from Narr. *wunne*, Del. *wulit*, Chip. *gwanatsch* = beautiful, handsome, good, pretty, etc.

The Indian who had artistically bedaubed his skin with red, ochreous clay, was esteemed in full dress, and delightful to look upon. Hence the term *wulit*, fine, pretty, came to be applied to the paint itself.

The custom of using such sticks, painted or notched, was by no means peculiar to the Delawares. They were familiar to the Iroquois, and the early travelers found them in common employment among the southern tribes.[2]

As the art advanced, in place of simple sticks, painted or notched, wooden tablets came into use, on which the symbols were scratched or engraved with a sharp flint or knife. Such are those still in use among the Chipeway, described by Dr. James as " rude pictures carved on a flat piece of wood;"[3] by the native Copway, as " board plates;"[4] and more precisely

---

[1] *Key into the Language of America*, p. 206.

[2] Lawson, in his *New Account of Carolina*, p. 180, says that the natives there bore in mind their traditions by means of a " Parcel of Reeds of different Lengths, with several distinct Marks, known to none but themselves." James Adair writes of the Southern Indians : "They count certain very remarkable things by notched square sticks, which are distributed among the head warriors and other chieftains of different towns." *History of the Indians*, p. 75.

[3] Dr. Edwin James, *Narrative of John Tanner*, p. 341.

[4] George Copway, *Traditional History of the Ojibway Nation*, pp. 130, 131.

by Mr. Schoolcraft, as "a tabular piece of wood, covered on both sides with a series of devices cut between parallel lines."[1]

The Chipeway terms applied to these devices or symbols are, according to Mr. Schoolcraft, *kekeewin*, for those in ordinary and common use, and *kekeenowin*, for those connected with the mysteries, the "meda worship" and the "great medicine." Both words are evidently from a radical signifying a mark or sign, appearing in the words given in Baraga's "Otchipwe Dictionary," *kikinawadjiton*, I mark it, I put a certain mark on it, and *kikinoamawa*, I teach, instruct him.

Moral and Mental Character.

The character of the Delawares was estimated very differently, even by those who had the best opportunities of judging. The missionaries are severe upon them. Brainerd described them as " unspeakably indolent and slothful. They have little or no ambition or resolution ; not one in a thousand of them that has the spirit of a man."[2] No more favorable was the opinion of Zeisberger. He speaks of their alleged bravery with the utmost contempt, and morally he puts them down as "the most ordinary and the vilest of savages."[3]

Perhaps these worthy missionaries measured them by the standard of the Christian ideal, by which, alas, we all fall wofully short.

Certainly, other competent observers report much more

---

[1] Schoolcraft, *Indian Tribes*, Vol. I, p. 339.

[2] Brainerd, *Life and Journal*, p. 410.

[3] E. de Schweinitz, *Life and Times of Zeisberger*, p. 92.

cheerfully. One of the first explorers of the Delaware, Captain Thomas Young (1634), describes them as "very well proportioned, well featured, gentle, tractable and docile."[1]

Of their domestic affections, Mr. Heckewelder writes: "I do not believe that there are any people on earth who are more attached to their relatives and offspring than these Indians are."[2]

Their action toward the Society of Friends in Pennsylvania indicates a sense of honor and a respect for pledges which we might not expect. They had learned and well understood that the Friends were non-combatants, and as such they never forgot to spare them, even in the bloody scenes of border warfare.

"Amidst all the devastating incursions of the Indians in North America, it is a remarkable fact that no Friend who stood faithful to his principles in the disuse of all weapons of war, the cause of which was generally well understood by the Indians, ever suffered personal molestation from them."[3]

The fact that for more than forty years after the founding of Penn's colony there was not a single murder committed on a settler by an Indian, itself speaks volumes for their self-control and moral character. So far from seeking quarrels

---

[1] *Mass. Hist. Soc. Colls.*, 4th series, Vol. IX, where Captain Young's journal is printed.

[2] *Heckewelder MSS.* in Amer Phil. Soc. Lib.

[3] *An Account of the Conduct of the Society of Friends toward the Indian Tribes*, p. 72 (London, 1844).

with the whites they extended them friendly aid and comfort.[1]

Even after they had become embittered and corrupted by the gross knavery of the whites (for example, the notorious "long walk,") and the debasing influence of alcohol, such an authority as Gen. Wm. H. Harrison could write these words about the Delawares : "A long and intimate knowledge of them, in peace and war, as enemies and friends, has left upon my mind the most favorable impression of their character for bravery, generosity and fidelity to their engagements."[2] More than this, and from a higher source, could scarcely be asked.

That intellectually they were by no means deficient is acknowledged by Brainerd himself. "The children," he

---

[1] The records of my own family furnish an example of this. My ancestor, William Brinton, arrived in the fall of 1684, and, with his wife and children, immediately took possession of a grant in the unbroken wilderness, about twenty miles from Philadelphia. A severe winter set in ; their food supply was exhausted, and they would probably have perished but for the assistance of some neighboring lodges of Lenape, who provided them with food and shelter. It is, therefore, a debt of gratitude which I owe to this nation to gather its legends, its language, and its memories, so that they,

> "In books recorded,
> May, like hoarded
> Household words, no more depart !"

[2] *A Discourse on the Aborigines of the Valley of the Ohio*, p. 25 (Cinn., 1838). I add the further testimony of John Brickell, who was a captive among them from 1791 to 1796. He speaks of them as fairly virtuous and temperate, and adds : "Honesty, bravery and hospitality are cardinal virtues among them." *Narrative of Captivity among the Delaware Indians*, in the *American Pioneer*, Vol. I, p. 48 (Cincinnati, 1844).

writes, "learn with surprising readiness; their master tells me he never had an English school that learned, in general, so fast."[1]

Religious Beliefs.

With the hints given us in various authors, it is not difficult to reconstruct the primitive religious notions of the Delawares. They resembled closely those of the other Algonkin nations, and were founded on those general mythical principles which, in my "Myths of the New World," I have shown existed widely throughout America. These are, the worship of Light, especially in its concrete manifestations of fire and the sun; of the Four Winds, as typical of the cardinal points, and as the rain bringers; and of the Totemic Animal.

As the embodiment of Light, some spoke of the sun as a deity,[2] while their fifth and greatest festival was held in honor of Fire, which they personified, and called the Grandfather of all Indian nations. They assigned to it twelve divine assistants, who were represented by so many actors in the ceremony, with evident reference to the twelve moons or months of the year, the fire being a type of the heavenly blaze, the sun.[3]

But both Sun and Fire were only material emblems of the mystery of Light. This was the " body or fountain of deity," which Brainerd said they described to him in terms that he could not clearly understand; something "all light;" a being

---

[1] *Life and Journal*, p. 381.

[2] " Others imagined the Sun to be the only deity, and that all things were made by him." David Brainerd, *Life and Journal*, p. 395.

[3] Loskiel, *Geschichte der Mission*, p. 55.

"*in* whom the earth, and all things in it, may be seen;" a "great man, clothed with the day, yea, with the brightest day, a day of many years, yea, a day of everlasting continuance." From him proceeded, in him were, to him returned, all things and the souls of all things.

Such was the extraordinary doctrine which a converted priest of the native religion informed Brainerd was the teaching of the medicine men.[1]

The familiar Algonkin myth of the "Great Hare," which I have elsewhere shown to be distinctively a myth of Light,[2] was also well known to the Delawares, and they applied to this animal, also, the appellation of the "Grandfather of the Indians."[3] Like the fire, the hare was considered their ancestor, and in both instances the Light was meant, fire being its symbol, and the word for hare being identical with that of brightness and light.

As in Mexico and elsewhere, this light or bright ancestor was the culture hero of their mythology, their pristine instructor in the arts, and figured in some of their legends as a white man, who, in some remote time, visited them from the east, and brought them their civilization.[4]

I desire to lay especial stress on these proofs of Light worship among the Delawares, for it has an immediate bearing on several points in the WALAM OLUM. There are no com-

[1] David Brainerd, *Life and Journal*, pp. 395, 399.

[2] D. G. Brinton, *The Myths of the New World*, chap. vi; *American Hero Myths*, chap. ii.

[3] Loskiel, *Geschichte der Mission*, p. 53.

[4] He is thus spoken of in Campanius, *Account of New Sweden*, Book III, chap. xi. Compare my *Myths of the New World*, p. 190.

pounds more frequent in that document than those with the root signifying "light," "brightness," etc. ; and this is one of the evidences of its authenticity.

Next in order, or rather, parallel with and a part of the worship of Light, was that of the Four Cardinal Points, always identified with the Four Winds, the bringers of rain and sunshine, the rulers of the weather.

"After the strictest inquiry respecting their notions of the Deity," says David Brainerd, "I find that in ancient times, before the coming of the white people, some supposed there were four invisible powers, who presided over the four corners of the earth."[1]

The Montauk Indians of Long Island, a branch of the Mohegans, also worshiped these four deities, as we are informed by the Rev. Sampson Occum ;[2] and Captain Argoll found them again in 1616 among the accolents of the Potomac, close relatives of the Delawares. Their chief told him : "We have five gods in all; our chief god appears often unto us in the form of a mighty great hare ; the other four have no visible shape, but are indeed the four winds, which keep the four corners of the earth."[3]

These are the fundamental doctrines, the universal *credo*, of not only all the Algonkin faiths, but of all or nearly all primitive American religions.

This is very far from the popular conception of Indian religion, with its "Good Spirit" and "Bad Spirit." Such

---

[1] Brainerd, *Life and Journal*, p. 395.

[2] His statements are in the *Colls. of the Mass. Hist. Soc.*, Vol. X (1st Series), p. 108.

[3] Wm. Strachey, *Historie of Travaile into Virginia*, p. 98.

ideas were not familiar to the native mind. Heckewelder,
Brainerd and Loskiel all assure us in positive terms that the
notion of a bad spirit, a "Devil," was wholly unknown
to the aborigines, and entirely borrowed from the whites.
Nor was the Divinity of Light looked upon as a benefi-
cent father, or anything of that kind. The Indian did not
appeal to him for assistance, as to his *totemic and personal
gods.*

These were conceived to be in the form of animals, and
various acts of propitiation to them were performed. Such
acts were not a worship of the animals themselves. Brainerd
explains this very correctly when he says: "They do not
suppose a divine power essential to or inhering in these
creatures, but that some invisible beings, not distinguished
from each other by certain names, but only notionally,
communicate to these animals a great power, and so make
these creatures the immediate authors of good to certain
persons. Hence such a creature becomes *sacred* to the
person to whom he is supposed to be the immediate author
of good, and through him they must worship the invisible powers, though to others he is no more than another
creature." [1]

They rarely attempted to set forth the divinity in image.
The rude representation of a human head, cut in wood, small
enough to be carried on the person, or life size on a post, was
their only idol. This was called *wsinkhoalican.* They also
drew and perhaps carved emblems of their totemic guardian.
Mr. Beatty describes the head chief's home as a long building
of wood: "Over the door a turtle is drawn, which is the

---

[1] Brainerd, *Life and Travels,* p. 394.

ensign of this particular tribe. On each door post was cut the face of a grave old man."[1]

Occasionally, rude representations of the human head, chipped out of stone, are exhumed in those parts of Pennsylvania and New Jersey once inhabited by the Lenape.[2] These are doubtless the *wsinkhoalican* above mentioned.

Doctrine of the Soul.

There was a general belief in a soul, spirit or immaterial part of man. For this the native words were *tschipey* and *tschitschank* (in Brainerd, *chichuny*). The former is derived from a root signifying to be separate or apart, while the latter means " the shadow."[3]

Their doctrine was that after death the soul went *south*, where it would enjoy a happy life for a certain term, and then could return and be born again into the world. In moments of spiritual illumination it was deemed possible to

---

[1] Charles Beatty, *Journal*, p. 44.

[2] One, about five inches in height, of a tough, argillaceous stone, is figured and described by Dr. C. C. Abbott, in the *American Naturalist*, October, 1882. It was found in New Jersey.

[3] From the same root, *tschip*, are derived the Lenape *tschipilek*, something strange or wonderful ; *tschepsit*, a stranger or foreigner ; and *tschapiet*, the invocation of spirits. Among the rules agreed upon by Zeisberger's converted Indians was this: " We will use no *tschapiet*, or witchcraft, when hunting." (De Schweinitz, *Life of Zeisberger*, p. 379.)

The root *tschitsch* indicates repetition, and applied to the shadow or spirit of man means as much as his double or counterpart.

A third word for soul was the verbal form *w'tellenapewoagan*, " man— his substance ;" but this looks as if it had been manufactured by the missionaries.

recall past existences, and even to remember the happy epoch passed in the realm of bliss.[1]

The path to this abode of the blessed was by the Milky Way, wherein the opinion of the Delawares coincided with that of various other American nations, as the Eskimos, on the north, and the Guaranis of Paraguay, on the south.

The ordinary euphemism to inform a person that his death was at hand was: "You are about to visit your ancestors;"[2] but most observers agree that they were a timorous people, with none of that contempt of death sometimes assigned them.[3]

The Native Priests.

An important class among the Lenape were those called by the whites doctors, conjurers, or medicine men, who were really the native priests. They appear to have been of two schools, the one devoting themselves mainly to divination, the other to healing.

According to Brainerd, the title of the former among the Delawares, as among the New England Indians, was *powwow*, a word meaning "a dreamer;" Chip., *bawadjagan*, a dream; *nind apawe*, I dream; Cree, *pawa-miwin*, a dream. They were the interpreters of the dreams of others, and themselves claimed the power of dreaming truthfully of the future and the absent.[4] In their visions their guardian spirit visited

---

[1] Compare Loskiel, *Geschichte*, pp. 48, 49; Brainerd, *Life and Journal*, pp. 314, 396, 399, 400.

[2] Schweinitz, *Life of Zeisberger*, p. 472.

[3] Heckewelder, MSS., says that he has often heard the lamentable cry, *matta wingi angeln*, "I do not want to die."

[4] "As for the Powaws," says the native Mohegan, the Rev. Sampson Occum, in his account of the Montauk Indians of Long Island, "they

them ; they became, in their own words, "all light," and
they "could see through men, and knew the thoughts of
their hearts."[1]   At such times they were also instructed at
what spot the hunters could successfully seek game.

The other school of the priestly class was called, as we are
informed by Mr. Heckewelder, *medeu*.[2] This is the same
term which we find in Chipeway as *mide* (*medaween*, Schoolcraft), and in Cree as *mitew*, meaning a conjurer, a member
of the Great Medicine Lodge.[3] I suspect the word is from
m'iteh, heart (Chip. *k'ide*, thy heart), as this organ was considered the source and centre of life and the emotions, and
is constantly spoken of in a figurative sense in Indian conversation and oratory.

Among the natives around New York Bay there was a body
of conjurers who professed great austerity of life. They had
no fixed homes, pretended to absolute continence, and both
exorcised sickness and officiated at the funeral rites. Their
name, as reported by the Dutch, was *kitzinacka*, which is
evidently Great Snake (*gitschi*, *achkook*). The interesting
fact is added, that at certain periodical festivals a sacrifice

<hr />

say they get their art from dreams." *Mass. Hist. Soc. Colls.*, Vol. X,
p. 109. Dr. Trumbull's suggested affinity of powaw with Cree *táp-
wayoo*, he speaks the truth; Nar., *taupowauog*, wise speakers, is, I
think, correct; but the latter are secondary senses. They were wise, and
gave true counsel, who could correctly interpret dreams. Compare the
Iroquois *katetsens*, to dream; *katetsiens*, to practice medicine, Indian
fashion. Cuoq, *Lexique de la Langue Iroquoise.*

[1] David Brainerd, *Life and Journal*, pp. 400, 401.

[2] *Hist. Ind. Nations*, p. 280.

[3] *Hist. and Statistics of the Indian Tribes*, Vol. I, p. 358, seq.

was prepared, which it was believed was carried off by a huge serpent.[1]

When the missionaries came among the Indians, the shrewd and able natives who had been accustomed to practice on the credulity of their fellows recognized that the new faith would destroy their power, and therefore they attacked it vigorously. Preachers arose among them, and claimed to have had communications from the Great Spirit about all the matters which the Christian teachers talked of. These native exhorters fabricated visions and revelations, and displayed symbolic drawings on deerskins, showing the journey of the soul after death, the path to heaven, the twelve emetics and purges which would clean a man of sin, etc.

Such were the famed prophets Papunhank and Wangomen, who set up as rivals in opposition to David Zeisberger; and such those who so constantly frustrated the efforts of the pious Brainerd. Often do both of these self-sacrificing apostles to the Indians complain of the evil influence which such false teachers exerted among the Delawares.[2]

The existence of this class of impostors is significant for the appreciation of such a document as the WALAM OLUM. They were partially acquainted with the Bible history of

---

[1] Wassenaer's *Description of the New Netherlands* (1631), in *Doc. Hist. of New York*, Vol. III, pp. 28, 40. Other signs of serpent worship were common among the Lenape. Loskiel states that their cast-off skins were treasured as possessing wonderful curative powers (*Geschichte*, p. 147), and Brainerd saw an Indian offering supplications to one (*Life and Journal*, p. 395).

[2] See Brainerd, *Life and Journal*, pp. 310, 312, 364, 398, 425, etc., and E. de Schweinitz, *Life of Zeisberger*, pp. 265, 332, etc.

creation; some had learned to read and write in the mission schools; they were eager to imitate the wisdom of the whites, while at the same time they were intent on claiming authentic antiquity and originality for all their sayings.

Religious Ceremonies.

The principal sacred ceremony was the dance and accompanying song. This was called *kanti kanti*, from a verbal found in most Algonkin dialects with the primary meaning to sing (Abnaki, *skan*, je danse et chante en même temps, Rasles; Cree, *nikam;* Chip., *nigam*, I sing). From this noisy rite, which seems to have formed a part of all the native celebrations, the settlers coined the word *cantico*, which has survived and become incorporated into the English tongue.

Zeisberger describes other festivals, some five in number. The most interesting is that called *Machtoga*, which he translates "to sweat." This was held in honor of "their Grandfather, the Fire." The number twelve appears in it frequently as regulating the actions and numbers of the performers. This had evident reference to the twelve months of the year, but his description is too vague to allow a satisfactory analysis of the rite.

CHAPTER IV.

THE LITERATURE AND LANGUAGE OF THE LENAPE.

§ 1. Literature of the Lenape Tongue.—Campanius; Penn; Thomas; Zeisberger; Heckewelder; Roth; Ettwein; Grube; Dencke; Luckenbach; Henry; Vocabularies; a native letter.

§ 2. General Remarks on the Lenape.

§ 3. Dialects of the Lenape.

§ 4. Special Structure of the Lenape.—The Root and the Theme; Prefixes; Suffixes; Derivatives; Grammatical Notes.

§ 1. *Literature of the Lenape Tongue.*

The first study of the Delaware language was undertaken by the Rev. Thomas Campanius (Holm), who was chaplain to the Swedish settlements, 1642-1649. He collected a vocabulary, wrote out a number of dialogues in Delaware and Swedish, and even completed a translation of the Lutheran catechism into the tongue. The last mentioned was published in Stockholm, in 1696, through the efforts of his grandson, under the title, LUTHERI CATECHISMUS, *Ofwersatt på American-Virginiskè Språket*, 1 vol., sm. 8vo, pp. 160. On pages 133–154 it has a *Vocabularium Barbaro-Virgineorum*, and on pages 155–160, *Vocabula Mahakuassica*. The first is the Delaware as then current on the lower river, the second the dialect of the Susquehannocks or Minquas, who frequently visited the Swedish settlements.

Although he managed to render all the Catechism into something which looks like Delaware, Campanius' knowledge of the tongue was exceedingly superficial. Dr. Trumbull says of his work: "The translator had not learned even so

much of the grammar as to distinguish the plural of a noun
or verb from the singular, and knew nothing of the "transitions" by which the pronouns of the subject and object are
blended with the verb." [1]

At the close of his "History of New Sweden," Campanius
adds further linguistic material, including an imaginary conversation in Lenape, and the oration of a sachem.   It is of
the same character as that found in the Catechism.

After the English occupation very little attention was given
to the tongue beyond what was indispensable to trading.
William Penn, indeed, professed to have acquired a mastery
of it.   He writes: "I have made it my business to understand it, that I might not want an interpreter on any occasion."[2]   But it is evident, from the specimens he gives,
that all he studied was the trader's jargon, which scorned
etymology, syntax and prosody, and was about as near
pure Lenape as pigeon English is to the periods of Ma-
caulay.

An ample specimen of this jargon is furnished us by Gabriel
Thomas, in his "Historical and Geographical Account of
the Province and Country of Pensilvania; and of West-New-
Jersey in America," London, 1698, dedicated to Penn.
Thomas tells us that he lived in the country fifteen years,
and supplies, for the convenience of those who propose visiting the province, some forms of conversation, Indian and
English.   I subjoin a short specimen, with a brief commentary :—

---

[1] *Transactions of the American Philological Association*, 1872, p. 158.

[2] Penn, Letter to the Free Society of Traders, 1683, Sec. xii.

1. *Hitah takoman?*	Friend, from whence com'st?
2. *Andogowa nee weekin.*	Yonder.
3. *Tony andogowa kee weekin?*	Where yonder?
4. *Arwaymouse.*	At Arwaymouse.
5. *Keco kee hatah weekin?*	What hast got in thy house?
6. *Nee hatah huska weesyouse og huska chetena chase og huska orit chekenip.*	I have very fat venison and good strong skins, with very good turkeys.
7. *Chingo kee beto nee chasa ag yousa etka chekenip?*	When wilt thou bring me skins and venison, with turkeys?
8. *Halapa etka nisha kishquicka.*	To-morrow, or two days hence.

1. *Hitah* for *n'ischu* (Mohegan, *nitap*), my friend; *takoman*, Zeis. *takomun*, from *ta*, where, *k*, 2d pers. sing.

2. *Andogowa*, similar to *undachwe*, he comes, Heck.; *nee*, pron. possess. 1st person; *weekin = wikwam*, or wigwam. "I come from my house."

3. *Tony*, = Zeis. *tani*, where? *kee*, pron. possess. 2d person.

4. *Arwaymouse* was the name of an Indian village, near Burlington, N. J.

5. *Keco*, Zeis. *koccu*, what? *hatah*, Zeis. *hattin*, to have.

6. *Huska*, Zeis. *husca*, "very, truly;" *wees*, Zeis. *wisu*, fatty flesh, *youse*, R. W. *jous*, deer meat; *og*, Camp.. *ock*, Zeis. *woak* and; *chetena*, Zeis. *tschitani*, strong; *chase*, Z. *chessak*, deerskin; *orit*, Zeis. *wulit*, good; *chekenip*, Z. *tschekenum*, turkey.

7. *Chingo*, Zeis. *tschingatsch*, when; *beto*, Z. *peten*, to bring; *etka*, R. W., *ka*, and.

8. *Halapa*, Z. *alappa*, to-morrow; *nisha*, two; *kishquicka*, Z. *gischgu*, day, *gischguik*, by day.

The principal authority on the Delaware language is the Rev. David Zeisberger, the eminent Moravian missionary, whose long and devoted labors may be accepted as fixing the standard of the tongue.

Before him, no one had seriously set to work to master the structure of the language, and reduce it to a uniform orthography. With him, it was almost a lifelong study, as for more than sixty years it engaged his attention. To his devotion to the cause in which he was engaged, he added considerable natural talent for languages, and learned to speak, with almost equal fluency, English, German, Delaware and the Onondaga and Mohawk dialects of the Iroquois.

The first work he gave to the press was a "Delaware Indian and English Spelling Book for the Schools of the Mission of the United Brethren," printed in Philadelphia, 1776. As he did not himself see the proofs, he complained that both in its arrangement and typographical accuracy it was disappointing. Shortly before his death, in 1806, the second edition appeared, amended in these respects. A "Hymn Book," in Delaware, which he finished in 1802, was printed the following year, and the last work of his life, a translation into Delaware of Lieberkuhn's "History of Christ," was published at New York in 1821.

These, however, formed but a small part of the manuscript materials he had prepared on and in the language. The most important of these were his Delaware Grammar, and his Dictionary in four languages, English, German, Onondaga and Delaware.

The MS. of the Grammar was deposited in the Archives of the Moravian Society at Bethlehem, Pa. A translation of it was prepared by Mr. Peter Stephen Duponceau, and published

in the "Transactions of the American Philosophical Society,"
in 1827.

The quadrilingual dictionary has never been printed. The
MS. was presented, along with others, in 1850, to the library
of Harvard College, where it now is. The volume is an
oblong octavo of 362 pages, containing about 9000 words
in the English and German columns, but not more than half
that number in the Delaware.

A number of other MSS. of Zeisberger are also in that
library, received from the same source. Among these are a
German-Delaware Glossary, containing 51 pages and about
600 words; a Delaware-German Phrase Book of about 200
pages; Sermons in Delaware, etc., mostly incomplete studies,
but of considerable value to the student of the tongue.[1]

Associated with Zeisberger for many years was the genial
Rev. John Heckewelder, so well known for his pleasant
"History of the Indian Nations of Pennsylvania," his in-
terpretations of the Indian names of the State, and his correspondence with Mr. Duponceau. He certainly had a fluent,
practical knowledge of the Delaware, but it has repeatedly
been shown that he lacked analytical power in it, and that
many of his etymologies as well as some of his grammatical
statements are erroneous.

Another competent Lenapist was the Rev. Johannes Roth.
He was born in Prussia in 1726, and educated a Catholic.
Joining the Moravians in 1748, he emigrated to America in
1756, and in 1759 took charge of the missionary station called

---

[1] On the literary works of Zeisberger, see Rev. E. de Schweinitz, *Life
of Zeisberger*, chap. xlviii, who gives a full account of all the printed
works, but does not describe the MSS.

Schechschiquanuk, on the west bank of the Susquehanna, opposite and a little below Shesequin, in Bradford county, Pennsylvania.   There he remained until 1772, when, with his flock, fifty-three in number, he proceeded to the new Gnadenhütten, in Ohio.   There a son was born to him, the first white child in the area of the present State of Ohio.   In 1774 he returned to Pennsylvania, and after occupying various pastorates, he died at York, July 22d, 1791.

Roth has left us a most important work, and one hitherto entirely unknown to bibliographers.   He made an especial study of the *Unami dialect* of the Lenape, and composed in it an extensive religious work, of which only the fifth part remains.   It is now in the possession of the American Philosophical Society, and bears the title :—

Ein Versuch !

der Geschichte unsers Herrn u. Heylandes

Jesu Christi

in dass Delawarische übersetzt der *Unami*

von der Marter Woche an

bis zur

Himmelfahrt unsers Herrn

im

Yahr 1770 u. 72 zu Tschechschequanüng

an

der Susquehanna.

Wuntschi mesettschawi tipatta lammowewoagan sekauchsianup. Wulapensuhalinēn, Woehowaolan Nihillalijeng mPatamauwoss.

The next page begins, "Der fünfte Theil," and § 86, and proceeds to § 139.   It forms a quarto volume, of title, 9 pages of contents in German and English, and 268 pages of text in Unami, written in a clear hand, with many corrections and interlineations.

This is the only work known to me as composed distinctively in the Unami, and its value is proportionately great as providing the means of studying this, the acknowledged most cultivated and admired of the Lenape dialects.

It will be the task of some future Lenape scholar to edit its text and analyze its grammatical forms. But I believe that Algonkin students will be glad to see at this time an extract from its pages.

I select § 96, which is the parable of the marriage feast of the king's son, as given in Matthew xxii, 1-14.

1. Wonk   Jesus   wtabptonalawoll   woak   lapi   nuwuntschi
   And   Jesus   he-spoke-with-them   and   again   he-began

Enendhackewoagannall   nelih*   woak   wtellawoll.
   parables   them-to   and   he-said-to-them.

2. Ne   Wusakimawoagan   Patamauwoss   { wtellgigui / mallaschi }
   The   his-kingdom   God   it-is-like

mejauchsid*   Sakima,   na Quisall   mall'nitauwan   Witach-
   certain   king,   his-son   he-made-for-him   mar-

pungewiwuladtpoàgan.
   riage.

3. Woak   wtellallocàlan   wtallocacannall,   wentschitsch   nek
   And   he-sent-out   his-servants   the-bidding   the

Elendpannik   lih*   Witachpungewiwuladtpoàgannüng   wentsch-
   those-bidden   to   marriage   those-

imcussowoak;   tschuk   necamawa   schingipawak.
   who-were-bidden,   but   they   they-were-unwilling.

4. Woak   lapi   wtellallocàlan   pili   wtallocacannall   woak
   And   again   he-sent-out   other   servants   and

wtella { panni / wolli };   Mauwiloh   nen   Elendpannik,   { penna / schita }
   he-said-to-them   those   the-bidden

Nolachtüppoágan 'nkischachtüppui, nihillalachkik Wisuheng-
The-feast I-have-made-the-feast, they-are-killed they-fattened-

pannik auwessissak nemætschi nhillapannick woak weemi
them beasts the-whole I-killed-them and all

ktaköcku 'ngischachtüppui, peeltik lih Witachpungkewi-
I-have-finished come to mar-

wuladtpoàgannüng.
riage.

5. Tschuk necamawa mattelĕmawoawollnenni, woak ewak
But they they-esteemed-it-not and went

ika, mejauchsid enda wtakihàcannüng, napilli nihillatschi
away certain thither to-his-plantation-place other

{ M'hallamawachtowoagannüng }
{ Nundauchsowoagannüng }.
to-merchandise-place.

6. Tschuk allende wtahunnawoawoll neca allocacannall
But some they-seized-them those servants

{ quochkikimäwoawoll }
{ popochpoalimawoawoll } woak wunihillawoawoll necamawa.
they-beat-them and they-killed-them they.

7. Elinenni na* Sakima pentanke, nannen lachxu,
When the king heard therefore he-was-angry,

woak wtellallokalan Ndopaluwinūwak, woak wunihillawunga
and he-sent-them warriors and he-slew

jok Nehhillowetschik, woak wūlusümen Wtutèn'nejuwaowoll.
these murderers, and he-destroyed their-cities.

8. Nannen wtella { woll }
{ panni } nelih wtallocacannall : Ne
Then he-said-to-them to his-servants The

Witachpungkewiwuladtpoagan khella nkischachtüppui, tschuk
marriage truly I-have-prepared-it but

nek Elendpannick { attacu uchtàpsiwunewo }
{ wtopielgique juwunewo }.
the those-bidden are-not-to-sit-down-worthy.

9. Nowentschi allmŭssin ikali mengichüngi Ansijall, woak
Therefore go-ye-away thither to-some-places roads and

winawammoh   lih Witachpungkewiwuladtpoagan ;   na   natta
ask-ye-them   to   marriage   those

aween *kiluwa* mechkaweek (oh).
whom   ye   find.

10. Woak nek Allocacannak iwak ikali menggichüngi
     And   the   servants   they-went thither to-some-places

Aneijall, woak mawehawoawoll   peschuwoawak   na   natta
roads   and   they-brought-them-together those

aween machkawoachtid, Memannungsitschik woak Wewu-
whom   they-found-them   the-bad-ones   and   the-

lilossitschik, woak nel* Ehendachpuingkill weemi tæphikka-
good-ones   and   the   at-the-tables   all   they-

wachtinewo.
seated.

11. Nannen mattemikæùh na Sakima, nek Elendpannik
     Then   he-entered-in the king   the   those-bidden

mauwi pennawoawoll, woak wunewoawoll uchtenda me-
       he-saw-them   and   he-saw-him   there   cer-

jauchsid Lenno, na matta uchtellachquiwon witachpungkewi
tain   man   the not   wearing   a marriage

Schakhokquiwan.
coat.

12. Woak wtellawoll neli ;* Elanggomëllen, ktelgiquiki
     And   he-said-to-him to-him   Friend   like   .

matte attemikën jun (*or* tá elinàquo wentschi jun k'mattī-
not   ashamed   here   not   like   therefore here thou-art-

mikeen,) ; woak { müngachsa*   mattacu witachpungkewi
                    ilik*   }
ashamed   and   not   marriage

Schakhokquiwan ktellachquiwon ? Necama tschuk k'pettúneù.
coat   thou wearest   He   but   he-mouth-shuts.

13. Nannen w'tellawoll na Sakima nelih* Wtallocacan-
     Then   he-said-to-them the king   to-them   his-ser-

nüng; Kachpiluh { nan   Wunachkall woak W'sittall, woak
                    woan }
vants Fasten-ye-him   his-hands   and   his-feet   and

lannéhewik quatschemung   enda   achwipegnünk, nitschlenda
  throw-him   where in pitch-darkness even-some

Lipackcuwoagan   woak   Tschætschak   koalochinen.
 weeping   and   teeth-gnashing

 14. Ntîtechquoh   macheli   mœtschi   wentschimcussuwak,
    Because   many   they-are-called

tschuk   tatthiluwak   achnæknuksitschik.
but they-are-few   the-chosen.

The asterisk occurs in the original apparently to indicate
that a word is superfluous or doubtful.   The interlined
translation I have supplied from the materials in the mission-
Delaware dialect, but my resources have not been sufficient
to analyze each word ; and this, indeed, is not necessary for
my purpose, which is merely to present an example of the
true Unami dialect.

The Moravian Bishop, John Ettwein, was another of their
fraternity who applied himself to the study of the Delaware.
Born in Europe in 1712, he came to the New World in 1754,
and died at the great age of ninety years in 1802.   He prepared a small dictionary and phrase book, especially rich in
verbal forms.   It is an octavo MS. of 88 pages, without title,
and comprises about 1300 entries.   This manuscript exists in
one copy only, in the Moravian Archives at Bethlehem.

Bishop Ettwein also prepared for General Washington, in
1788, an account of the traditions and language of the natives,
including a vocabulary.   This was found among the Washington papers by Mr. Jared Sparks, and was published in the
"Bulletin of the Pennsylvania Historical Society," 1848.

One of the most laborious of the Moravian missionaries
was the Rev. Adam Grube.   His life spanned nearly a century, from 1715, when he was born in Germany, until 1808,

when he died in Bethlehem, Pa. Many years of this were spent among the Delawares in Pennsylvania and Ohio. He was familiar with their language, but the only evidence of his study of it that has come to my knowledge is a MS. in the Harvard College Library, entitled, "Einige Delawarische Redensarten und Worte." It has seventy-five useful leaves, the entries without alphabetic arrangement, some of the verbs accompanied by partial inflections. The only date it bears is "Oct. 10, 1800," when he presented it to the Rev. Mr. Luckenbach, soon to be mentioned.

After the War of 1812 the Moravian brother, Rev. C. F. Dencke, who, ten years before had attempted to teach the Gospel to the Chipeways, gathered together the scattered converts among the Delawares at New Fairfield, Canada West. In 1818 he completed and forwarded to the Publication Board of the American Bible Society a translation of the Epistles of John, which was published the same year.

He also stated to the Board that at that time he had finished a translation of John's Gospel and commenced that of Matthew, both of which he expected to send to the Board in that year. A donation of one hundred dollars was made to him to encourage him in his work, but for some reason the prosecution of his labors was suspended, and the translation of the Gospels never appeared (contrary to the statements in some bibliographies).

It is probable that Mr. Dencke was the compiler of the Delaware Dictionary which is preserved in the Moravian Archives at Bethlehem. The MS. is an oblong octavo, in a fine, but beautifully clear hand, and comprises about 3700 words. The handwriting is that of the late Rev. Mr. Kamp-

man, from 1840 to 1842 missionary to the Delawares on the
Canada Reservation.   On inquiring the circumstances connected with this MS., he stated to me that it was written at
the period named, and was a copy of some older work, probably by Mr. Dencke, but of this he was not certain.

While the greater part of this dictionary is identical in
words and rendering with the second edition of Zeisberger's
"Spelling Book" (with which I have carefully compared it),
it also includes a number of other words, and the whole is
arranged in accurate alphabetical order.

Mr. Dencke also prepared a grammar of the Delaware, as
I am informed by his old personal friend, Rev. F. R. Holland,
of Hope, Indiana ; but the most persistent inquiry through
residents at Salem, N. C., where he died in 1839, and at the
Missionary Archives at Bethlehem, Pa., and Moraviantown,
Canada, have failed to furnish me a clue to its whereabouts.
I fear that this precious document was "sold as paper stock,"
as I am informed were most of the MSS. which he left at his
decease!   A sad instance of the total absence of intelligent
interest in such subjects in our country.

The Rev. Abraham Luckenbach may be called the last of
the Moravian Lenapists.   With him, in 1854, died out the
traditions of native philology.   Born in 1777, in Lehigh
county, Pennsylvania, he became a missionary among the
Indians in 1800, and until his retirement, forty-three years
later, was a zealous pastor to his flock on the White river,
Indiana, and later, on the Canada Reservation.   His published work is entitled " Forty-six Select Scripture Narratives
from the Old Testament, embellished with Engravings, for
the Use of Indian Youth.   Translated into Delaware Indian,

by A. Luckenbach. New York. Printed by Daniel Fanshaw, 1838." 8vo, pp. xvi, 304.

After his retirement in Bethlehem, he edited, in 1847, the second edition of Zeisberger's "Collection of Hymns," the first of which has already been mentioned.

A short MS. vocabulary, in German and Delaware, is in the possession of his family, in Bethlehem, and some loose papers in the language.

One of the most recent students of the Delaware was Mr. Matthew G. Henry, of Philadelphia. In 1859 and 1860 he compiled, with no little labor, a "Delaware Indian Dictionary," the MS. of which, in the library of the American Philosophical Society, forms a thick quarto volume of 843 pages, with a number of maps. It is in three parts: 1, English and Delaware; 2, Delaware and English; 3, Delaware Proper Names and their Translations.

It includes, without analysis or correction, the words in Zeisberger's "Spelling Book," Roger William's "Key," Campanius' Vocabulary, those in Smith's and Strachey's "Virginia," and various Nanticoke, Mohegan, Minsi and other vocabularies. The derivations of the proper names are chiefly from Heckewelder, and in other cases are venturesome. The compilation, therefore, while often useful, lacks the salutary check of a critical, grammatical erudition, and in its present form is of limited value.

Some of the later vocabularies collected by various travelers offer points for comparison, and may be mentioned here.

In 1786 Major Denny,[1] at Fort McIntosh, Ohio, collected

---

[1] Major Ebenezer Denny's "Journal," in *Memoirs of the Hist. Soc. of Penna.*, Vol. VII, pp. 481-86.

a number of Delaware words, principally from Shawnee Indians. A comparison shows many of them to be in a corrupt form, owing either to the ignorance of the Shawnee authority, or to the inaccuracy of Major Denny in catching the sounds.

While engaged on the Pacific Railroad survey, in 1853, Lieut. Whipple[1] collected a vocabulary of a little over 200 words from a Delaware chief, named Black Beaver, in the Indian Territory, which was edited, in 1856, by Prof. Turner. It is evidently a pure specimen, and, as the editor observes, "agrees remarkably" with earlier authentic vocabularies.

In the second volume of Schoolcraft's large work[2] is a vocabulary of about 350 words, obtained by Mr. Cummings, U. S. Indian Agent. The precise source, date and locality are not given, but it is evidently from some trustworthy native, and is quite correct.

Some small works for the schools of the Baptist missions among the Delawares in Kansas were prepared by the Rev. J. Meeker. They appear to be entirely elementary in character.

It will be observed that in this list not a single native writer is named. So far as I have ascertained, though many learned to write their native tongue, not one attempted any composition in it beyond the needs of daily life.

To make some amends for this, and as I wished to obtain an example of the Lenape of to-day, I asked Chief Gottlieb Tobias, an educated native on the Moravian Reservation in

---

[1] *Report upon the Indian Tribes*, by Whipple, Ewbank and Turner, p. 56 (Washington, 1855).

[2] *History and Statistics of the Indian Tribes*, Vol. II, p. 470.

Canada, to give me in writing his opinion of the Delaware text of the WALUM OLUM, which I had sent him. This he obligingly did, and added a translation of his letter. The two are as follows, without alteration :—

MORAVIANTOWN, Sept. 26, 1884.

I, GOTTLIEB TOBIAS,

Nanne ni ngutschi nachguttemin, jun awen ect ma elekhigetup. Woak alende nenostamen woak alende taku eli wtallichsin elewondasik wiwonalatokowo pachsi wonamii lichsu woak pachsi pilli lichsoagan.   Taku ni nenostamowin.   Lamoe nemochomsinga achpami ect newinachke woak chash tichi kachtin nbibindameneb nin lichsoagan. Mauchso lenno woak mauchso chauchshissis woak juque mauchso chauchshissis achpo pomauchsu igabtshi lue wiwonallatokowo won bambil alachshe. Woak lue lamoe ni enda. Mimensiane ntelsitam alowi ayachichson won elhagewit woak ehelop ne likhiqui. Gichgi wonami lichso shuk tatcamse woak gichgi minsiwi lichso.

TRANSLATION.

Then I will try to answer this (which) some one at some time wrote. And some I understand, and some not, because his language is called Wonalatoko, half Unami and half another language.   I do not understand it.   Long ago my grandfather about 48 years ago I heard it that language.   One man and one old woman and now another old woman here lives yet who uses this Wonalatoko language just like this book and she said, I of old time when I was a child heard more difficult dialect than the present, and many at that time partly Unami he speak, but sometimes also partly Minsi he speak.

The drift of Chief Tobias' letter is highly important to this present work, though his expressions are not couched in the most perfect English. It will be noted that he recognizes the text of the WALUM OLUM to be a native production composed in one of the ancient southern dialects of the tongue, the Unami (Wonami) or the Unalachtgo (Wonalatoko). I shall recur to this when discussing the authenticity of that document on a later page.

§ 2. *General Remarks on the Lenape.*

The Lenape language is a well-defined and quite pure member of the great Algonkin stock, revealing markedly the linguistic traits of this group, and standing philologically, as well as geographically, between the Micmac of the extreme east and the Chipeway of the far West.

These linguistic traits, common to the whole stock, I may briefly enumerate as follows :—

1. All words are derived from simple, monosyllabic roots, by means of affixes and suffixes.

2. The words do not come within the grammatical categories of the Aryan language, as nouns, adjectives, verbs and other "parts of speech," but are "indifferent themes," which may be used at will as one or the other. To this there appear to be a few exceptions.

3. Expressions of being (*i. e.*, nominal themes) undergo modifications depending on the ontological conception as to whether the thing spoken of is a living or a lifeless object. This forms the "animate and inanimate," or the "noble and ignoble" declensions and conjugations. The distinction is not strictly logical, but largely grammatical, many lifeless objects being considered living, and the reverse. This is the only modification of the kind known,

G

true grammatical gender not appearing in any of these tongues.

4. Expressions of action (*i. e.*, verbal themes) undergo modifications depending on the abstract assumption as to whether the action is real or conjectural. If the latter, it is indicated by a change in the vowel of the root. This leads to a fundamental division of verbal modes into *positive* and *suppositive* modes.

5. The expression of action is subordinate to that of being, so that the verbal elements of a proposition are secondary to the nominal or pronominal elements, and the subjective relation becomes closely akin to, or identical with, that of possession.[1]

6. The conception of number is feebly developed in its application to inanimate objects, which often have no grammatical plurals. The inclusive and exclusive plurals are used in the first person.

7. The genius of the language is *holophrastic*—that is, its effort is to express the relationship of several ideas by combining them in one word. This is displayed: 1, in nominal themes, by *polysynthesis*, by which several such themes are

---

[1] I am aware that in this proposition I am following the German and French linguists, Steinthal, F. Müller, Adam, Henry, etc., and not our own distinguished authority on Algonkin grammar, Dr. J. Hammond Trumbull, who, in his essay "On the Algonkin Verb," has learnedly maintained another opinion (*Transactions of the American Philological Association*, 1876, p. 146). I have not been able, however, to convince myself that his position is correct. The formative elements of the Algonkin paradigms appear to me simply attached particles, and not true inflections. Their real character is obscured by phonetic laws, just as in the Finnish when compared with the Hungarian.

welded into one, according to fixed laws of elision and euphony; and 2, by *incorporation*, where the object (or a pronoun representing it) and the subject are united with the verb, forming the so-called "transitions," or "objective conjugations."

8. There is no relative pronoun, so that the relation of minor to major clauses is left to be indicated either by position or the offices of a simple connective.

9. The language of both sexes is identical, those differences of speech between the males and females, so frequently observed in other American tongues, finding no place in the Algonkin.

10. No independent verb-substantive is found, and, as might be anticipated, no means of predicating existence apart from quality and attribute.

§ 3. *Dialects of the Lenape.*

Two slightly different dialects prevailed among the Delawares themselves, the one spoken by the Unami and Unalachtgo, the other by the Minsi. The former is stated by the Moravian missionaries to have had an uncommonly soft and pleasant sound to the ear,[1] and William Penn made the same remark. It was also considered to be the purer and more elegant dialect, and was preferred by the missionaries as the vehicle for their translations.

The Minsi was harsher and more difficult to learn, but

---

[1] "Ungemein wohlklingend." Loskiel, *Geschichte der Mission*, p. 24. An early traveler of English nationality pronounced it "sweet, of noble sound and accent." Gabriel Thomas, *Hist. and Geog. Account of Pensilvania and West New Jersey*, p. 47 (London, 1698).

would seem to have been the more archaic branch, as it is stated to be a key to the other, and to preserve many words in their integrity and original form, which in the Unami were abbreviated or altogether dropped. The Minsi dialect was closely akin to the Mohegan.

How far the separation of the Delaware dialects had extended may be judged from the subjoined list of words. They are selected, as showing the greatest variation, from a list of over one hundred, prepared by Mr. Heckewelder for the American Philosophical Society, and preserved in MS. in its library.

The comparison proves that the differences are far from extensive, and chiefly result from a greater use of gutturals.

COMPARISON OF THE UNAMI AND MINSI DIALECTS.

	Unami.	*Minsi.*
God	Patamawos	Pachtamawos
Earth	hacki	achgi
Valley	pasaeck	pachsajech
Beard	wuttoney	wuchtoney
Tooth	wipit	wichpit
Blood	mocum	mochcum
Night	ipocu	ipochcu
Pretty	schiki	pschickki
Small	tangeto	tschankschisu
Stone	assinn	achsün
The Sea	kithanne	gichthanne
Light	woacheu	woashe'jeek
Black	süksit	neesachgissit
Chief	saki'ma	wajauwe
Green	asgask	asgasku
No, not	matta	machta

What differences there were have been retained and perhaps accentuated in modern times, if we may judge from the names of consanguinity obtained by Mr. Lewis H. Morgan on the Kansas Reservation in 1860. These are given in part in the annexed table, and the Mohegan is added for the sake of extending the comparison.

	Delaware.	Minsi.	Mohegan.
My grandfather	nu mohómus	na mãhomis'	nuh mãhome'
My grandmother	noo home'	na nóhome	no ome'
My father	noh'h	na no'uh	noh
My mother	ngã'hase	nain guk'	n'guk
My son	n'kweese'	nain,gwase'	n'diome'
My daughter	n'dãnuss	nain dãness'	ne chune'
My grandchild	noh whese'	nain no whasé	nã hise'
My elder brother	nah hãns	nain n'hans	n tã kun'
My elder sister	na mese'	nain nawasé	nã mees
My younger brother	nah eese umiss	nain hisesamus'	nhisum

A noteworthy difference in the Northern and Southern Lenape dialects was that the latter possessed the three phonetic elements *n*, *l* and *r*, while the former could not pronounce the *r*, and their neighbors, the Mohegans, neither the *l* nor the *r*.

The dialect studied by Campanius and Penn, and that in southern New Jersey presented the *r* sound where the Upper Unami and Minsi had the *l*. Thus Campanius gives *rhenus*, for *lenno*, man ; and Penn *oret*, for the Unami *wulit*, good.

The dialectic substitution of one of these elements for another is a widespread characteristic of Algonkin phonology.

Roger Williams early called attention to it among the tribes of New England.[1]

Tracing it to its origin, it clearly arises from the use of "alternating consonants," so extensive in American languages. In very many of them it is optional with the speaker to employ any one of several sounds of the same class. This is the case with these letters in Cree, which, for various reasons, may be considered the most archaic of all the Algonkin dialects. In its phonetics, the *th, y, l, n* and *r* are "permuting" or "alternating" letters.[2]

Often, too, the sound falls between these letters, so that the foreign ear is left in doubt which to write.

That this is the case with the Delaware is evident from some of the more recent vocabularies where the *r* is not infrequent. The following words, from the vocabulary in Major Denny's *Memoir*, illustrate this :—

Stone	*seegriana*
Buffalo	*serelea*
Beaver	*thomagru*
Above	*hoqrunog*, etc.

Even Mr. Lewis A. Morgan, who had considerable practice in writing the sounds of the Indian languages, inserts the *r* in a number of pure Delaware words he collected in Kansas.[3]

Another difficulty presents itself in the sibilants. They are not always distinguished.

---

[1] *Key into the Language of North America*, p. 129. See, also, Mr. Pickering's remarks on the same subject, in his Appendix to Rasles' *Dictionary of the Abnaki*.

[2] Howse, *Grammar of the Cree Language*, p. 316.

[3] See his *Ancient Society*, pp. 172–73.

Mr. Horatio Hale writes me on this point: "In Minsi, and perhaps in all the Lenape dialects, the sound written *s* is intermediate between *s* and *th* (the Greek *θ*). This element is pronounced by placing the tongue and teeth in the position of the theta, and then endeavoring to utter *s*."

The guttural, represented in the Moravian vocabularies by *ch*, was softened by the English likewise to the *s* sound, as it appears also to have been by the New Jersey tribes.[1]

In connection with dialectic variation, the interesting question arises as to the rapidity of change in language. With regard to the Lenape we are enabled to compare this for a period covering more than two centuries. To test it, I have arranged the subjoined table of words culled from three writers at about equidistant points in this period. Each wrote in the orthography of his own tongue, and this I have not altered. The words from Campanius are from the southern dialect, which preferred the *r* to the *l*, and this substitution should be allowed for in a fair comparison.

---

[1] The native name of William Penn offers an instance of this phonetic alteration. It is given as *Onas*. The proper form is *Wonach*. It literally means the tip or extremity of anything; as *wonach-sitall*, the tips of the toes; *wonach-gulinschall*, the tips of the fingers. The inanimate plural form *wolanniall*, means the tail feathers of a bird. To explain the name *Penn* to the Indians a feather was shown them, probably a quill pen, and hence they gave the translation *Wonach*, corrupted into *Onas*.

COMPARISON OF THE DELAWARE AT INTERVALS DURING 210
YEARS.

	Campanius. 1645. Swedish Orthography.	Zeisberger. 1778. German Orthography.	Whipple. 1855. English Orthography.
Man	rhenus	lenno	lenno
Woman	âquaeo	ochque	h'que'i
Father	nⱳk	nooch (my)	nuuh
Mother	kahaess	gahowes	gaiez
Head	kwijl	wil	wil
Hair	mijrack	milach	milakh
Ear	hittaock	w'hittawak (pl.)	howitow
Eye	schinck	w'ushgink	tukque'ling
Nose	wikiiwan	w'ikiwan	ouiki'o
Mouth	tⱳn	w'doon	ouitun
Tongue	hijrano	w'ilano	ouilano
Tooth	wippit	w'epit	ouipita
Hand	alænskan	w'anach	puck-alenge
Foot	zijt	sit	zit
Heart	chitto, kitte	ktee (thy)	huté
House	wickⱳmen	wiquoam	ouigwam
Pipe	hopockan	hopenican	haboca
Sun	chisogh	gischuch	kishu'h
Star	aranck	alank	alanq'
Fire	taenda	tindey	tundaih
Water	bij	mbi	bih
Snow	kuun	guhn	ku'no

COMPARISON OF DELAWARE NUMERALS.

	Campanius. 1645.	Thomas. 1695.	Zeisberger. 1750.	Whipple. 1855.
1	Ciútte	Kooty	Ngutti	Co'te
2	Nissa	Nisha	Nischa	Ni'sha
3	Náha	Natcha	Nacha	Naha'
4	Nævvo	Neo	Newo	Ne'ewah
5	Parcenach	Pelenach	Palenach	Pahle'nah'k
6	Ciuttas	Kootash	Guttasch	Cot'tasch
7	Nissas	Nishash	Nischasch	Ni'shasch
8	Haas	Choesh	Chasch	Hasch
9	Paeschum	Peshonk	Peschkonk	Pes'co
10	Thæren	Telen	Tellen	Te'len

I have no doubt that if a Swede, a German and an Englishman were to-day to take down these words from the mouth of a Delaware Indian, each writing them in the orthography of his own tongue, the variations would be as numerous as in the above list, except, perhaps, the ancient and now disused *r* sound.   The comparison goes to show that there has probably been but a very slight change in the Delaware, in spite of the many migrations and disturbances they have undergone.   They speak the language of their forefathers as closely as do the English, although no written documents have aided them in keeping it alive.   This is but another proof added to an already long list, showing that the belief that American languages undergo rapid changes is an error.

The dialect which the Moravian missionaries learned, and in which they composed their works, was that of the Lehigh Valley.   That it was not an impure Minsi mixed with Mohegan, as Dr. Trumbull seems to think,[1] is evident from the direct statements of the missionaries themselves, as well as from Heckewelder's Minsi vocabularies, which show many points of divergence from the printed books.   Moreover, among the first converts from the Delaware nation were members of the Unami or Turtle tribe, and Zeisberger was brought into immediate contact with them.[2]   We may fairly consider it to have been the upper or inland Unami, which, as I have said, was recognized by the nation as the purest, or at least the most polished dialect of their tongue.   It stood midway between the Unalachtgo and Southern Unami and the true Minsi.

[1] *Trans. Am. Philol. Assoc.*, 1872, p. 157.

[2] De Schweinitz, *Life of Zeisberger*, p. 131.

§ 4. *Special Structure of the Lenape.*

The Root and the Formation of the Theme.—As they appear in the language of to-day, the Lenape radicals are chiefly monosyllables, which undergo more or less modifications in composition. They cannot be used alone, the tongue having long since passed from that interjectional condition where each of these roots conveyed a whole sentence in itself.

Whether they can be resolved back into a few elementary sounds, primitive elements of speech, I shall not discuss. This has been done for the Cree roots by Mr. Joseph Howse,[1] and most of the radicals of that tongue are identical with those of the Lenape. Some of his conclusions appear to me hazardous and hypothetical; and certainly many of his supposed analogies drawn from European tongues are extravagant.

As in other idioms, so in Lenape, two or more radicals may be compounded to form a combination, which, in turn, performs the offices of a radical in the construction of themes.

This combination is formed either by prefixes or suffixes. The prefixes are generally adjectival in signification, while the suffixes are usually classificatory. A number of these are secondary roots, which are themselves capable of further analysis.

As so much of the strength of the languages depends on this plan of word building, I have drawn off a list of a few

---

[1] *A Grammar of the Cree Language, with which is combined an Analysis of the Chippeway Dialect*, by Joseph Howse, Esq. (London, 1844).

of the more frequent affixes of the Lenape, with their signification :—

Lenape Prefixes.

awoss-, beyond, the other side of.

eluwi-, most, a superlative form.

gisch-, see page 102.

kit-, great, large.

lappi-, again, indicates repetition.

lenno-, male, man,

lippoe-, wise, shrewd ; as *lippoeweno*, a shrewd man.

mach-, evil, bad, hurt.

matt-, negative and depreciatory ; as *mattaptonen*, to speak uncivilly.

ni-, see page 101.

ochque-, she, female.

pach-, division, separation ; *pachican*, a knife ; *pachat*, to split.

pal-, negative, as dis- or in-, from *palli*, otherwheres.

tach-, pairs or doubles.

tschitsch-, indicates repetition.

wit-, with or in common.

wul-, or *wel-*, see page 104.

Many of these are abbreviated to the extent that a single significant letter is all that remains, as *min* in *msim*, hickory nut ; *pakihm*, cranberry ; and so *acki* to *k*, *hanne* to *an*, as *kitanink* (Kittanning), from *gitschi*, great ; *hanne*, flowing river ; *ink*, locative, "at the place of the great river."

Lenape Suffixes.

-ak, wood, from *tachan ; kuwenchak*, pine wood.

-aki, place, land.

-ammen, acceptance, adoption ; *wulistamen*, I accept it as good, I believe it. See page 104.

-ape, male, man. From a root *ap*, to cover (carnally). In Chipeway applied only to lower animals.

-atton, or *hatton*, to have, to put somewhere. The radical is *at*. Also a prefix, as, *hattape*, the bow; lit., what the man has.

-bi, tree; *machtschibi*, papaw tree.

-chum, a quadruped.

-elendam, a verbal termination, signifying a disposition of mind. The root is *en, ne, ni*, I; "it is to me so."

-gook, a snake; from *achgook*, a serpent.

-hanna, properly *hannek*, a river; from the root, which appears in Cree as *anask*, to stretch out along the ground; *mech-hannek*, a large stream.

> Heckewelder derives this from *amhamme*, a river. The terminal *k* is, however, part of the root, and not the locative termination. The word is allied to Del. *quenek*, long.

-hikan, tidal water; *kittahikan*, the ocean; *shajahikan*, the sea shore.

-hilleu, it is so, it is true; impersonal form from *lissin*.

-hittuck, river, water in motion.

-igan, instrumental; also *shican* and *can*. A participial termination used with inanimate objects.

-in or *ini*, of the kind; like; predicative form of the demonstrative pronoun.

-ink or *unk*, place where.

-is or *-it*, diminutive termination.

-leu, it is so, it is true.

-meek, a fish; *maschilamek*, a trout.

-min, a fruit.

-peek, a body of still water; *menuppek*, a lake.

-sacunk, an outlet of a stream into another; also *saquik*.

-sipu, stream; lit., stretched, extended.

-tin, with, or in common.

-tit, diminutive termination; *amentit*, a babe.

-*wagan*, abstract verbal termination ; *machelemuxowagan*, the being honored.

-*wehelleu*, a bird.

-*wi*, the verb-substantive termination, predicating being ; *tchek*, cold ; *tchekwi*, he or it is cold.

-*wi*, negative termination in certain verbal forms.

-*xit*, indicates the passive recipient of the action ; *machelemuxit*, the one who is honored.

The analysis of a series of derivatives from the same root offers a most instructive subject for investigation in the Lenape. Not only does it reveal the linguistic processes adapted, but it discloses the psychology of the native mind, and teaches us the associations of its ideas, and the range of its imaginative powers. By no other avenue can we gain access to the intimate thought-life of this people. Here it is unfolded to us by evidence which is irrefragable.

These considerations lead me to present a few examples of the derivatives from roots of different classes.

EXAMPLES OF LENAPE DERIVATIVES.

Subjective Root NI, *I, mine.*

   1. In a good sense.

      Nihilleu, it is I, *or*, mine.

      Nihillatschi, self, oneself.

      Nihillapewi, free (*ape*, man = I am my own man).

      Nihillapewit, a freeman.

      Nihillasowagan, freedom, liberty.

      Nihillapeuhen, to make free, to redeem.

      Nihillapeuhoalid, the Redeemer, the Saviour.

   2. In a bad sense.

      Ni'hillan, he is mine to beat, I beat him.

      Nihil'lan, I beat him to death, I kill him.

Nihillowen, I put him to death, I murder him.

Nihillowet, a murderer.

Nihillowewi, murderous.

3. In a demonstrative sense.

Ne, pl. *nek*, or *nell*, this, that, the.

Nall, nan, nanne, nanni, this one, that one.

Nill, these.

Naninga, those gone, with reference to the dead.

4. In a possessive sense.

Nitaton, in-my-having, I can, I am able, I know how.

Nitaus, of-my-family, sister-in-law.

Nitis, of-mine, a friend, a companion.

Nitsch ! my child! exclamation of fondness.

The strangely conflicting ideas evolved from this root already attracted the attention of Mr. Duponceau.[1] That the notions for freedom and servitude, murderer and Saviour, should be expressed by modifications of the same radical is indeed striking! But the psychological process through which it came about is evident on studying the above arrangement.

Objective-intensive root GISCH *or* KICH (*Cree*, KIS *or* KIK).

Signification—successful action.

1. Applied to persons.

A. Initial successful action.

Gischigin, to begin life, to be born.

Gischihan, to form, to make with the hands.

Gischiton, to make ready, to prepare.

Gischeleman, to create with the mind, to fancy.

Gischelendam, to meditate a plan, to lie.

B. Continuous successful action.

Gischikenamen, to increase, to produce fruit.

[1] In a note to Zeisberger's *Grammar of the Delaware*, p. 141.

Giken, to grow better in health.

Gikeowagan, life, health.

Gikey, long-living, old, aged.

c. Final successful action.

Gischatten, finished, ready, done, cooked.

Gischiton, to make ready, to finish.

Gischpuen, to have eaten enough.

Gischileu, it has proved true.

Gischatschimolsin, to have resolved, to have decreed.

Gischachpoanhe, baked, cooked (the bread is).

2. Applied to things.

A. Initial successful action.

Gischuch, sun, moon, day, month. The idea appears
to be the beginning of a period of time, with the collateral notion of prosperous activity. The correctness
of the derivation is shown by the next word.

Gischapan, day-break, beginning day-light. From
wapan, the east, or light.

Gischuchwipall, the rays of the sun.

Gischeu, or *Gischquik*, day.

B. Continuous successful action.

Gischten, clear, light, shining.

Gischachsummen, to shine, to enlighten.

Gischuten, warm, tepid.

Numerous other derivatives could be added, but the above
are sufficient to show the direction of thoughts flowing from
this root. Howse considers it identical with the root *kitch*,
great, large.[1] This would greatly increase its derivatives.
They certainly appear allied. In Cree, Lacombe gives *kitchi*,

---

[1] *A Grammar of the Cree Language*, p. 175.

great, and *kije*, finished, perfect, both being terms applied to divinity.[1]

General Algonkin root 8 $\begin{Bmatrix} L \\ N \\ R \end{Bmatrix}$ I. *Abnaki,* 8RI; *Micmac,* 8E'LI, *Chippeway,* GWAN-; *Del., two forms,* WUL *and* WIN. *It conveys the idea of pleasurable sensation.*

A. First form, *wul.*

Wulit, well, good, handsome, fine.

Wullihilleu, it is good, etc.

Wuliken, it grows well.

Wulamoe, he truth-speaks.

Wulamoewagan, truth.

Wulistamen, to believe, to accept as truth.

Wulenensin, to be fine in appearance, to dress.

Wulenensen, to be fine to oneself, to be proud.

B. Second form, *won* or *win.*

Winu, ripe, good to eat.

Wonita, he is ripe for it, he can, he is able.

Wingan, sweet, savory.

Winktek, done, boiled, fit to eat.

Winak, sassafras. From its sweet leaves.

Wingi, gladly, willingly.

Winginamen, to delight in.

The figure 8 in the above represents the "whistled *w*," like the *wh* in "which," when strongly pronounced.

From this root, as I have already said, is derived also the word WALAM, red paint, from the sense "to be fine in appearance, to dress," as the Indian accomplished that object by painting himself.

---

[1] *Dictionnaire de la Langue des Cris,* sub voce.

Grammatical Structure of the Lenape.

It would not be worth while for me to enter into the intricacies of Lenape grammar, particularly as I can add little to what is already known.

The Delaware Grammar of Zeisberger remains our only authority, and in spite of its manifest shortcomings and state of incompletion, the unprejudiced student must acknowledge, with Albert Gallatin,[1] that it is "most honestly done," and showed the Delaware as it actually was spoken, though perhaps not as scientific linguists think it ought to have been spoken.

A few general observations will be sufficient.

As in other languages of the class, the theme is indifferently nominal, verbal or adjectival; that is, it performs the functions of either of these grammatical categories, according to its connection.

Nominal themes are either animate or inanimate. The characteristic of all animate plurals is *k* (*ak*, *ik*, *ek*). Inanimate plurals are in *al*, *wall* or *a*. As usual, the distinction between animate and inanimate nouns is partly logical, partly grammatical, various objects being conceived as animate which are in fact not so.

The possessive relation is generally indicated by placement

---

[1] In *Trans. Amer. Antiq. Society*, Vol. II, p. 223. Zeisberger's statements were criticised by Joseph Howse, *Grammar of the Cree Language*, pp. 109, 310, 313. His strictures and those of the Abbé Cuoq, in his *Etudes Philologiques sur Quelques Langues Sauvages*, Chap. I, were collected and extended by Dr. J. Hammond Trumbull, in his paper on "Some Mistaken Notions of Algonquin Grammar," *Trans. of the American Philological Association*, 1874. There is a needless degree of severity in both these last named productions.

H

alone, the possessor preceding the thing possessed, as *lenno quisall*, the man's son ; but one could also say *lenno w'quisall*, the man his son.

Adjectives precede nouns, and when used attributively assume a verbal form by adding the termination *wi*, which indicates objective existence (like the Chip. *-win*). Thus, *scattek*, burning ; *scattewi w'dehin*, a burning heart—literally, it-is-a-burning-thing his-heart.

The degrees of comparison are formed by prefixing *allo-wiwi*, more, and *eluwi*, most. Both of these are from the same radical *ali*, which may perhaps come from the *admirationis particula*, *ala'* (Abnaki, *ara'*) found in the northern dialects as expressive of astonishment.[1]

There being no relative pronoun in Delaware, dependent clauses are either included in the verbal of the major clause, or include it as a secondary.

The scheme of the simple sentence is usually subject-verb-object; but emphasis allows departures from this, as in the following sentence from Bishop Ettwein's MSS. :—

> *Jesus wemi amemensall w'taholawak.*
>
> Jesus all children   he-loved-them.

Of the formal affixes, the inseparable pronouns are the most prominent. They are the same for nouns and verbs, and are—

1st. *n*, I, my, we, our.

2d. *k*, thou, thy, you, your.

3d. *w* or *o*, he, she, it, his, their.

---

[1] Rasles, *Dictionary of the Abnaki*, p. 550. Dr. Trumbull compares the Mass. *anue*, more than. *Trans. American Philological Association*, 1872, p. 168.

Past time is indicated by the terminal *p*, with a connective vowel, and future time by *tsch*, which may be either a prefix or suffix, as—

> *N'dellsin*, I am thus.
>
> *N'dellsineep*, I was thus.
>
> or $\left.\begin{array}{l}\textit{N'dellsintschi,}\\\textit{Nantsch n'dellsin,}\end{array}\right\}$ I shall be thus.

The change or "flattening" of the vowel of the root in suppositive propositions, was recognized as a fact of speech, but not grammatically analyzed by Zeisberger.

Its effect on verbal forms may be seen from the following examples from his *Grammar :*—

Examples of Vowel Change in Lenape.

N'dappin, I am there.	*Achpiya*, if I am there.
	Epia, where I am.
N'dellsin, I am so.	*Lissiye*, if I am so.
N'gauwi, I sleep.	*Gewi*, he who sleeps.
N'pommauchsi, I walk or live.	*Pemauchsit*, living.
N'da, I go.	*Eyaya*, when I go.
	Eyat, going.

Another omission in his Grammar is that of the "obviative" and "super-obviative" forms of nouns. These are used in the Algonkin dialects to define the relations of third persons. They prevent such obscurity as appears in the following English sentence: "John's brother called at Robert's, to see his wife." Whose wife is referred to is left ambiguous; but in Algonkin these third persons would have different forms, and there would be no room for ambiguity. In his writings in Lenape, Zeisberger makes use of obviatives, with the terminations *al* and *l*, but does not treat of them in his Grammar.

As a question in philosophical grammar, it may be doubted whether the Lenape has any true passive voice. Cardinal Mezzofanti was accustomed to deny the presence of any real passives in American languages; and he had studied the Delaware among others.

The sign of the Delaware passive is the suffix *gussu* or *cusso*. In the Cree dialect, which, as I have already said, preserves the ancient forms most closely, this is *k-ussu*, and is a particle expressing likeness or similarity in animate objects.[1] Hence, probably, the original sense of the Lenape word translated, "I am loved," is "I am like the object of the action of loving."

[1] J. Howse, *Grammar of the Cree Language*, p. 111.

CHAPTER V.

HISTORICAL SKETCHES OF THE LENAPE.

§ 1. The Lenape as "Women."
§ 2. Recent Migrations of the Lenape.
§ 3. Missionary Efforts in the Provinces of Pennsylvania and New Jersey.

The Lenape as "Women."

A unique peculiarity of the political condition of the Lenape was that for a certain time they occupied a recognized position as non-combatants—as "women," as they were called by the Iroquois.

Indian customs and phraseology attached a two-fold significance to this term.

The more honorable was that of peace-makers. Among the Five Nations and Susquehannocks, certain grave matrons of the tribe had the right to sit in the councils, and, among other privileges, had that of proposing a cessation of hostilities in time of war. A proposition from them to drop the war club could be entertained without compromising the reputation of the tribe for bravery. There was an official orator and messenger, whose appointed duty it was to convey such a pacific message from the matrons, and to negotiate for peace.[1]

Another and less honorable sense of the term arose from a custom prevalent throughout America, and known also among the ancient Scythians. Its precise purpose remains obscure,

---

[1] II. R. Schoolcraft, *Notes on the Iroquois*, pp. 135–36.

109

although it has been made the subject of a careful study by one of our most eminent surgeons, who had facilities of observation among the Western tribes.[1] Certain young men of the tribe, apparently vigorous and of normal development, were deprived of the accoutrements of the male sex, clothed like women, and assigned women's work to do. They neither went out to hunt nor on the war-path, and were treated as inferiors by their male associates. Whether this degradation arose from superstitious rites or sodomitic practices, it certainly carried to its victims the contempt of both sexes.

In their account of the transaction the Delawares claimed that they were appointed as peace-makers in an honorable manner, although the Iroquois deceived them as to their object.

The Lenape account is as follows :—

"The Iroquois sent messengers to the Delawares with the following speech :—

"'It is not well that all nations should war; for that will finally bring about the destruction of the Indians. We have thought of a means to prevent this before it is too late. Let one nation be The Woman. We will place her in the middle, and the war nations shall be the Men and dwell around the Woman. No one shall harm the Woman; and if one does, we shall speak to him and say, 'Why strikest thou the Woman?' Then all the Men shall attack him who has

---

[1] *The Disease of the Scythians (Morbus Feminarum) and Certain Analogous Conditions.* By William A. Hammond, M. D. (New York, 1882). Dr. Hammond found that the *hombre mujerado* of the Pueblo Indians " is the chief passive agent in the pederastic ceremonies which form so important a part in their religious performances," p. 9.

struck the Woman. The Woman shall not go to war, but shall do her best to keep the peace. When the Men around her fight one another, and the strife waxes hot, the Woman shall have power to say: ' Ye Men ! what do ye that ye thus strike one another ?   Remember that your wives and children must perish, if ye do not cease. Will ye perish from the face of the earth ?' Then the Men shall listen to the Woman and obey her.'

" The Delawares did not at once perceive the aim of the Iroquois, and were pleased to take this position of the Woman.

" Then the Iroquois made a great feast, and invited the Delawares, and spoke to their envoys an address in three parts.

" First, they declared the Delaware nation to be the Woman in these words :—

" ' We place upon you the long gown of a woman, and adorn you with earrings.'

" This was as much as to say that thenceforward they were not to bear arms.

" The second sentence was in these words :—

" ' We hang on your arm a calabash of oil and medicine. With the oil you shall cleanse the ears of other nations that they listen to good and not to evil. The medicine you shall use for those nations who have been foolish, that they may return to their senses, and turn their hearts to peace.'

" The third sentence intimated that the Delawares should make agriculture their chief occupation. It was :—

" ' We give herewith into your hands a corn pestle and a hoe.'

" Each sentence was accompanied with a belt of wampum.

These belts have ever since been carefully preserved and their meanings from time to time recalled." [1]

Opinions of historians about this tradition have been various. It has generally been considered a fabrication of the Delawares, to explain their subjection in a manner consoling to their national vanity. Gen. Harrison dismisses it as impossible ; [2] Albert Gallatin says, " it is too incredible to require serious discussion ; [3] Mr. Hale characterizes it as " preposterous ;" [4] and Bishop de Schweinitz as " fabulous and absurd." [5]

On the other hand, it is vouched for by Zeisberger, who furnished the account to Loskiel, and who would not have said that the wampum belts with their meaning were still preserved unless he knew it to be a fact. It is repeated emphatically by Heckewelder, who adds that his informants were not only Delawares but Mohegans as well, who could not have shared the motive suggested above. [6]

There can be no question but that the neutral position of the Delawares was something different from that of a conquered nation, and that it meant a great deal more. They undoubtedly were the acknowledged peace-makers over a wide area, and this in consequence of some formal ancient

[1] Loskiel, *Geschichte der Mission, etc.*, s. 161–2.

[2] Wm. Henry Harrison, *A Discourse on the Aborigines of the Valley of the Ohio*, pp. 24, 25 (Cincinnati, 1838).

[3] Gallatin, *Trans. Amer. Antiq. Soc.*, Vol. II, p. 46.

[4] Horatio Hale, *The Iroquois Book of Rites*, p. 92.

Edmund de Schweinitz, *Life and Times of David Zeisberger*, p. 46.

Heckewelder, *Indian Nations*, pp. xxxii and 60.

treaty. This is distinctly stated by the Stockbridge Indian, Hendrick Aupaumut, in his curious Narrative :—[1]

"The Delawares, who we calld *Wenaumeen,* are our Grandfathers, according to the ancient covenant of their and our ancestors, to which we adhere without any deviation in these near 200 years, to which nation the 5 nations and British have commit the whole business. For this nation has the greatest influence with the southern, western and northern nations."

Hence Aupaumut undertook his embassy directly to them, so as to secure their influence for peace in 1791.

To the fact that they exerted this influence during the Revolutionary War, may very plausibly be attributed the success of the Federal cause in the dark days of 1777 and 1778 ; for, as David Zeisberger wrote : " If the Delawares had taken part against the Americans in the present war, America would have had terrible experiences ; for the neutrality of the Delawares kept all the many nations that are their grandchildren neutral also, except the Shawanese, who are no longer in close union with their grandfathers."[2]

---

[1] *Narrative of Hendrick Aupaumut, Mems. Hist. Soc. Pa.,* Vol. II, pp. 76–77. Wenaumeen for Unami, the Mohegan form of the name. This seems to limit the peace-making power to that gens. He may mean, " Those of the Delawares who are called the Unamis are our Grandfathers," etc.

The Chipeways, Ottawas, Shawnees, Pottawattomies, Sacs, Foxes and Kikapoos, all called the Delawares " Grandfather." J. Morse, *Report on Indian Affairs,* pp. 122, 123, 142. The term was not intended in a genealogical, but solely in a political, sense. Its origin and precise meaning are alike obscure.

[2] *History of the Indians,* MS., quoted by Bishop Schweinitz, *Life of Zeisberger,* p. 444, note.

When at the close of the French War, in 1758, the treaty of Easton put a stop to the bloody feuds of the border, "the *peace-belt* was sent to our brethren, the Delawares, that they might send it to all the nations living toward the setting sun,"[1] and they carried it as the recognized pacific envoys.

The Iroquois, however, assumed a most arrogant and contemptuous tone toward the Delawares, about the middle of the eighteenth century. In 1756 they sent a belt to them, with a most insulting message:[2] "You will remember that you are our women; our forefathers made you so, and put a petticoat on you, and charged you to be true to us, and lie with no other man; but now you have become a common bawd," etc.

Two years later, the Cayuga chief, John Hudson, said, at a council at Burlington,[3] "The Munseys are women, and cannot make treaties for themselves."

These were but repetitions of the famous diatribe of the Onondaga chieftain, Canassatego, at a council at Philadelphia, in 1742. Turning to the representatives of the Lenape, he broke out upon them with the words :—

"How came you to take upon you to sell land? We conquered you. We made women of you. You know you are women, and can no more sell land than women.   *   *   *   We charge you to remove instantly. We don't give you the liberty to think about it. We assign you two places to go

---

[1] The words are those of George Croghan, Esq., at the treaty of Pittsburg, 1759, with the Six Nations and Wyandots. *History of Western Penna.*, App. p. 135.

[2] *Records of the Council at Easton*, 1756, in Lib. Amer. Philos. Soc.

[3] Smith, *History of New Jersey*, p. 451 (2d ed.)

to, either Wyoming or Shamokin. Don't deliberate, but remove away ; and take this belt of wampum."

And as he handed the belt to the Lenape head chief he seized him by his long hair and pushed him out of the door of the council room !

It was notorious at the time, however, that this was a scene arranged between the Governor of the Province, Mr. George Thomas, and the Iroquois deputation. The Lenape had been grossly cheated out of their lands by the trick of the so-called "Long Walk," in 1735, and they refused to vacate their hunting grounds. The Governor sent secret messengers to the powerful and dreaded Six Nations to exert their pretended rights, and paid them well for it.[1]

What could the Lenape do ? They were feeble, and undoubtedly had been brought under the authority of their warlike northern neighbors. They found themselves in the position of the Persian chieftain Harmosar, as he stood before the caliph Omar, and heard the latter revile the patriot cause:

"In deinen Händen ist die Macht,
  Wer einem Sieger widerspricht, der widerspricht mit Unbedacht."
                                        —Von Platen-Hallermunde.

Such were the respective claims of the Lenape and Iroquois. Instead of discussing the antecedent probability of one or the other being true, I shall endeavor to ascertain from the early records the precise facts about this curious transaction.

[1] See the *Narrative of the Long Walk*, by John Watson, father and son, in Hazard's *Register of Penna.*, 1830, reprinted in Beach's *Indian Miscellany*, pp. 90–94; also the able discussion of the question in Dr. Charles Thompson's *Inquiry into the Causes of the Alienation of the Delaware and Shawnee Indians*, pp. 30–34 and 42–46. (London, 1759.)

It is certain that toward the close of the sixteenth century the unending wars between the Delaware confederacy and the Iroquois had reduced the latter almost to destruction.   The Jesuit missionaries tell us this.[1]   The turning point in their affairs was the settlement of the Dutch on the Hudson. Quick to appreciate the value of firearms, they bought guns and powder at any price, and soon had rendered themselves formidable to all their neighbors.[2]   About 1670 they attacked successfully that family of the Minsi called the *Minisink.*

This was probably the victory to which the Five Nations referred at a treaty at Philadelphia, in 1727, when they stated that their conquest of the Delawares was about the time William Penn first landed, and that he sent congratulations to them on their success—an obvious falsehood.[3]

They were certainly at that period pressing hard on the Susquehannocks and destroying their remnant in the valley of that river.   Mr. William P. Foulke is quite correct in his conclusion that, "Upon the whole we may conclude that the

[1] *Relations des Jesuites,* 1660, p. 6.   Some confusion has arisen in this matter, from confounding the Susquehannocks with the Iroquois, both of whom were called " Mengwe " by the Delawares, corrupted into " Mingoes."   Thus, a writer in the first half of the 17th century says of the " Mingoes " that the river tribes " are afraid of them, so that they dare not stir, much less go to war against them."   Thomas Campanius, *Description of the Province of New Sweden,* p. 158.

[2] See Mr. E. M. Ruttenber's able discussion of the subject in his *History of the Indian Tribes of Hudson's River,* p. 66 (Albany, 1872).

[3] Dr. Charles Thompson, *An Inquiry into the Causes of the Alienation of the Delaware and Shawnee Indians,* pp. 11, 12.   (London, 1759.)

Lancaster lands fell into the power of the Five Nations at some time between 1677 and 1684."[1]

Yet their conquest of the Minsi was not complete. The latter had the mind and the will to renew the combat. In 1692 they appealed to the government of Pennsylvania to aid them in an attack on the Senecas, but the Quakers declined the foray. The next year the Minsi asked Governor Benjamin Fletcher at least to protect them against these Senecas, adding that with assistance they were ready to attack them, for "although wee are a small number of Indians, wee are Men, and know fighting."[2]

Evidently there was neither subjection nor womanhood with the Minsi at that date.

There is also positive evidence that the Five Nations at that time regarded the Delawares as a combatant nation, and worthy of an invitation to join a war. On July 6th, 1694, Governor Wm. Markham met in conference the famous chief Tamany and others; and the Delaware orator, Hithquoquean, laid down a belt of wampum, and said :—[3]

" This belt is sent us by the Onondagas and Senecas, who say: 'You Delaware Indians do nothing but stay at home and boil your pots, and are like women ; while we, Onondagas and Senecas, go abroad and fight the enemy.'

" The Senecas would have us Delaware Indians to be part-ners with them, and fight against the French, but we, having

---

[1] See his " Notes Respecting the Indians of Lancaster County, Penna.," in the *Collections of the Historical Society of Penna.*, Vol. IV, Part p. 198.

[2] *Minutes of the Provincial Council of Pennsylvania*, Vol. I, p. 333.

[3] Ibid, Vol. I, p. 410–11.

always been a peaceful people, and resolving to live so; and being but weak and verie few in number, cannot assist them, and having resolved among ourselves not to go, doe intend to send back, this their Belt of Wampum.''

The Lenape, therefore, did not, at that date, occupy any degrading position, although they were under the general domination of the Iroquois League.

Both these points are proved yet more conclusively by the proceedings at a conference at White Marsh, May 19th, 1712, between Governor C. Gookin and the Delaware chiefs. Gollitchy, orator of the latter, exhibited thirty-two belts of wampum, which they were on their way to deliver to the Five Nations, adding " that many years ago they had been made tributaries to the Mingoes.'' He also shewed " a long Indian pipe, with a stone head, a wooden shaft, and feathers fixt to it like wings. This pipe, they said, upon making their submission to the Five Nations, who had subdued them, and obliged them to be their tributaries, those Nations had given to these Indians, to be kept by them.'' All the tribute belts, however, were sent by the women and children, as the speaker explained at length, "as the Indian reckons the paying of tribute becomes none but women and children.''[1]

Fortunately, however, we are able to fix the exact date and circumstances of the political transformation of the Delawares into women. It is by no means so remote as Mr. Heckewelder thought, who located the occurrence at Norman's Kill, on the Hudson, between 1609 and 1620;[2]

---

[1] *Minutes of the Provincial Council*, Vol. II, pp. 572–73.

[2] *History of the Indian Nations*, p. xxix.

and it was long after 1670, which is the date assigned by Mr. Ruttenber,[1] from a study of the New York records.

It was in the year 1725, and was in consequence of the Delawares refusing to join the Iroquois in an attack on the English settlements.

These data come to light in a message of the Shawnee chiefs, in 1732, to Governor Gordon, who had inquired their reasons for migrating to the Ohio Valley.

Their reply was as follows : —

"About nine years agoe the 5 nations told us att Shallyschohking, wee Did nott Do well to Setle there, for there was a Greatt noise In the Greatt house and thatt in three years time, all Should know whatt they had to Say, as far as there was any Setlements or the Sun Sett.

"About ye Expiration of 3 years affore S^d, the 5 nations Came and Said our Land is goeing to bee taken from us, Come brothers assistt us. Lett us fall upon and fightt with the English. Wee answered them no, wee Came here for peace and have Leave to Setle here, and wee are In League with them and Canott break itt.

"Aboutt a year after they, ye 5 nations, Told the Delawares and us, Since you have nott hearkened to us, nor Regarded whatt we have said, now wee will pettycoatts on you, and Look upon you as women for the future, and nott as men. Therefore, you Shawanese Look back toward Ohioh, The place from whence you Came, and Return thitherward, for now wee Shall Take pitty on the English and Lett them have all this Land.

"And further Said now Since you are Become women, Ile Take Peahohquelloman, and putt itt on Mcheahoaming and Ile Take Mcheahoaming and putt itt on Ohioh, and Ohioh Ile putt on Woabach, and thatt shall bee the warriours Road for the future." (*Penna. Archives*, Vol. I.)

---

[1] The *Indian Tribes of Hudson's River*, p. 69.

The circumstances attending the ceremony were probably pretty much as Loskiel relates.

The correctness of this account is borne out by an examination of law titles.

That the river tribes at the time of Penn's treaties (1680–1700) could not sell their lands without the permission of the Iroquois has never been established. Mr. Gallatin states that William Penn "always purchased the right of possession from the Delawares, and that of sovereignty from the Five Nations."[1] This may have been the case in some later treaties of the colony, but certainly there is no intimation of it in the celebrated "First Indian Deed" to Penn, July 15th, 1682.[2] Furthermore, in the Release which the Iroquois did give of their Pennsylvania lands in 1736, the boundaries are defined as "Westward to the Setting of the Sun, and Eastward to the furthest springs of the Waters running into the said River," i. e., the Susquehannah;[3] and to do away with any doubt that the tract thus defined included all the land in this part to which they had a claim, the Release goes on to recite that "our true intent and meaning was and is to release all our Right, Claim and Pretensions whatsoever to all and every the Lands lying within the Bounds and Limits of the Government of Pennsylvania, Beginning Eastward on the River Delaware, as far Northward as the sᵈ Ridge or Chain of Endless Mountains." In other words, although the Six Nations advanced no claim to land east of the Susquehanna watershed, the Proprietors chose to include the Delaware watershed so as to

---

[1] *Trans. Am. Antiq. Soc.*, Vol. II, p. 46.

[2] *Pennsylvania Archives*, Vol. I, p. 47.

[3] *Pennsylvania Archives*, Vol. I, p. 498.

avoid any future complication. It seems to me this Release does away with any "right of sovereignty" of the Iroquois over the Delaware Valley south of the mountains, and brands Canassatego's remarks above quoted as braggart falsehoods.

As for land east of the Delaware river, Mr. Ruttenber correctly observes: "The Iroquois never questioned the sales made by the Lenapes or Minsis east of that river. * * The findings of Gallatin in this particular are confirmed by all the title deeds in New York and New Jersey."[1]

It was only to the Susquehannock lands, purchased by Penn in 1699, that the confirmation of the Iroquois was required.[2]

The close of this condition of subjection was in 1756. In that year Sir William Johnson formally "took off the petticoat" from the Lenape, and "handed them the war belt."[3] The year subsequent they made the public declaration that "they would not acknowledge but the Senecas as their superiors."[4]

Even their supremacy was soon rejected. At the Treaty of Fort Pitt, October, 1778, Captain White Eyes, when reminded by the Senecas that the petticoats were still on his people, scornfully repudiated the imputation, and made good his words by leading a war party against them the following year.

[1] *The Indian Tribes of Hudson's River*, p. 69.

[2] See *Penna. Archives*, Vol. I, p. 144, and Du Ponceau, *Memoir on the Treaty at Shackamaxon, Collections of the Penna. Hist. Soc.*, Vol. III, Part II, p. 73.

[3] *New York Colonial Documents*, Vol. VII, p. 119.

[4] Thompson, *Inquiry into the Causes of the Alienation of the Delaware and Shawnee Indians*, p. 107.

I

The Iroquois, however, released their hold unwillingly, and it was not until 1794, shortly before the Treaty of Greenville, that their delegates came forward and "officially declared that the Lenape were no longer women, but *men*," and the famous chief, Joseph Brant, placed in their hands the war club.[1]

§ 2. *Historic Migrations of the Lenape.*

It does not form part of my plan to detail the later history of the Lenape. But some account of their number and migrations will aid in the examination of the origin and claims of the WALUM OLUM.

The first estimate of the whole number of native inhabitants of the province was by William Penn. He stated that there were ten different nations, with a total population of about 6000 souls.[2]

This was in 1683. Very soon after this they began to diminish by disease and migration. As early as 1690, a band of the Minsi left for the far West, to unite with the Ottawas.[3] In 1721 the Frenchman Durant speaks of them as "exceedingly decreased."[4] Already they had yielded to the pressure of the whites, and were seeking homes on the head-waters of the Ohio, in Western Pennsylvania. Their first cabins are said to have been built there in 1724.[5]

---

[1] Heckewelder, *Indian Nations*, p. 70; E. de Schweinitz, *Life of Zeisberger*, pp. 430, 641.

[2] Janney, *Life of Penn*, p. 247.

[3] Ruttenber, *Indians of the Hudson River*, p. 177.

[4] Durant's *Memorial*, in *New York Colonial Documents*, Vol. V, p. 623.

[5] *Early History of Western Pennsylvania*, p. 31 (Pittsburg, 1846); and see *Penna. Archives*, Vol. I, pp. 322, 330.

All that remained in the Delaware valley were ordered by the Iroquois, at the treaty of Lancaster, 1744, to leave the waters of their river, and remove to Shamokin (now Sunbury) and Wyoming, on the Susquehanna, and most of them obeyed.   The former was their chief town, and the residence of their "king," Allemœbi.

When the interpreter, Conrad Weiser, visited their Ohio settlements, in 1748, he reported their warriors there at 165, which was probably about one-fourth of the nation.

In the "French War," 1755, the Delawares united with the French against the Iroquois and English, and suffered considerable losses.   At its close they were estimated to have, both on the Susquehanna and in Ohio, a total of 600 available fighting men.[1]

After this date they steadily migrated from the Susquehannah to the streams in central and eastern Ohio, establishing their chief fire on the Tuscarawas river, at Gekelemukpechunk, and hunting on the Muskingum, the Licking, etc.[2]

When the war of the Revolution broke out, Zeisberger used all his efforts to have them remain neutral, and at least prevented them from joining in a general attack on the settlements.   Their distinguished war-chief, Koquethagachton, known to the settlers as "Captain White Eyes," declared, in 1775, in favor of the Federal cause, and renounced for himself and his people all dependence on the Iroquois. These friendly relations were confirmed at the treaty of

[1] Loskiel, *Geschichte der Mission*, p. 54.   The treaty of Lancaster 1762, was the last treaty held with the Indians in eastern Pennsylvania.

[2] Schweinitz, *Life of Zeisberger*, p. 90.

Fort Pitt (1778), and the next year a number of Delawares accompanied Col. Brodhead in an expedition against the Senecas.

The massacre of the unoffending Christian natives of Gnadenhütten, in 1788, was but one event in the murderous war between the races that continued in Ohio from 1782 to the treaty of peace at Greenville, in 1795.

To escape its direful scenes, a part of the Delawares removed south, to upper Louisiana, in 1789, where they received official permission from Governor Carondelet, in 1793, to locate permanent homes.[1] Zeisberger also, in 1791, conducted his colony of Christian Indians to Canada, and founded the town of Fairfield, on the Retrenche river. Thus, in both directions the Delawares were driven off the soil of the United States. Yet those that remained in Ohio, if we may accept the account of John Brickell, who was a captive among them from 1791 to 1796, attempted to live a peaceable and agricultural life.[2]

Peace restored, the Delawares made their next remove to the valley of White Water river, Indiana, where they attempted to rekindle the national council fire, under the head chief Tedpachxit. They founded six towns, the largest of which was *Woapikamikunk* or *Wapeminskink*, "Place of Chestnut Trees." This tract was guaranteed them "in perpetuity"

---

[1] *New York Colonial Documents*, Vol. VII, p. 583.

[2] On the locations of the Delawares in Ohio, and the boundaries of their tract, see Ed. de Schweinitz, *Life of Zeisberger*, p. 374, and an article by the Rev. Stephen D. Peet, entitled "The Delaware Indians in Ohio," in the *American Antiquarian*, Vol. II.

by the treaty of Vincennes, 1808.[1] Nevertheless, just ten years later, at the treaty of St. Mary's, they released the whole of their land, "without reserve," to the United States, the government agreeing to remove them west of the Mississippi, and grant them land there.

At this time they numbered about 1000 souls, of whom 800 were Delawares, the others being Mohegans and Nanticokes.[2] Their head chief was Thahutoowelent, of the Turkey tribe, Tedpachxit having been assassinated, at the instigation of Tecumseh.

They are described as "having a peculiar aversion to white people," and "more opposed to the Gospel and the whites than any other Indians,"[3] which is small matter of wonder, when they had seen the peaceful Christian converts of their nation massacred three times, in cold blood, once at Gnadenhütten, in Pennsylvania (1756); again at Gnadenhütten, in Ohio (1788), and finally at Fairfield, Canada (1813).

The Rev. Isaac McCoy, who visited them on the White Water, in the winter of 1818–19, states that they lived in log huts and bark shanties, and were fearfully deteriorated by whisky drinking.[4]

The last band of the Delawares that appeared in Ohio was in 1822.[5]

---

[1] The position of the Delawares in Indiana is roughly shown on Hough's Map of the Tribal Districts of Indiana, in the *Report on the Geology and Natural History of Indiana*, 1882.

[2] J. Morse, *Report on the Indian Tribes*, p. 110.

[3] Mr. John Johnston, Indian Agent, in *Trans. of the Amer. Antiquarian Society*, Vol. I, p. 271.

[4] *History of the Baptist Indian Missions*, p. 53, etc.

[5] *Captivity of Christian Fast*, in Beach, *Indian Miscellany*, p. 63.

The location assigned to the Delawares was near the mouth of the Kansas river, Kansas. They were reported, in 1850, as possessing there 375,000 acres and numbering about 1500 souls. Four years later they "ceded" this land, and were moved to various reservations in the Indian Territory.

There still remain about sixty natives at New Westfield, near Ottawa, Kansas, under the charge of the Moravian Church. The same denomination has about 300 of the tribe on the reservation at Moraviantown, in the province of Ontario, Canada. A second reservation in Canada is under the charge of the Anglican Church. The majority of the tribe are scattered in different agencies in the Indian Territory.

§ 3. *Missionary Efforts in the Provinces of New Jersey and Pennsylvania.*

None of the American colonies enjoyed a more favorable opportunity to introduce the Christian religion to the natives than that located on the Delaware river. What use was made of it?

The Rev. Thomas Campanius, of Stockholm, a Lutheran clergyman, attached to the Swedish settlement from 1642 to 1649, made a creditable effort to acquire the native tongue and preach Christianity to the savages about him. He translated the Catechism into the traders' dialect of Lenape, but we have no record that he succeeded in his attempts at conversion.

One might suppose that so very religious a body as the early Friends would have taken some positive steps in this direction. Such was not the case. I have not found the record of any one of them who set seriously to work to learn the native tongue, without which all effort would have been fruitless.

William Penn was not wholly unmindful of the spiritual condition of his native wards. In 1699 he offered to provide the Friends' Meeting at Philadelphia with interpreters to convey religious instruction to the Indians. But the Meeting took no steps in this direction. He himself, when in the colony in 1701, made some attempts to address them on religious subjects, as did also Friend John Richardson, who was with him, availing themselves of interpreters. The latter reports a satisfactory response to his words, but not being followed up, their effect was ephemeral.[1]

Nothing further was done for nearly half a century, and when the enthusiastic young David Brainerd began his mission in 1742, he distinctly states that there was not another missionary in either province.[2] His labors extended over four years, and were productive of some permanent good results among the New Jersey Indians, and this in spite of the suspicions, opposition and evil example of the whites around him. The little society of Christian Indians which he gathered in Burlington County, New Jersey, was even reported as a congregation of rioters and enemies of the State![3]

[1] See the work entitled, *Account of the Conduct of the Society of Friends toward the Indian Tribes*, pp. 55 seq. (London, 1844.)

[2] "I have likewise been wholly alone in my work, there being no other missionary among the Indians, in either of these Provinces." He wrote this in 1746. *Life of David Brainerd*, p. 409.

[3] See "A State of Facts about the Riots," in *New Jersey Archives*, Vol. VI, pp. 406–7, where the writer speaks with great suspicion of "the cause pretended for such a number of Indians coming to live there is that they are to be taught the Christian religion by one Mr. *Braniard*." Well he might! Any such occurrence was totally unprecedented in the annals of the colony.

Nor was the province of Penn inclined to greater favors toward Christianized natives. When the Indians were cheated out of their lands by the "Long Walk," a few who had been converted, among others the chief Moses Tatemy, petitioned the Council to remain on their lands, some of which were direct personal gifts from the Proprietaries. Their request was refused, and Moses Tatemy, who did remain, was shot down like a dog, in the road, by a white man.[1]

Unknown to Brainerd, however, the seeds of a Christian harvest had already been sown, in 1742, in the wilderness of Pennsylvania, by the ardent Moravian leader, Count Nicholas Lewis Zinzendorf; already, in 1744, the fervent Zeisberger, prescient of his long and marvelous service in the church militant, had registered himself as *destinirter Heidenbote*—"appointed messenger to the heathen"—in the corner-stone of the Brethren's House, at Bethlehem; already the pious Rauch had collected a small but earnest congregation of Mohegans at Shekomeko, who soon removed to the Lehigh valley, and pitched the first of those five *Gnadenhütten*, "Tents of Grace," destined successively to mark the unwearied efforts of the Moravian missionaries, and their frustration through the treachery of the conquering whites.[2]

---

[1] See *Minutes of the Provincial Council of Penna.*, Nov., 1742, Vol. IV, 624–5. Further, on Tatemy, who had been converted by Brainerd and served him as interpreter, see Heckewelder, *Indian Nations*, second edition, p. 302, note of the editor.

[2] The Heckewelder MSS., in the library of the Am. Philos. Society, give the results of the first twenty years, 1741–61, of the labors of the Moravian brethren. In that period 525 Indians were converted and baptized. Of these—163 were Connecticut Wampanos; 111 were Mahicanni proper; 251 were Lenape. Some of the latter were of the New Jersey Wapings.

It is not my purpose to tell the story of this long struggle. Its thrilling events are recounted, with all desirable fullness, in the vivid narrative of Bishop Edmund de Schweinitz, grouped around the marked individuality of the devoted Zeisberger—pages which none can read without amazement at the undaunted courage of these Christian heroes, without sorrow at the sparse harvest gleaned from such devotion.[1]

When, after sixty-two years of missionary labors, the venerable Zeisberger closed his eyes in death (1808), the huts of barely a score of converted Indians clustered around his little chapel. His aspiration that the Lenape would form a native Christian State, their ancient supremacy revived and applied to the dissemination of peace, piety and civilization among their fellow-tribes—this cherished hope of his life had forever disappeared. He had lived to see the Lenape, a mere broken remnant, "steeped in all the abominations of heathenism, eke out their existence far away from their former council fires."

[1] *The Life and Times of David Zeisberger, the Western Pioneer and Apostle of the Indians.* By Edmund de Schweinitz, Philadelphia, 1871.

CHAPTER VI.

Myths and Traditions of the Lenape.

Cosmogonical and Culture Myths.—The Culture-hero, Michabo.—Myths from Lindstrom, Ettwein, Jasper Donkers, Zeisberger.—Native Symbolism.—The Saturnian
Age.—Mohegan Cosmogony and Migration Myth.

National Traditions.—Beatty's Account.—The Number Seven.—Heckewelder's Account.—Prehistoric Migrations.—Shawnee Legend.—Lenape Legend of the Naked
Bear.

Cosmogonical and Culture Myths.

The Algonkins, as a stock, had a well developed creation-
myth and a culture legend, found in more or less completeness
in all their branches.

Their culture hero, their ancestor and creator, he who made
the earth and stocked it with animals, who taught them the
arts of war and the chase, and gave them the Indian corn,
beans and squashes, was generally called *Michabo*, The Great
Light, but was also known among the Narragansetts of New
England as *Wetucks*, The Common Father; among the Cree
as *Wisakketjâk*, the Trickster; by the Chippeways as Nanabozho (*Nenâboj*), the Cheat; by the Black Feet as *Natose*,
Our Father, or *Napiw*; and by the Micmacs and Penobscots
as *Glus-Kap*, the Liar.

I have given the details of this myth and analyzed them
in previous works;[1] here it is sufficient to say that it is a

---

[1] D. G. Brinton, *Myths of the New World*, Chap. VI. (N. Y., 1876), and
American Hero Myths, Chap. II (Phila., 1882). The seeming incongruity
of applying such terms as Trickster, Cheat and Liar to the highest divinity
I have explained in a paper in the *American Antiquarian* for the current
year (1885) and will recur to later.

Light-myth, and one of noble proportion and circumstance, quite worthy of comparison with those of the Oriental world.

Traces of it are reported among the Lenape, and I doubt not that had we their ancient stories in their completeness, we should find that they had preserved it as wholly as the Chipeways. These related of their Nanabozho that he was the son of a maiden who had descended from heaven. She conceived without knowledge of man, and having given birth to twins, she disappeared. One of these twins was Nanabozho. Having formed the earth by his miraculous powers, and done many wonderful things, he disappeared toward the east, where he still dwells beyond the sunrise.

It was undoubtedly a fragment of this legend that the Swedish engineer, Lindstrom heard among the Lenape, on the Delaware, about 1650. They told him, or rather he understood them, as follows :—

"Once, one of your women (*i. e.*, a white woman) came among us, and she became pregnant, in consequence of drinking out of a creek ; an Indian had connection with her, and she became pregnant, and brought forth a son, who, when he came to a certain size, was so sensible and clever, that there never was one who could be compared to him, so much and so well he spoke, which excited great wonder ; he also performed many miracles. When he was quite grown up, he left us, and went up to heaven, and promised to come again, but has never returned."[1]

This is but a mistranslation of the general Algonkin legend, in which the virgin mother bears a white and dark

[1] Thomas Campanius, *Account of New Sweden*, Book III, cap. xi.

twin, the former of whom becomes the tribal culture hero and demiurgic deity.

Its interpretation is, that the virgin is the Dawn, who brings forth the Day, which assures safety and knowledge, and the Night, which departs with her. The Day leaves us, and in its personified form returns no more, though ever expected.

That such were the original form and significance of the myth, we have the testimony of Bishop Ettwein,[1] himself a Delaware scholar, and who drew his information from the natives as well as the missionaries. He tells us that their legend ran, that in the beginning the first woman fell from heaven and bore twins; that it was toward the east that they directed their children to turn their faces when they prayed to the spirits; and that their old men had said that it was an ancient belief that from that quarter some one would come to them to benefit them. Therefore, said they, when our ancestors saw the first white men, they looked upon them as divine, and adored them.

The Dutch travelers, Jasper Donkers and Peter Sluyter, relate a part of this myth as they heard it from New Jersey Indians in 1679. These informed them that all things came from a tortoise. It had brought forth the world, and from the middle of its back had sprung up a tree, upon whose branches men had grown.

This tortoise "had a power and a nature to produce all things, such as earth, trees and the like." But it was not the *primum mobile*, not the ultimate energy of the universe. "The first and great beginning of all things was *Kickeron*

---

[1] *Traditions and Language of the Indians*, in *Bulletin Hist. Soc. Pa.*, Vol. I, pp. 30–31.

or *Kickerom*, who is the original of all, who has not only once produced or made all things, but produces every day." The tortoise brought forth what this primal divinity "wished through it to produce."[1]

This is a very interesting statement. It reveals a depth of thought on the part of the native philosophers for which we were scarcely prepared. The worthy Dutch travelers do not pretend to explain the myth. But its sense can be clearly interpreted.

The turtle or tortoise is everywhere in Algonkin pictography the symbol of the earth.[2] From the earth, from the soil, all organic life, the whole realm of animate existence— ever sharply defined in Algonkin grammar and thought from inanimate existence—proceeds, directly as vegetable life, or indirectly as animal life. The earth is the All-Mother, ever-producing, inexhaustible.

As for *Kikeron*, the eternally active, hidden spirit of the universe, I have but to refer the reader to the list of ideas associated around this root *kik*, which I have given on a previous page (p. 102) to reveal the significance of this word. We may, with equal correctness, translate it Life, Light, Action or Energy. It is the abstract conception back of all these.

The distinction was the same as that established by the

---

[1] *Journal of a Voyage to New York in 1679-80.* By Jasper Donkers and Peter Sluyter, p. 268. Translation in Vol. I of the *Transactions of the Long Island Historical Society* (Brooklyn, 1867).

[2] Schoolcraft says of the Chipeway pictographic symbols: "The turtle is believed to be, in all instances, a symbol of the earth, and is addressed as mother." *History and Statistics of the Indian Tribes*, Vol. I, p. 390.

scholastic philosophers between the *mundus* and the *anima mundi*; between the *essentia* and the *existentia;* between *natura naturans* and *natura naturata.* But who expected to find it among the Lenape?

This creation myth of the Delawares is also given in brief by Zeisberger. It dated back to that marvelous overflow which is heard of in many mythologies. The whole earth was submerged, and but a few persons survived. They had taken refuge on the back of a turtle, who had reached so great an age that his shell was mossy, like the bank of a rivulet. In this forlorn condition a loon flew that way, which they asked to dive and bring up land. He complied, but found no bottom. Then he flew far away, and returned with a small quantity of earth in his bill. Guided by him, the turtle swam to the place, where a spot of dry land was found. There the survivors settled and repeopled the land.[1]

This is more a tale of reconstruction than a creation myth. It is that which has generally been supposed to refer to the Deluge. But, as I have explained in my "Myths of the New World," all these so-called Deluge Myths are but developments of crude cosmogonical theories.

To understand the significance of this myth we must examine the Indian notion of the earth. This is the more germane to my theme, as the meaning of the original text which is printed in this volume can only be grasped by one acquainted with this notion.

The Indians almost universally believed the dry land they knew to be a part of a great island, everywhere surrounded

[1] Zeisberger, MSS., in E. de Schweinitz, *Life and Times of Zeisberger*, pp. 218, 219; Heckewelder, *Indian Nations*, p. 253.

by wide waters whose limits were unknown.[1] Many tribes
had vague myths of a journey from beyond this sea; many
placed beyond it the home of the Sun and of Light, and the
happy hunting grounds of the departed souls. The Delawares
believed that the whole was supported by a fabled turtle, whose
movements caused earthquakes and who had been their first
preserver.[2] As above mentioned, the turtle in its amphibious
character and rounded back represented the earth or the land
itself, as distinguished from water. Like the turtle, the land
lies at times under the water and at times above it. The
spirit of the earth was the practical and visible developmental
energy of nature.

The medicine men, or conjurers, who professed to be in
personal relations with this power, made their "medicine
rattle" of a turtle shell (Loskiel), and when they died,
such a shell was suspended from their tomb posts (Zeisberger).

The Delawares also shared the belief, common to so many
nations the world over, that the pristine age was one of un-
alloyed prosperity, peace and happiness, an Age of Gold, a
Saturnian Reign. Their legends asseverated that at that time
"the killing of a man was unknown, neither had there been
instances of their dying before they had attained to that age
which causes the hair to become white, the eyes dim, and the
teeth to be worn away."

This happy time was brought to a close by the advent of

[1] "The Indians call the American continent an island; believing it to
be entirely surrounded by water." Heckewelder, *Hist. Indian Nations*,
p. 250.

[2] Ibid, p. 308.

certain evil beings who taught men how to kill each other by sorcery.[1]

Their kinsmen, the Mohegans, varied this cosmogonical tradition, though retaining some of its main features. They taught that in the beginning there was nought but water and sky. At length from the sky a woman descended, our common mother. As she approached the boundless ocean, a small point of land rose above the watery surface, and supplied her with firm footing. She was pregnant by some mysterious power, and she brought forth on this island animal triplets— a bear, a deer and a wolf. From these all men and animals are descended. The island grew to a main land, and the mother of all, her mission accomplished, returned to her home in the sky.[2]

This creation-myth, obtained from the Indians around New York harbor in the first generation after the advent of the whites, has every mark of a genuine native production, and coincides closely with that generally believed by the early Algonkins.

It is followed by a migration myth, which ran to the effect that their early forefathers came out of the northwest, forsaking a tide-water country, and crossing over a great watery tract, called *ukhkok-pek*, "snake water, or water where snakes are abundant," (*ákhgook*, snake, and *pek*, standing water,

---

[1] Heckewelder, MSS. in the Library of the American Philosophical Society. It is one of the points in favor of the authenticity of the WALAM OLUM that this halcyon epoch is mentioned in its lines, though no reference to it is contained in printed books relating to the Lenape legends.

[2] Van der Donck, *Description of the New Netherlands, Coll. N. Y. Hist. Soc.*, Ser. II, Vol. I, pp. 217–18.

probably from *n'pey*, water, *akek*, place or country). They crossed many streams, but none in which the water ebbed and flowed, until they reached the Hudson. "Then they said, one to another, 'This is like the Muhheakunnuck (tidal ocean) of our nativity.' Therefore they agreed to kindle a fire there and hang a kettle, whereof they and their children after them might dip out their daily refreshment." Hence came their name, the Tide-water People (see ante, p. 20).

National Traditions.

Many early writers attest the passionate fondness of the Delawares for their ancestral traditions and the memory of their ancient heroes. The missionary, David Brainerd, mentions this as one of the leading difficulties in the way of "evangelizing the Indians." "They are likewise much attached," he writes, "to the traditions and fabulous notions of their fathers, which they firmly believe, and thence look upon their ancestors to have been the best of men."[1]

To the same effect, Loskiel informs us that the Delawares "love to relate what great warriors their ancestors had been, and how many heroic deeds they had performed. It is a pleasure to them to rehearse their genealogies. They are so skilled at it that they can repeat the chief and collateral lines with the utmost readiness. At the same time, they characterize their ancestors, by describing this one as a wise or skillful man, as a great chieftain, a renowned warrior, a rich man, and the like. This they teach to their children,

[1] *Life and Journal of the Rev. David Brainerd*, pp. 397, 425 (Edinburgh, 1826).

J

and *embody it in pictures, so as to make it more readily remembered.*"[1]

The earliest writer who gives us any detailed description of what these traditions were, is the Rev. Charles Beatty, who visited the Delaware settlements in Ohio in 1767. On his way there, he met a white man, Benjamin Sutton, who for years had been a captive among the natives. He related to Beatty the following tradition, which he had heard recited by some old men among the Delawares:—

"That of old time their people were divided by a river, nine parts of ten passing over the river, and one part remaining behind; that they knew not, for certainty, how they came to this continent; but account thus for their first coming into these parts where they are now settled; that a king of their nation, where they formerly lived, far to the west, left his kingdom to his two sons; that the one son making war upon the other, the latter thereupon determined to depart and seek some new habitation; that accordingly he sat out, accompanied by a number of his people, and that, after wandering to and fro for the space of forty years, they at length came to Delaware river, where they settled 370 years ago. The way, he says, they keep an account of this is by putting on a black bead of wampum every year on a belt they keep for that purpose."[2]

---

[1] So we may understand Loskiel to mean when he says, "Das bringen sie ihren Kindern ebenfalls bey, und kleiden es in Bilder ein, um es noch eindrücklicher zu machen." *Geschichte der Mission*, etc., s. 32. I think Zeisberger, who was Loskiel's authority, meant *Bilder* in its literal, not rhetorical, sense.

[2] Charles Beatty, *Journal of a Two Months' Tour; with a View of*

From another source Mr. Beatty obtained the traditions of the Nanticokes, which is apparently a version of that of their relatives, the Delawares. It ran to this effect: At some remote age, while on their way to their present homes, "They came to a great water. One of the Indians that went before them tried the depth of it by a long pole or reed, which he had in his hand, and found it too deep for them to wade. Upon their being non-plussed, and not knowing how to get over it, their God made a bridge over the water in one night, and the next morning, after they were all over, God took away the bridge."[1]

A curious addition to this story is mentioned by Loskiel.[2] The number of the mythical ancestors of their race who thus were left on the shore of the great water was *seven*. This at once recalls the seven caves (*Chicomoztoc*) or primitive stirpes of the Mexican tribes, the seven clans (*vuk amag*) of the Cakchiquels, the seven ancestors of the Qquechuas, etc., and strongly intimates that there must be some common natural occurrence to give rise to this wide-spread legend.[3]

Some peculiar sacredness must have attached to this number among the Delawares also, as we are informed that the period

---

Promoting Religion among the Frontier Inhabitants of Pennsylvania, and of Introducing Christianity among the Indians to the Westward of the Alleghgeny Mountains, p. 27 (London, 1768).

[1] Ibid, p. 91.

[2] *Geschichte der Mission*, etc., p. 31.

[3] The Mohegans seem also to have at one time had a sevenfold division. At least a writer speaks of the "seven tribes" into which those in Connecticut were divided. *Mass. Hist. Soc. Colls.*, Vol. IX (1 ser.), p. 90.

of isolation of their women at the catamenial period was seven days.[1]

The lunar month of 28 days, if divided and assigned equally to each of the four cardinal points, would give a week of seven days to each. Something of this kind seems to have been done by another Algonkin tribe, the Ottawas, who declared that the winds are caused (alternately?) by seven genii or gods who dwelt in the air.[2]

The seven day period is also a natural, physical one, whose influence is felt widely by vertebrate and invertebrate animals, as Darwin has pointed out,[3] and hence its appearance among these people, who lived entirely subject to the operation of their physical surroundings, is not so surprising.

The most complete account of the Delaware tradition is that preserved by Heckewelder. In his pages it appears, not as a reminiscence of tribal history, but as the tradition of the whole eastern Algonkin race, and it claims for the three Delaware tribes an antiquity of organization surpassing that of any of their neighbors.

It holds such an important place that I quote all the essential passages:—

"The Lenni Lenape (according to the traditions handed down to them by their ancestors) resided many hundred years ago in a very distant country in the western part of the American continent. For some reason, which I do not find accounted for, they determined on migrating to the eastward, and accordingly set out together in a body. After a very

---

[1] Charles Beatty, *Journal*, etc., p. 84.

[2] *Relation des Jesuites*, 1648, p. 77.

[3] *The Descent of Man*, p. 165, note.

long journey, and many nights' encampments by the way, they at length arrived on the *Namæsi Sipu*, where they fell in with the Mengwe, who had likewise emigrated from a distant country, and had struck upon this river somewhat higher up. Their object was the same with that of the Delawares ; they were proceeding on to the eastward, until they should find a country that pleased them. The spies which the Lenape had sent forward for the purpose of reconnoitring, had long before their arrival discovered that the country east of the Mississippi was inhabited by a very powerful nation, who had many large towns built on the great rivers flowing through their land. Those people (as I was told) called themselves Talligeu or Talligewi. Colonel John Gibson, however, a gentleman who has a thorough knowledge of the Indians, and speaks several of their languages, is of opinion that they were not called Talligewi, but Alligewi. * * *

" Many wonderful things are told of this famous people. They are said to have been remarkably tall, and stout, and there is a tradition that there were giants among them, people of a much larger size than the tallest of the Lenape. It is related that they had built to themselves regular fortifications or entrenchments, from whence they would sally out, but were generally repulsed. * * *

" When the Lenape arrived on the banks of the Mississippi, they sent a message to the Alligewi to request permission to settle themselves in their neighbourhood. This was refused them, but they obtained leave to pass through the country and seek a settlement farther to the eastward. They accordingly began to cross the Namæsi Sipu, when the Alligewi, seeing that their numbers were so very great, and in fact they

consisted of many thousands, made a furious attack on those
who had crossed, threatening them all with destruction, if
they dared to persist in coming over to their side of the
river. * * *

"Having united their forces, the Lenape and Mengwe declared war against the Alligewi, and great battles were fought,
in which many warriors fell on both sides. The enemy fortified their large towns and erected fortifications, especially on
large rivers and near lakes, where they were successively attacked and sometimes stormed by the allies. An engagement
took place in which hundreds fell, who were afterwards buried
in holes or laid together in heaps and covered over with earth.
No quarter was given, so that the Alligewi, at last, finding
that their destruction was inevitable if they persisted in their
obstinacy, abandoned the country to the conquerors, and
fled down the Mississippi river, from whence they never returned. * * *

"In the end the conquerors divided the country between
themselves; the Mengwe made choice of the lands in the
vicinity of the great lakes and on their tributary streams, and
the Lenape took possession of the country to the south. For
a long period of time—some say many hundred years—the
two nations resided peaceably in this country, and increased
very fast; some of their most enterprising huntsmen and
warriors crossed the great swamps, and falling on streams
running to the eastward, followed them down to the great
Bay river, thence into the Bay itself, which we call Chesa-
peak. As they pursued their travels, partly by land and
partly by water, sometimes near and at other times on the
great Salt-water Lake, as they call the sea, they discovered

the great river, which we call the Delaware; and thence exploring still eastward, the *Scheyichbi* country, now named New Jersey, they arrived at another great stream, that which we call the Hudson or North river. * * *

"At last they settled on the four great rivers (which we call Delaware, Hudson, Susquehannah, Potomack), making the Delaware, to which they gave the name of '*Lenape-wihittuck*' (the river or stream of the Lenape), the centre of their possessions.

"They say, however, that the whole of their nation did not reach this country; that many remained behind, in order to aid and assist that great body of their people which had not crossed the Namæsi Sipu, but had retreated into the interior of the country on the other side. * * *

"Their nation finally became divided into three separate bodies; the larger body, which they suppose to have been one-half the whole, was settled on the Atlantic, and the other half was again divided into two parts, one of which, the strongest, as they suppose, remained beyond the Mississippi, and the remainder where they left them, on this side of that river.

"Those of the Delawares who fixed their abodes on the shores of the Atlantic divided themselves into three tribes. Two of them, distinguished by the names of the *Turtle* and the *Turkey*, the former calling themselves *Unâmi*, and the other *Unalâchtgo*, chose those grounds to settle on which lay nearest to the sea, between the coast and the high mountains. As they multiplied, their settlements extended from the *Mohicanittuck* (river of the Mohicans, which we call the North or Hudson river) to the Potomack. * * *

"The third tribe, the *Wolf*, commonly called the *Minsi*, which we have corrupted into *Monseys*, had chosen to live back of the other two. * * * They extended their settlements from the Minisink, a place named after them, where they had their council seat and fire, quite up to the Hudson, on the east; and to the west or southward far beyond the Susquehannah.

"From the above three tribes, the *Unami, Unalachtgo* and the *Minsi*, had, in the course of time, sprung many others, * * * the *Mahicanni*, or Mohicans, who spread themselves over all that country which now composes the Eastern States, * * * and the *Nanticokes*, who proceeded far to the south, in Maryland and Virginia."

On their conquests during the period of their western migrations, the Delawares based a claim for hunting grounds in the Ohio valley. It is stated that when they had decided to remove to the valley of the Muskingum, their chief, Netawatwes, presented this claim to the Hurons and Miamis, and had it allowed.[1] They also claimed lands on White River, Indiana, and their settlement in that region at the close of the last century was regarded as a return to their ancient seats.

Nevertheless, in the earliest historic times, when the whites first came in contact with the Lenape tribes, none of them dwelt west of the mountains, nor, apparently, had they any towns in the valley of the west branch of the Susquehanna or of its main stream.

Although the above mentioned facts point to a migration in prehistoric times from the West toward the East, there are

[1] Heckewelder, *Trans. Amer. Philos. Soc.*, Vol. III, p. 388.

indications of a yet older movement from the northeast westward and southward to the upper Mississippi valley. A legend
common to the western Algonkin tribes, the Kikapoos, Sacs,
Foxes, Ottawas and Pottawatomies, located their original
home north of the St. Lawrence river, near or below where
Montreal now stands. In that distant land their ancestors
were created by the Great Spirit, and they dwelt there, "all
of one nation." Only when they removed or were driven
west did they separate into tribes speaking different dialects.[1]

The Shawnees, who at various times were in close relation
with the Delawares, also possessed a vague migration myth,
according to which, at some indefinitely remote past, they
had arrived at the main land after crossing a wide water.
Their ancestors succeeded in this by their great control of
magic arts, their occult power enabling them to walk over the
water as if it had been land. Until within the present century
this legend was repeated annually, and a yearly sacrifice offered
up in memory of their safe arrival.[2] It is evidently a version
of that which appears in the third part of the WALAM OLUM.

---

[1] This legend was told by the Sac Chief Masco, to Major Marston, about
1819. See J. Morse, *Report on Indian Affairs*, p. 138.

[2] This myth was obtained in 1812, from the Shawnees in Missouri
(Schoolcraft, *Indian Tribes*, Vol. IV, p. 254), and independently in 1819,
from those in Ohio (Mr. John Johnston, in *Trans. of the Amer. Antiq.
Soc.*, Vol. I, p. 273). Those of the tribe who now live on the Quapaw
Reservation, Indian Territory, repeat every year a long, probably mythical
and historical, chant, the words of which I have tried, in vain, to obtain.
They say that to repeat it to a white man would bring disasters on their
nation. I mention it as a piece of aboriginal composition most desirable
to secure.

One of the curious legends of the Lenape was that of the Great Naked or Hairless Bear. It is told by the Rev. John Heckewelder, in a letter to Dr. B. S. Barton.[1] The missionary had heard it both among the Delawares and the Mohicans. By the former, it was spoken of as *amangachktiātmachque*, and in the dialect of the latter, *ahamagachktiāt mechqua*.[2]

The story told of it was that it was immense in size and the most ferocious of animals. Its skin was bare, except a tuft of white hair on its back. It attacked and ate the natives, and the only means of escape from it was to take to the water. Its sense of smell was remarkably keen, but its sight was defective. As its heart was very small, it could not be easily killed. The surest plan was to break its back-bone; but so dangerous was an encounter with it, that those hunters who went in pursuit of it bade their families and friends farewell, as if they never expected to return.

Fortunately, there were few of these beasts. The last one known was to the east, somewhere beyond the left bank of the Mahicanni Sipu (the Hudson river). When its presence was learned a number of bold hunters went there, and mounted a rock with precipitous sides. They then made a noise, and attracted the bear's attention, who rushed to the attack with great fury. As he could not climb the rock, he tore at it

---

[1] Published in the *Transactions of the American Philosophical Society*, 1st ser., Vol. IV, pp. 260, sqq.

[2] From *amangi*, great or big (in composition *amangach*), with the accessory notion of terrible, or frightful; Cree, *amansis*, to frighten; *tiāt*, an abbreviated form of *tawa*, naked, whence the name *Tawatawas*, or Twightees, applied to the Miami Indians in the old records. (See *Minutes of the Provincial Council of Penna.*, Vol. VIII, p. 418.)

with his teeth, while the hunters above shot him with arrows and threw upon him great stones, and thus killed him.

Though this was the last of the species, the Indian mothers still used his name to frighten their children into obedience, threatening them with the words, " The Naked Bear will eat you."

CHAPTER VII.

The Walam Olum: Its Origin, Authenticity and Contents.

Biographical Sketch of Rafinesque.—Value of his Writings.—His Account of the Walam Olum.—Was it a Forgery?—Rafinesque's Character.—The Text pronounced Genuine by Native Delawares.—Conclusion Reached.

Phonetic System of the Walam Olum —Metrical Form.—Pictographic System.— Derivation and Precise Meaning of Walam Olum.—The MS. of the Walam Olum.—General Synopsis of the Walum Olum.—Synopsis of its Parts.

Rafinesque and his Writings.

Constantine Samuel Rafinesque-Schmaltz, to whom we owe the preservation and first translation of the Walam Olum, was born in Galata, a suburb of Constantinople, Oct. 22d, 1783, and died in Philadelphia, of cancer of the stomach, Sept. 18th, 1840.

His first visit to this country was in 1802. He remained until 1804, when he went to Sicily, where he commenced business. As the French were unpopular there, he added "Schmaltz" to his name, for "prudent considerations," that being the surname of his mother's family.

In 1815 he returned to America, but had the misfortune to be shipwrecked on the coast, losing his manuscripts and much of his property. On his arrival, he supported himself by teaching, occupying his leisure time in scientific pursuits and travel. In 1819 he was appointed "Professor of Historical and Natural Sciences," in Transylvania University, Kentucky.

This position he was obliged to resign, for technical reasons, in 1826, when he returned to Philadelphia, which city he made his home during the rest of his life.

From his early youth he was an indefatigable student, collector and writer in various branches of knowledge, especially in natural history. On the title-page of the last work that he published, "The Good Book and Amenities of Nature" (Philadelphia, 1840), he claims to be the author of "220 books, pamphlets, essays and tracts." Including his contributions to periodicals, there is no reason to doubt the correctness of this estimate. They began when he was nineteen, and were composed in English, French, Italian and Latin, all of which he wrote with facility.

His earlier essays were principally on botanical subjects; later, he included zoölogy and conchology; and during the last fifteen years of his life the history and antiquities of America appear to have occupied his most earnest attention.

The value of his writings in these various branches has been canvassed by several eminent critics in their respective lines.

First in point of time was Prof. Asa Gray, who in the year following Rafinesque's death published in the "American Journal of Science and Arts," Vol. XI, an analysis of his botanical writings. He awards him considerable credit for his earlier investigations, but much less for his later ones. To quote Dr. Gray's words: "A gradual deterioration will be observed in Rafinesque's botanical writings from 1819 to 1830, when the passion for establishing new genera and species appears to have become a complete *monomania*."[1] But modern believers in the doctrine of the evolution of plant forms and

[1] *American Journal of Science*, Vol. XL, p. 237.

the development of botanical species will incline to think
that there was a method in this madness, when they read the
passage from Rafinesque's writings, about 1836, which Dr.
Gray quotes as conclusively proving that, in things botanical,
Rafinesque had lost his wits. It is this: "But it is needless
to dispute about new genera, species and varieties. Every
variety is a deviation, which becomes a species as soon as it
is permanent by reproduction. Deviations in essential organs
may thus gradually become new genera." This is really an
anticipation of Darwinianism in botany.

The next year, in the same journal, appeared a "Notice of
the Zoölogical Writings of the late C. S. Rafinesque," by
Prof. S. S. Haldeman. It is, on the whole, depreciatory, and
convicts Rafinesque of errors of observation as well as of inference; at the same time, not denying his enthusiasm and
his occasional quickness to appreciate zoölogical facts.

In 1864 the conchological writings of Rafinesque were
collected and published, in Philadelphia, by A. G. Binney
and Geo. W. Tryon, Jr., without comments. One of
the editors informs me that they have positive merit,
although the author was too credulous and too desirous
of novelties.

The antiquarian productions of Rafinesque, which interest
us most in this connection, were reviewed with caustic severity
by Dr. S. F. Haven,[1] especially the "Ancient Annals of
Kentucky," which was printed as an introduction to Mar-
shall's History of that State, in 1824. It is, indeed, an
absurd production, a reconstruction of alleged history on the
flimsiest foundations; but, alas! not a whit more absurd than

---

[1] Samuel F. Haven, *Archæology of the United States*, p. 40.

the laborious card houses of many a subsequent antiquary of renown.

His principal work in this branch appeared in Philadelphia in 1836, entitled: "The American Nations; or, Outlines of a National History; of the Ancient and Modern Nations of North and South America." It was printed for the author, and is in two parts. Others were announced but never appeared, nor did the maps and illustrations which the title page promised. Its pages are filled with extravagant theories and baseless analogies. In the first part he prints with notes his translation of the WALAM OLUM, and his explanation of its significance.

History of the Walam Olum.

Rafinesque's account of the origin of the WALAM OLUM may be introduced by a passage in the last work he published, "The Good Book." In that erratic volume he tells us that he had long been collecting the signs and pictographs current among the North American Indians, and adds :—

"Of these I have now 60 used by the Southern or Floridian Tribes of Louisiana to Florida, based upon their language of Signs—40 used by the Osages and Arkanzas, based on the same—74 used by the Lenàpian (Delaware and akin) tribes in their WALLAMOLUM or Records—besides 30 simple signs that can be traced out of the NEOBAGUN or Delineation of the Chipwas or Ninniwas, a branch of the last." [1]

[1] *The Good Book; or the Amenities of Nature. Printed for the Eleutherium of Knowledge.* Philadelphia, 1840, pp. 77, 78. This "Eleutherium," so far as I can learn, consisted of nobody but Monsieur Rafinesque himself. Among his manifold projects was a "Divitial Sys-

In these lines Rafinesque makes an important statement, which has been amply verified by the investigations of Col. Garrick Mallery, Dr. W. J. Hoffman and Capt. W. P. Clark, within the last decade, and that is, that the Indian pictographic system was based on their gesture speech.

So far as I remember, he was the first to perceive this suggestive fact ; and he had announced it some time before 1840. Already, in "'The American Nations" (1836), he wrote, " the Graphic Signs correspond to these Manual Signs." [1]

Here he anticipates a leading result of the latest archæological research ; and I give his words the greater prominence, because they seem to have been overlooked by all the recent writers on Indian Gesture-speech and Sign-language.

The *Neobagun*, the Chipeway medicine song to which he alludes, is likewise spoken of in " The American Nations," where he says: " The Ninniwas or Chipiwas * * have such painted tales or annals, called Neobagun (male tool) by the former." [2] I suspect he derived his knowledge of this from the Shawnee " Song for Medicine Hunting," called " Nah-o-bah-e-gun-num," or, The Four Sticks, the words and figures of which were appended by Dr. James to Tanner's *Narrative*, published in 1830. [3]

---

tem," by which all interested could soon become large capitalists. He published a book on it (of course), which might be worth the attention of a financial economist. The solid men of Philadelphia, however, like its scholars, turned a deaf ear to the words of the eccentric foreigner.

[1] *The American Nations*, etc., p. 78.

[2] Ibid, p. 123.

[3] Tanner's *Narrative*, p. 359.

Discovery of the Walam Olum.

As for the Lenape records, he gives this not very clear account of his acquisition of them :—

" Having obtained, through the late Dr. Ward, of Indiana, some of the original Wallam-Olum (painted record) of the Linápi Tribe of Wapihani or White River, the translation will be given of the songs annexed to each."[1]

On a later page he wrote :—[2]

" *Olum* implies *a record, a notched stick*, an engraved piece of wood or bark. It comes from *ol*, hollow or graved record. * * * These actual *olum* were at first obtained in 1820, as a reward for a medical cure, deemed a curiosity; and were unexplicable. In 1822 were obtained from another individual the songs annexed thereto in the original language; but no one could be found by me able to translate them. I had therefore to learn the language since, by the help of Zeisberger, Heckewelder and a manuscript dictionary, on purpose to translate them, which I only accomplished in 1833. The contents were totally unknown to me in 1824, when I published my 'Annals of Kentucky.' "

I have attempted to identify this "Dr. Ward, of Indiana;" but no such person is known in the early medical annals of that State. There is, however, an old and well-known Kentucky family of that name, who, about 1820, resided, and still do reside, in the neighborhood of Cynthiana. One of these, in 1824–25, was a friend of Rafinesque, invited him to his house, and shared his archæological tastes, as Rafinesque

---

[1] *American Nations*, p. 122.   [2] Ibid, p. 151.

K

mentions in his autobiography.[1] It was there, no doubt, that he copied the signs and the original text of the Walam Olum. My efforts to learn further about the originals from living members of the family have been unsuccessful. From a note in Rafinesque's handwriting, on the title page of his MS. of 1833, it would appear that he had at least seen the wooden tablets. This note reads :—

" This Mpt & the wooden original was (*sic*) procured in 1822 in Kentucky—but was inexplicable till a deep study of the Linapi enabled me to translate them with explanations. (Dr. Ward.)"

The name of Dr. Ward added in brackets is, I judge, merely a note, and is not intended to imply that the sentence is a quotation.

Was it a Forgery?

The crucial question arises: Was the WALAM OLUM a forgery by Rafinesque?

It is necessary to ask and to answer this question, though it seems, at first sight, an insult to the memory of the man to do so. No one has ever felt it requisite to propound such an inquiry about the pieces of the celebrated Mexican collection of the Chevalier Boturini, who, as an antiquary, was scarcely less visionary than Rafinesque.

But, unquestionably, an air of distrust and doubt shadowed Rafinesque's scientific reputation during his life, and he was not admitted on a favorable footing to the learned circles of

---

[1] " My friend, Mr. Ward, took me to Cynthiana in a gig, where I surveyed other ancient monuments." Rafinesque, *A Life of Travels and Researches*," p. 74. (Phila., 1836.)

the city where he spent the last fifteen years of his life. His articles were declined a hearing in its societies; and the learned linguist, Mr. Peter Stephen Duponceau, whose specialty was the Delaware language, wholly and deliberately ignored everything by the author of "The American Nations."

Why was this?

Rafinesque was poor, eccentric, negligent of his person, full of impractical schemes and extravagant theories, and manufactured and sold in a small way a secret nostrum which he called " pulmel," for the cure of consumption. All these were traits calculated to lower him in the respect of the citizens of Philadelphia, and the consequence was, that although a member of some scientific societies, he seems to have taken no part in their proceedings, and was looked upon as an undesirable acquaintance, and as a sort of scientific outcast.

As early as 1819 Prof. Benjamin Silliman declined to publish contributions from him in the "American Journal of Science,"[1] and returned him his MSS. Dr. Gray strongly intimates that Rafinesque's assertions on scientific matters were at times intentionally false, as when he said that he had seen Robin's collection of Louisiana plants in France, whereas that botanist never prepared dried specimens; and the like.

I felt early in this investigation that Rafinesque's assertions were, therefore, an insufficient warranty for the authenticity of this document.

As I failed in my efforts to substantiate them by local researches in Kentucky and Indiana, I saw that the evidence must come from the text itself. Nor would it be sufficient to

[1] *American Journal of Science*, Vol. XL, p. 237, note.

prove that the words of the text were in the Lenape dialect. With Zeisberger and Heckewelder at hand, both of whose works had been years in print, it were easy to string together Lenape words.

But what Rafinesque certainly had not the ability to do, was to write a sentence in Lenape, to compose lines which an educated native would recognize as in the syntax of his own speech, though perhaps dialectically different.

This was the test that I determined to apply. I therefore communicated my doubts to my friend, the distinguished linguist, Mr. Horatio Hale, and asked him to state them to the Rev. Albert Anthony, a well educated native Delaware, equally conversant with his own tongue and with English.

Mr. Anthony considered the subject fully, and concluded by expressing the positive opinion that the text as given was a genuine *oral* composition of a Delaware Indian. In many lines the etymology and syntax are correct; in others there are grammatical defects, which consist chiefly in the omission of terminal inflections.

The suggestion he offered to explain these defects is extremely natural. The person who wrote down this oral explanation of the signs, or, to speak more accurately, these chants which the signs were intended to keep in memory, was imperfectly acquainted with the native tongue, and did not always catch terminal sounds. The speaker also may have used here and there parts of that clipped language, or "white man's Indian," which I have before referred to as serving for the trading tongue between the two races.

This was also the opinion of the Moravian natives who examined the text. They all agreed that it impressed them as being of aboriginal origin, though the difference of the forms of words left them often in the dark as to the meaning.

This very obscurity is in fact a proof that Rafinesque did not manufacture it. Had he done so, he would have used the "Mission Delaware" words which he found in Zeisberger. But the text has quite a number not in that dialect, nor in any of the mission dictionaries.

Moreover, had he taken the words from such sources, he would in his translation have given their correct meanings; but in many instances he is absurdly far from their sense. Thus he writes: "The word for angels, *angelatawiwak*, is not borrowed, but real Linapi, and is the same as the Greek word *angelos*;"[1] whereas it is a verbal with a future sense from the very common Delaware verb *angeln*, to die. Many such examples will be noted in the vocabulary on a later page.

In several cases the figures or symbols appear to me to bear out the corrected translations which I have given of the lines, and not that of Rafinesque. This, it will be observed, is an evidence, not merely that he must have received this text from other hands, but the figures also, and weighs heavily in favor of the authentic character of both.

That it is a copy is also evident from some manifest mistakes in transcription, which Rafinesque preserves in his printed version, and endeavored to translate, not perceiving their erroneous form. Thus, in the fourth line of the first chant, he wrote *owak*, translating it "much air or clouds," when it is clearly a mere transposition for *woak*, the Unami form of the conjunction "and," as the sense requires. No such blunder would appear if he had forged the document.

[1] *The American Nations*, p. 151.

It is true that a goodly share of the words in the earlier chants occur in Zeisberger. Thus it seems, at first sight, suspicious to find the three or four superlatives in III, 5, all given under examples of the superlatives, in Zeisberger's *Grammar*, p. 105. It looks as if they had been bodily transferred into the song. So I thought; but afterwards I found these same superlatives in Heckewelder, who added specifically that "the Delawares had formed them to address or designate the Supreme being."[1]

If we assume that this song is genuine, then Zeisberger was undoubtedly familiar with some version of it; had learned it probably, and placed most of its words in his vocabulary.

Some other collateral evidences of authenticity I have referred to on previous pages (pp. 67, 89, 136).

From these considerations, and from a study of the text, the opinion I have formed of the WALAM OLUM is as follows:—

It is a genuine native production, which was repeated orally to some one indifferently conversant with the Delaware language, who wrote it down to the best of his ability. In its present form it can, as a whole, lay no claim either to antiquity, or to purity of linguistic form. Yet, as an authentic modern version, slightly colored by European teachings, of the ancient tribal traditions, it is well worth preservation, and will repay more study in the future than is given it in this volume. The narrator was probably one of the native chiefs or priests, who had spent his life in the Ohio and

[1] *Correspondence between the Rev. John Heckewelder and Peter S. Duponceau, Esq.,* p. 410.

Indiana towns of the Lenape, and who, though with some knowledge of Christian instruction, preferred the pagan rites, legends and myths of his ancestors. Probably certain lines and passages were repeated in the archaic form in which they had been handed down for generations.

Phonetic System.

The phonetic system adopted by the writer, whoever he was, is not that of the Moravian brethren. They employed the German alphabet, which does not obtain in the present text. On this point Rafinesque says: "The orthography of the Linapi names is reduced to the Spanish or French pronunciation, except *sh*, as in English; *u*, as in French; *w*, as in *how*."[1] A comparison of the words with their equivalents in Zeisberger's spelling shows that this is generally true.

It is obvious that the gutturals are few and soft, and that the process of synthesis is carried further than in the Minsi dialect. For this reason, from the introduction of peculiar words, and from the loss of certain grammatical terminations, the Minsi Delawares of to-day, to whom I have submitted it, are of the opinion that it belongs to one of the southern dialects of their nation; perhaps to the Unalachtgo, as suggested by Chief Gabriel Tobias, in his letter printed on a preceding page (p. 88).

Metrical Form.

Even to an ear not acquainted with the language, the chants of the WALAM OLUM are obviously in metrical arrangement. The rhythm is syllabic and accentual, with frequent

---

[1] *The American Nations*, p. 125.

effort to select homophones (to which the correct form of the words is occasionally sacrificed), and sometimes alliteration. Iteration is also called in aid, and the metrical scheme is varied in the different chants.

All these rhythmical devices appear in the native American songs of many tribes, though I cannot point to any other strictly aboriginal production in Algonkin, where a tendency toward rhyme is as prominent as in the WALAM OLUM. It is well to remember, however, that our material for comparison is exceedingly scanty, and also that for nearly three-fourths of a century before this song was obtained, the music-loving Moravian missionaries had made the Delawares familiar with numerous hymns in their own tongue, correctly framed and rhymed.

Pictographic System.

The pictographic system which the WALAM OLUM presents is clearly that of the Western Algonkins, most familiar to us through examples from the Chipeways and Shawnees. It is quite likely, indeed, that it was the work of a Shawnee, as we know that they supplied such songs, with symbols, to the Chipeways, and were intimately associated with the Delawares.

At the time Rafinesque wrote, Tanner's *Narrative* had been in print several years, and the numerous examples of Algonkin pictography it contains were before him. Yet it must be said that the pictographs of the WALAM OLUM have less resemblance to these than to those published by the Chipeway chief, George Copway, in 1850, and by Schoolcraft, in his "History and Statistics of the Indian Tribes."

There is generally a distinct, obvious connection between the symbol and the sense of the text, sufficient to recall the latter to one who has made himself once thoroughly familiar with it. I have not undertaken a study of the symbols; but have confined myself to a careful reproduction of them, and the suggestion of their more obvious meanings, and their correspondences with the pictographs furnished by later writers. I shall leave it for others to determine to what extent they should be accepted as a pure specimen of Algonkin pictographic writing.

Derivation of Walam Olum.

The derivation of the name WALAM OLUM has been largely anticipated on previous pages. I have shown that *wǎlǎm* (in modern Minsi, *wǎlumin*) means "painted," especially "painted *red*." This is a secondary meaning, as the root *wǎli* conveys the idea of something pleasant, in this connection, pleasant to the eye, fine, pretty. (See ante p. 104.)

Olum was the name of the scores, marks, or figures in use on the tally-sticks or record-boards. The native Delaware missionary, Mr. Albert Anthony, says that the knowledge of these ancient signs has been lost, but that the word *olum* is still preserved by the Delaware boys in their games when they keep the score by notches on a stick. These notches— not the sticks—are called to this day *olum*—an interesting example of the preservation of an archaic form in the language of children.

The name *Wǎlǎm Olum* is therefore a highly appropriate one for the record, and may be translated "RED SCORE."

The MS. of the WALAM OLUM.

The MS. from which I have printed the WALAM OLUM is a small quarto of forty unnumbered leaves, in the handwriting of Rafinesque. It is in two parts with separate titles. The first reads :—

WALLAMOLUM.

First Part of the painted-engraved [traditions of the Linni linapi, &c.] containing [the 3 original traditional poems.] 1. on the Creation and Ontogony, 24 verses.] 2. on the Deluge, &c. 16 v.] 3. on the passage to America, 20 v.] Signs and Verses, 60 [with the original glyphs or signs] for each verse of the poems or songs] translated word for word [by C. S. Rafinesque [1833.

The title of the second part is :—

WALLAM-OLUM.

First and Second Parts of the [Painted and engraved traditions] of the Linni linapi.

II. Part.

Historical Chronicles or Annals [in two Chronicles.

I. From arrival in America to settlement in Ohio, &c. 4 chapters each of 16 verses, each of 4 words, 64 signs.

2d. From Ohio to Atlantic States and back to Missouri, a mere succession of names in 3 chapters of 20 verses—60 signs.

Translated word for word by means of Zeisberger and Linapi Dictionary. With explanations, &c.

By C. S. Rafinesque. 1833.

When Rafinesque died, his MSS. were scattered and passed into various hands. Prof. Haldeman, in his notice above referred to (p. 150), stated that he and " Mr. Poulson of Philadelphia " had a large part of them.

This particular one, and also others descriptive of Rafinesque's archæological explorations in the southwest, his surveys of the earthworks of Kentucky and the neighboring states, and the draft of a work on "The Ancient Monuments of North and South America," came into the possession of the Hon. Brantz Mayer, of Baltimore, distinguished as an able public man and writer on American subjects, from whose family I obtained them.

He loaned them all to Mr. E. G. Squier, who made extensive use of Rafinesque's surveys, in the "Ancient Monuments of the Mississippi Valley," giving due credit.

In June, 1848, Mr. Squier read before the New York Historical Society a paper entitled, "Historical and Mythological Traditions of the Algonquins; with a translation of the 'Walum-Olum,' or Bark Record of the Linni-Lenape." This was published in the "American Review," February, 1849, and has been reprinted by Mr. W. W. Beach, in his "Indian Miscellany" (Albany, 1877), and in the fifteenth edition of Mr. S. G. Drake's "Aboriginal Races of North America."

This paper gave the symbols, original text and Rafinesque's translation of the first two songs, and a free translation only, of the remainder. The text was carelessly copied, whole words being omitted, and no attempt was made to examine the accuracy of the translation; the symbols were also imperfect, several being reversed. Hence, as material for a critical study of the document, Squier's essay is of little value.

At the close of the second part of the MS. there are four pages, closely written, with the title :—

"Fragment on the History of the Linapis since abt 1600 when the *Wallamolum* closes. translated from the Linapi by John Burns."

This was printed by Rafinesque and Squier, but as it has no original text, as nothing is known of "John Burns," and as the document itself, even if reasonably authentic, has no historic value, I omit it.

General Synopsis of the Walam Olum.

The myths embodied in the earlier portion of the WALAM OLUM are perfectly familiar to one acquainted with Algonkin mythology. They are not of foreign origin, but are wholly within the cycle of the most ancient legends of that stock. Although they are not found elsewhere in the precise form here presented, all the figures and all the leading incidents recur in the native tales picked up by the Jesuit missionaries in the seventeenth century, and by Schoolcraft, McKinney, Tanner and others in later days.

In an earlier chapter I have collected the imperfect fragments of these which we hear of among the Delawares, and these are sufficient to show that they had substantially the same mythology as their western relatives.

The cosmogony describes the formation of the world by the Great Manito, and its subsequent despoliation by the spirit of the waters, under the form of a serpent. The happy days are depicted, when men lived without wars or sickness, and food was at all times abundant. Evil beings, of mysterious power, introduced cold and war and sickness and premature death. Then began strife and long wanderings.

However similar this general outline may be to European and Oriental myths, it is neither derived originally from them, nor was it acquired later by missionary influence. This similarity is due wholly to the identity of psychological action, the same ideas and fancies arising from similar impressions in New as well as Old World tribes. No sound ethnologist, no thorough student in comparative mythology, would seek to maintain a genealogical relation of cultures on the strength of such identities. They are proofs of the oneness of the human mind, and nothing more.

As to the historical portion of the document, it must be judged by such corroborative evidence as we can glean from other sources. I have quoted, in an earlier chapter, sufficient testimony to show that the Lenape had traditions similar to these, extending back for centuries, or at least believed by their narrators to reach that far. What trust can be reposed in them is for the archæologist to judge.

Authentic history tells us nothing about the migrations of the Lenape before we find them in the valley of the Delaware. There is no positive evidence that they arrived there from the west; still less concerning their earlier wanderings.

Were I to reconstruct their ancient history from the WALAM OLUM, as I understand it, the result would read as follows:—

At some remote period their ancestors dwelt far to the northeast, on tide-water, probably at Labrador (Compare ante, p. 145). They journeyed south and west, till they reached a broad water, full of islands and abounding in fish, perhaps the St. Lawrence about the Thousand Isles. They crossed and dwelt for some generations in the pine and hemlock regions of New York, fighting more or less with the Snake people, and the Talega, agricultural nations, living in stationary villages to the southeast of them, in the area of Ohio and Indiana. They drove out the former, but the latter remained on the upper Ohio and its branches. The Lenape, now settled on the streams in Indiana, wished to remove to the East to join the Mohegans and other of their kin who had moved there directly from northern New York. They, therefore, united with the Hurons (Talamatans) to drive out the

Talega (Tsalaki, Cherokees) from the upper Ohio. This they only succeeded in accomplishing finally in the historic period (see ante p. 17). But they did clear the road and reached the Delaware valley, though neither forgetting nor giving up their claims to their western territories (see ante p. 144).

In the sixteenth century the Iroquois tribes seized and occupied the whole of the Susquehanna valley, thus cutting off the eastern from the western Algonkins, and ended by driving many of the Lenape from the west to the east bank of the Delaware (ante p. 38).

Synopsis of the separate parts.

I.

The formation of the universe by the Great Manito is described. In the primal fog and watery waste he formed land and sky, and the heavens cleared. He then created men and animals. These lived in peace and joy until a certain evil manito came, and sowed discord and misery.

This canto is a version of the Delaware tradition mentioned in the Heckewelder MSS. which I have given previously, p. 135. The notion of the earth rising from the primal waters is strictly a part of the earliest Algonkin mythology, as I have amply shown in previous discussions of the subject. See my *Myths of the New World*, p. 213, and *American Hero Myths*, Chap. II.

II.

The Evil Manito, who now appears under the guise of a gigantic serpent, determines to destroy the human race, and for that purpose brings upon them a flood of water. Many perish, but a certain number escape to the turtle, that is, to solid land, and are there protected by Nanabush (Manibozho or Michabo). They pray to him for assistance, and he caused the water to disappear, and the great serpent to depart.

This canto is a brief reference to the conflict between the Algonkin hero god and the serpent of the waters, originally, doubtless, a meteorological myth. It is an ancient and authentic aboriginal legend, shared both by Iroquois and Algonkins, under slightly different forms. In one aspect, it is the Flood or Deluge Myth. For the general form of this myth, see my *Myths of the New World*, pp. 119, 143, 182, and *American Hero Myths*, p. 50, and authorities there quoted; also, E. G. Squier, "Manabozho and the Great Serpent; an Algonquin Tradition," in the *American Review*, Vol. II, Oct., 1848.

III.

The waters having disappeared, the home of the tribe is described as in a cold northern clime. This they concluded to leave in search of warmer lands. Having divided their people into a warrior and a peaceful class, they journeyed southward, toward what is called the "Snake land." They approached this land in winter, over a frozen river. Their number was large, but all had not joined in the expedition with equal willingness, their members at the west preferring their ancient seats in the north to the uncertainty of southern conquests. They, however, finally united with the other bands, and they all moved south to the land of spruce pines.

IV.

The first sixteen verses record the gradual conquest of most of the Snake land. It seems to have required the successive efforts of six or seven head chiefs, one after another, to bring this about, probably but a small portion at a time yielding to the attacks of these enemies. Its position is described as being to the southwest, and in the interior of the country. Here they first learned to cultivate maize.

The remainder of the canto is taken up with a long list of chiefs, and with the removal of the tribe, in separate bands and at different times, to the east. In this journey from the Snake land to the east, they encountered and had long wars with the Talega. These lived in strong towns, but by the aid of the Hurons (Talamatans), they overcame them and drove them to the south.

V.

Having conquered the Talegas, the Lenape possessed their land and that of the Snake people, and for a certain time enjoyed peace and abundance. Then occurred a division of their people, some, as Nanticokes and Shawnees, going to the south, others to the west, and later, the majority toward the east, arriving finally at the Salt sea, the Atlantic ocean. Thence a portion turned north and east, and encountered the Iroquois. Still later, the three sub-tribes of the Lenape settled themselves definitely along the Delaware river, and received the geographical names by which they were known, as Minsi, Unami and Unalachtgo (see ante, p. 36). They were often at war with the Iroquois, generally successfully. Rumors of the whites had reached them, and finally these strangers approached the river, both from the north (New York bay) and the south. Here the song closes.

THE WALAM OLUM,

OR

RED SCORE,

OF THE

LENÂPÉ.

I.

1. Sayewi talli wemiguma wokgetaki,

2. Hackung kwelik owanaku
   wak yutali Kitanitowit-
   essop.

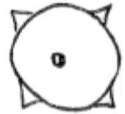

3. Sayewis hallemiwis nolemiwi
   elemamik Kitanitowit-es-
   sop.

4. Sohalawak kwelik hakik
   owak[1] awasagamak.

5. Sohalawak gishuk nipahum
   alankwak.

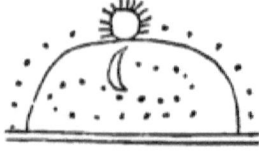

6. Wemi-sohalawak yulik yuch-
   aan.

7. Wich-owagan kshakan moshakwat[2] kwelik kshipehelep.

8. Opeleken mani-menak delsin-epit.

---

[1] Read, *woak.*   [2] Var. *moshakguat.*

I.

1. At first, in that place, at all times, above the earth,

2. On the earth, [was] an extended fog, and there the great Manito was.

3. At first, forever, lost in space, everywhere, the great Manito was.

4. He made the extended land and the sky.

5. He made the sun, the moon, the stars.

6. He made them all to move evenly.

7. Then the wind blew violently, and it cleared, and the water flowed off far and strong.

8. And groups of islands grew newly, and there remained.

9. Lappinup Kitanitowit manito manitoak.

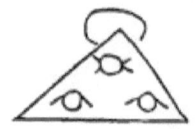

10. Owiniwak   angelatawiwak chichankwak wemiwak.

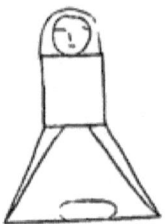

11. Wtenk manito jinwis lenno-wak mukom.

12. Milap netami gaho owini gaho.

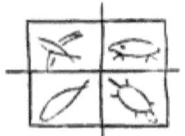

13. Namesik milap, tulpewik mi-lap, awesik milap, cholen-sak milap.

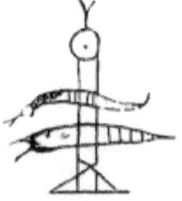

14. Makimani shak sohalawak makowini nakowak aman-gamek.

9. Anew spoke the great Manito, a manito to manitos,

10. To beings, mortals, souls and all,

11. And ever after he was a manito to men, and their grandfather.

12. He gave the first mother, the mother of beings.

13. He gave the fish, he gave the turtles, he gave the beasts, he gave the birds.

14. But an evil Manito made evil beings only, monsters,

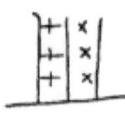

15. Sohalawak uchewak, sohalawak pungusak.

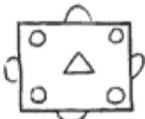

16. Nitisak wemi owini w'delsi-
newuap.

17. Kiwis, wunand wishimani-
toak essopak.

18. Nijini netami lennowak, nigoha netami okwewi, nan-
tinéwak.

19. Gattamin netami mitzi nijini
nantiné.

20. Wemi wingi-namenep, wemi
ksin-clendamep, wemi wul-
latemanuwi.

21. Shukand eli-kimi mekenikink
wakon powako init'ako.

15. He made the flies, he made the gnats.

16. All beings were then friendly.

17. Truly the manitos were active and kindly

18. To those very first men, and to those first mothers;
    fetched them wives,

19. And fetched them food, when first they desired it.

20. All had cheerful knowledge, all had leisure, all
    thought in gladness.

21. But very secretly an evil being, a mighty magician,
    came on earth,

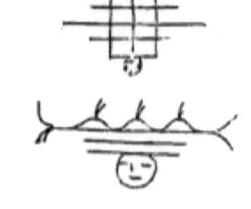

22. Mattalogas pallalogas maktaton owagan payat-chik
yutali.

23. Maktapan   payat,   wihillan
payat, mboagan payat.

24. Won wemi wiwunch kamik
atak kitahikan netamaki
epit.

II.

1. Wulamo maskanako anup
lennowak makowini esso-
pak.

2. Maskanako shingalusit nijini
essopak   shawelendamep
eken shingalan.

3. Nishawi   palliton,   nishawi
machiton, nishawi matta
lungundowin.

4. Mattapewi wiki nihanlowit
mekwazoan.

22. And with him brought badness, quarreling, unhappiness,

23. Brought bad weather, brought sickness, brought
death.

24. All this took place of old on the earth, beyond the
great tide-water, at the first.

II.

1. Long ago there was a mighty snake and beings evil
to men.

2. This mighty snake hated those who were there (and)
greatly disquieted those whom he hated.

3. They both did harm, they both injured each other,
both were not in peace.

4. Driven from their homes they fought with this murderer.

5. Maskanako gishi penauwelendamep lennowak owini
   palliton.

6. Nakowa petonep, amangam
   petonep, akopehella petonep.

7. Pehella pehella, pohoka pohoka, eshohok eshohok,
   palliton palliton.

8. Tulapit menapit Nanaboush
   maskaboush owinimokom
   linowimokom.

9. Gishikin-pommixin tulagis-
   hatten-lohxin.

10. Owini linowi wemoltin,
    Pehella gahani pommixin,
    Nahiwi tatalli tulapin.

5. The mighty snake firmly resolved to harm the men.

6. He brought three persons, he brought a monster, he brought a rushing water.

7. Between the hills the water rushed and rushed, dashing through and through, destroying much.

8. Nanabush, the Strong White One, grandfather of beings, grandfather of men, was on the Turtle Island.

9. There he was walking and creating, as he passed by and created the turtle.

10. Beings and men all go forth, they walk in the floods and shallow waters, down stream thither to the Turtle Island.

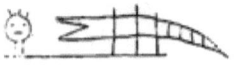
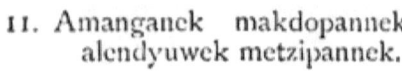

11. Amanganek makdopannek alendyuwek metzipannek.

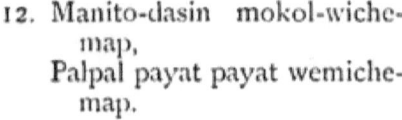

12. Manito-dasin mokol-wiche-map,
Palpal payat payat wemiche-map.

13. Nanaboush Nanaboush we-mimokom,
Winimokom linnimokom tu-lamokom.

14. Linapi-ma tulapi-ma tulape-wi tapitawi.

15. Wishanem tulpewi pataman tulpewi poniton wuliton.

16. Kshipehelen penkwihilen,
Kwamipokho sitwalikho,
Maskan wagan palliwi pal-liwi.

III.

1. Pehella wtenk lennapewi tu-lapewini psakwiken woli-wikgun wittank talli.

2. Topan-akpinep, wineu-akpi-nep, kshakan-akpinep, thu-pin akpinep.

11. There were many monster fishes, which ate some of them.

12. The Manito daughter, coming, helped with her canoe, helped all, as they came and came.

.

13. [And also] Nanabush, Nanabush, the grandfather of all, the grandfather of beings, the grandfather of men, the grandfather of the turtle.

14. The men then were together on the turtle, like to turtles.

15. Frightened on the turtle, they prayed on the turtle that what was spoiled should be restored.

16. The water ran off, the earth dried, the lakes were at rest, all was silent, and the mighty snake departed.

III.

1. After the rushing waters (had subsided) the Lenape of the turtle were close together, in hollow houses, living together there.

2. It freezes where they abode, it snows where they abode, it storms where they abode, it is cold where they abode.

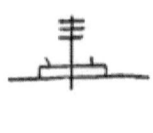

3. Lowankwamink   wulaton wtakan tihill kelik me-shautang sili ewak.

4. Chintanes-sin   powalessin peyachik wikhichik pok-wihil.

5. Eluwi-chitanesit eluwi takau-wesit, elowi chiksit, elowi-chik delsinewo.

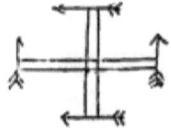

6. Lowaniwi, wapaniwi, shawa-niwi, wunkeniwi, elowichik apakachik.

7. Lumowaki, lowanaki tulpe-naki elowaki tulapiwi lina-piwi.

8. Wemiako yagawan tendki lakkawelendam nakopowa wemi owenluen atam.

9. Akhokink wapaneu wemoltin palliaal kitelendam apte-lendam.

3. At this northern place they speak favorably of mild, cool (lands), with many deer and buffaloes.

4. As they journeyed, some being strong, some rich, they separated into house-builders and hunters;

5. The strongest, the most united, the purest, were the hunters.

6. The hunters showed themselves at the north, at the east, at the south, at the west.

7. In that ancient country, in that northern country, in that turtle country, the best of the Lenape were the Turtle men.

8. All the cabin fires of that land were disquieted, and all said to their priest, "Let us go."

9. To the Snake land to the east they went forth, going away, earnestly grieving.

10. Pechimuin shakowen[1] nungihillan lusasaki pikihil pok-
wihil akomenaki.

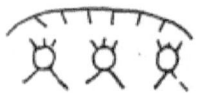

11. Nihillapewin   komelendam
lowaniwi wemiten chihillen
winiaken.

12. Namesuagipek   pokhapock-
hapek   guneunga   wapla-
newa   ouken   waptumewi
ouken.

13. Amokolon nallahemen agunouken pawasinep wapasi-
nep akomenep.[2]

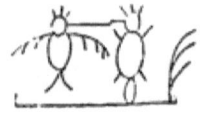

14. Wihlamok kicholen luchundi,
Wematam akomen luchundi.

15. Witehen wemiluen wemaken
nihillen.

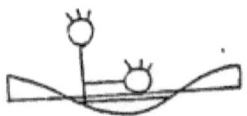

16. Nguttichin lowaniwi,
Nguttichin wapaniwi,
Agamunk topanpek
Wulliton epannek.

17. Wulelemil w'shakuppek,
Wemopannek hakhsinipek.
Kitahikan pokhakhopek.

---

[1] Var. *showoken.*   [2] Var. *menakinep.*

10. Split asunder, weak, trembling, their land burned,
they went, torn and broken, to the Snake Island.

11. Those from the north being free, without care, went
forth from the land of snow, in different directions.

12. The fathers of the Bald Eagle and the White Wolf
remain along the sea, rich in fish and muscles.

13. Floating up the streams in their canoes, our fathers
were rich, they were in the light, when they were
at those islands.

14. Head Beaver and Big Bird said,
"Let us go to Snake Island," they said.

15. All say they will go along to destroy all the land.

16. Those of the north agreed,
Those of the east agreed.
Over the water, the frozen sea,
They went to enjoy it.

17. On the wonderful, slippery water,
On the stone-hard water all went,
On the great Tidal Sea, the muscle-bearing sea.

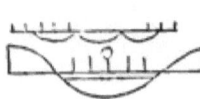

18. Tellenchen kittapakki nillawi,
Wemoltin gutikuni nillawi,
Akomen wapanawaki nillawi,
Ponskan, ponskan, wemiwi
olini.

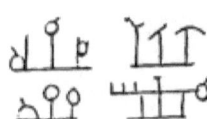

19. Lowanapi, wapanapi, shawa-
napi,
Lanewapi, tamakwapi, tume-
wapi,
Elowapi, powatapi, wilawapi,
Okwisapi, danisapi, allumapi,

20. Wemipayat gunéunga shinaking,
Wunkenapi chanelendam
payaking,
Allowelendam kowiyey tul-
paking.

IV.

1. Wulamo linapioken manup
shinaking.

2. Wapallanewa sittamaganat
yukepechi wemima,

3. Akhomenis michihaki wellaki kundokanup.

18. Ten thousand at night,
    All in one night,
    To the Snake Island, to the east, at night,
    They walk and walk, all of them.

19. The men from the north, the east, the south,
    The Eagle clan, the Beaver clan, the Wolf clan,
    The best men, the rich men, the head men,
    Those with wives, those with daughters, those with
      dogs,

20. They all come, they tarry at the land of the spruce
      pines;
    Those from the west come with hesitation,
    Esteeming highly their old home at the Turtle land.

IV.

1. Long ago the fathers of the Lenape were at the land
   of spruce pines.

2. Hitherto the Bald Eagle band had been the pipe
   bearer,

3. While they were searching for the Snake Island, that
   great and fine land.

4. Angomelchik elowichik elmusichik menalting.

5. Wemilo kolawil sakima lis-
silnia.

6. Akhopayat kihillalend akhopokho askiwaal.

7. Showihilla akhowemi gandhaton mashkipokhing.

8. Wtenkolawil shinaking sakimanep wapagokhos.

9. Wtenk nekama sakimanep
janotowi enolowin.

10. Wtenk nekama sakimanep
chilili shawaniluen.

4. They having died, the hunters, about to depart, met
    together.

5. All say to Beautiful Head, " Be thou chief."

6. " Coming to the Snakes, slaughter at that Snake hill,
    that they leave it."

7. All of the Snake tribe were weak, and hid them-
    selves in the Swampy Vales.

8. After Beautiful Head, White Owl was chief at Spruce
    Pine land.

9. After him, Keeping-Guard was chief of that people.

10. After him, Snow Bird was chief; he spoke of the
    south,

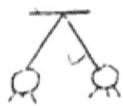

11. Wokenapi nitaton wullaton apakchikton.

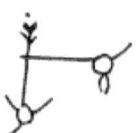

12. Shawaniwaen chilili, wapaniwaen tamakwi.

13. Akolaki shawanaki, kitshinaki shabiyaki.

14. Wapanaki namesaki, pemapaki sisilaki.

15. Wtenk chilili sakimanep ayamek weminilluk.

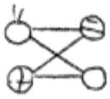

16. Chikonapi akhonapi makatapi assinapi.

17. Wtenk ayamek tellen sakimak machi tonanup shawapama.

11. That our fathers should possess it by scattering abroad.

12. Snow Bird went south, White Beaver went east.

13. The Snake land was at the south, the great Spruce Pine land was toward the shore ;

14. To the east was the Fish land, toward the lakes was the buffalo land.

15. After Snow Bird, the Seizer was chief, and all were killed,

16. The robbers, the snakes, the evil men, the stone men.

---

17. After the Seizer there were ten chiefs, and there was much warfare south and east.

18. Wtenk nellamawa sakimanep
    langundowi akolaking.

19. Wtenk nekama sakimanep
    tasukamend shakagapipi.

20. Wtenk nekama sakimanep
    pemaholend wulitowin.

21. Sagimawtenk matemik, sagi-
    mawtenk pilsohalin.

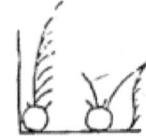

22. Sagimawtenk gunokeni, sagi-
    mawtenk mangipitak.

23. Sagimawtenk olumapi, lek-
    sahowen sohalawak.

24. Sagimawtenk taguachi sha-
    waniwaen minihaking.

25. Sakimawtenk huminiend mi-
    nigeman sohalgol.

18. After them, the Peaceable was chief at Snake land.

19. After him, Not-Black was chief, who was a straight man.

20. After him, Much-Loved was chief, a good man.

21. After him, No-Blood was chief, who walked in cleanliness.

22. After him, Snow-Father was chief, he of the big teeth.

23. After him, Tally-Maker was chief, who made records.

24. After him, Shiverer-with-Cold was chief, who went south to the corn land.

25. After him, Corn-Breaker was chief, who brought about the planting of corn.

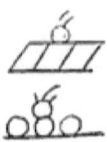

26. Sakimawtenk alkosohit saki-
    machik apendawi.

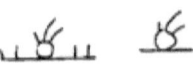

27. Sawkimawtenk shiwapi, saki-
    matenk penkwonwi.

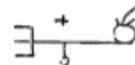

28. Attasokelan attaminin wapa-
    niwaen italissipek.

29. Oligonunk sisilaking nalli-
    metzin kolakwaming.

30. Wtenk penkwonwi wekwo-
    chella, wtenk nekama chin-
    galsuwi.

31. Wtenk nekama kwitikwond,
    slangelendam attagatta,

32. Wundanuksin wapanickam[1]
    allendyachick kimimikwi.

33. Gunehunga wetatamowi wa-
    kaholend sakimalanop.

[1] Var. *wapanahan.*

26. After him, the Strong-Man was chief, who was useful to the chieftains.

27. After him, the Salt-Man was chief; after him the
Little-One was chief.

28. There was no rain, and no corn, so they moved further seaward.

29. At the place of caves, in the buffalo land, they at
last had food, on a pleasant plain.

30. After the Little-One (came) the Fatigued; after him,
the Stiff-One.

31. After him, the Reprover; disliking him, and unwilling (to remain),

32. Being angry, some went off secretly, moving east.

----

33. The wise ones who remained made the Loving-One
chief.

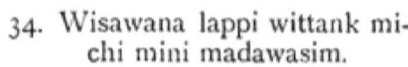

34. Wisawana lappi wittank mi-
chi mini madawasim.

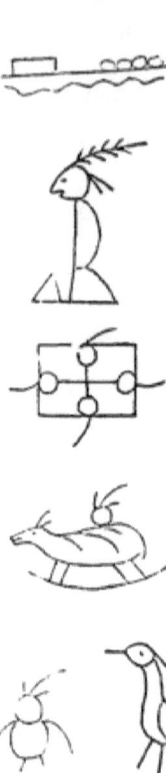

35. Weminitis tamenend sakimanep nekohatami.

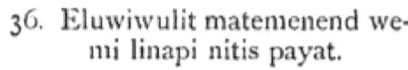

36. Eluwiwulit matemenend wemi linapi nitis payat.

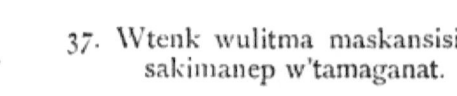

37. Wtenk wulitma maskansisil
sakimanep w'tamaganat.

38. Machigokloos sakimanep,
wapkicholen sakimanep.

39. Wingenund sakimanep powatanep gentikalanep.

40. Lapawin sakimanep, wallama
sakimanep.

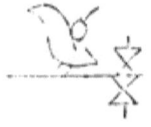

41. Waptipatit sakimanep, lappi
mahuk lowashawa.

34. They settled again on the Yellow river, and had much corn on stoneless soil.

35. All being friendly, the Affable was chief, the first of that name.

36. He was very good, this Affable, and came as a friend to all the Lenape.

37. After this good one, Strong-Buffalo was chief and pipe-bearer.

38. Big-Owl was chief; White-Bird was chief.

39. The Willing-One was chief and priest; he made festivals.

40. Rich-Again was chief; the Painted-One was chief.

41. White-Fowl was chief; again there was war, north and south.

42. Wewoattan menatting tuma-okan sakimanep.

43. Nitatonep wemi palliton mas-kansini nihillanep.

44. Messissuwi sakimanep ako-wini pallitonep.

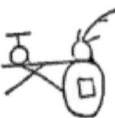

45. Chitanwulit sakimanep lowa-nuski pallitonep.

46. Alokuwi sakimanep towakon pallitonep.

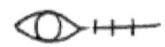

47. Opekasit sakimanep sakhe-lendam pallitonepit.

48. Wapagishik yuknohokluen makeluhuk wapaneken.

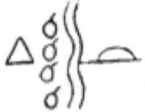

49. Tschepicken nemassipi[1] no-landowak gunehunga.

[1] Var. *mixtisipi*.

42. The Wolf-wise-in-Counsel was chief.

43. He knew how to make war on all; he slew Strong-Stone.

44. The Always-Ready-One was chief; he fought against the Snakes.

45. The Strong-Good-One was chief; he fought against the northerners.

46. The Lean-One was chief; he fought against the Tawa people.

47. The Opossum-Like was chief; he fought in sadness,

48. And said, "They are many; let us go together to the east, to the sunrise."

———————

49. They separated at Fish river; the lazy ones remained there.

 50. Yagawanend sakimanep tal-
ligewi wapawullaton.

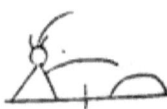 51. Chitanitis sakimanep wapa-
waki gotatamen.

 52. Wapallendi pomisinep tale-
gawil allendhilla.

 53. Mayoksuwi wemilowi palli-
ton palliton.

 54. Talamatan nitilowan payat-
chik wemiten.

 55. Kinehepend sakimanep ta-
maganat sipakgamen.

 56. Wulatonwi makelima palli-
hilla talegawik.

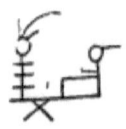 57. Pimokhasuwi   sakimanep
wsamimaskan talegawik.

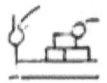 58. Tenchekentit sakimanep we-
milat makelinik.

50. Cabin-Man was chief; the Talligewi possessed the east.

51. Strong-Friend was chief; he desired the eastern land.

52. Some passed on east; the Talega ruler killed some of them.

53. All say, in unison, "War, war."

54. The Talamatan, friends from the north, come, and all go together.

55. The Sharp-One was chief; he was the pipe-bearer beyond the river.

56. They rejoiced greatly that they should fight and slay the Talega towns.

57. The Stirrer was chief; the Talega towns were too strong.

58. The Fire-Builder was chief; they all gave to him many towns.

N

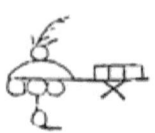

59. Pagan chihilla sakimanep
shawanewak wemi talega.

60. Hattan wulaton sakimanep,
wingelendam wemi lenno-
wak.

61. Shawanipekis gunehungind
lowanipekis talamatanitis.

62. Attabchinitis gishelendam
gunitakan sakimanep.

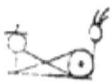

63. Linniwulamen sakimanep
pallitonep talamatan.

64. Shakagapewi sakimanep nungiwi talamatan.

V.

1. Wemilangundo wulamo talli
talegaking.

2. Tamaganend sakimanep wapalaneng.

3. Wapushuwi sakimanep kelitgeman.

59. The Breaker-in-Pieces was chief; all the Talega go south.

60. He-has-Pleasure was chief; all the people rejoice.

61. They stay south of the lakes; the Talamatan friends north of the lakes.

62. When Long-and-Mild was chief, those who were not his friends conspired.

63. Truthful-Man was chief; the Talamatans made war.

64. Just-and-True was chief; the Talamatans trembled.

V.

1. All were peaceful, long ago, there at the Talega land.

2. The Pipe-Bearer was chief at the White river.

3. White-Lynx was chief; much corn was planted.

4. Wulitshinik sakimanep makdopannik.

 5. Lekhihitin sakimanep wallamolumin.

 6. Kolachuisen sakimanep makeliming.

 7. Pematalli sakimanep makelinik.

 8. Pepomahenem sakimanep makelaning.

 9. Tankawon sakimanep makeleyachik,

 10. Nentegowi shawanowi shawanaking.

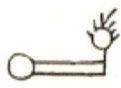 11. Kichitamak sakimanep wapahoning.

 12. Onowutok awolagan wunkenahep.

13. Wunpakitonis wunshawononis wunkiwikwotank.

4. Good-and-Strong was chief; the people were many.

5. The Recorder was chief; he painted the records.

6. Pretty-Blue-Bird was chief; there was much fruit.

7. Always-There was chief; the towns were many.

8. Paddler-up-Stream was chief; he was much on the rivers.

9. Little-Cloud was chief; many departed,

10. The Nanticokes and the Shawnees going to the south.

11. Big-Beaver was chief, at the White Salt Lick.

12. The Seer, the praised one, went to the west.

13. He went to the west, to the southwest, to the western villages.

 14. Pawanami sakimanep tale-
ganah.

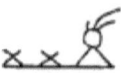 15. Lokwelend sakimanep mak-
palliton.

 16. Lappi towako lappi sinako
lappi lowako.

 17. Mokolmokom   sakimanep
mokolakolin.

 18. Winelowich sakimanep lo-
wushkakiang.

 19. Linkwekinuk sakimanep ta-
legachukang.

 20. Wapalawikwan   sakimanep
waptalegawing.

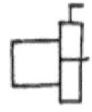 21. Amangaki amigaki wapaki-
sinep.

 22. Mattakohaki mapawaki ma-
wulitenol.

14. The Rich-Down-River-Man was chief, at Talega river.

15. The Walker was chief; there was much war.

16. Again with the Tawa people, again with the Stone people, again with the northern people.

17. Grandfather-of-Boats was chief; he went to lands in boats.

18. Snow-Hunter was chief; he went to the north land.

19. Look-About was chief; he went to the Talega moun- mountains.

20. East-Villager was chief; he was east of Talega.

———————

21. A great land and a wide land was the east land,

22. A land without snakes, a rich land, a pleasant land.

23. Gikenopalat sakimanep pekochilowan.

24. Saskwihanang   hanahólend
sakimanep.

25. Gattawisi sakimanep winakaking.

26. Wemi   lowichik gishikshawipek lappi kichipek.

27. Makhiawip sakimanep lapihaneng.

28. Wolomenap sakimanep maskekitong.

29. Wapanand tumewand waplowaan.

30. Wulitpallat sakimanep piskwilowan.

31. Mahongwi pungelika wemi
nungwi.

23. Great Fighter was chief, toward the north.

24. At the Straight river, River-Loving was chief.

25. Becoming-Fat was chief at Sassafras land.

26. All the hunters made wampum again at the great sea.

27. Red-Arrow was chief at the stream again.

28. The Painted-Man was chief at the Mighty Water.

29. The Easterners and the Wolves go northeast.

30. Good-Fighter was chief, and went to the north.

31. The Mengwe, the Lynxes, all trembled.

32. Lappi tamenend sakimanepit
    wemi langundit.

33. Wemi nitis wemi takwicken
    sakima kichwon.

36. Kichitamak sakimanep wina-
    kununda.

37. Wapahakey sakimanep shey-
    abian.

38. Elangomel sakimanep make-
    liwulit.

39. Pitenumen sakimanep unchi-
    hillen.

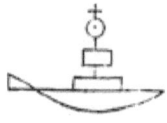

40. Wonwihil wapekunchi wap-
    sipayat.

----

41. Makelomush sakimanep wu-
    latenamen.

32. Again an Affable was chief, and made peace with all,

33. All were friends, all were united, under this great chief.

36. Great-Beaver was chief, remaining in Sassafras land.

37. White-Body was chief on the sea shore.

38. Peace-Maker was chief, friendly to all.

39. He-Makes-Mistakes was chief, hurriedly coming.

40. At this time whites came on the Eastern sea.

----

41. Much-Honored was chief; he was prosperous.

42. Wulakeningus   sakimanep
    shawanipalat.

43. Otaliwako akowetako ashki-
    palliton.

44. Wapagamoshki   sakimanep
    lamatanitis.

45. Wapashum sakimanep tale-
    gawunkik.

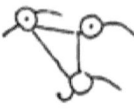

46. Mahiliniki mashawoniki ma-
    konowiki.

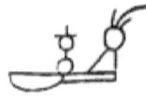

47. Nitispayat sakimanep kipe-
    mapekan,

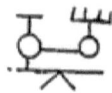

48. Wemiamik weminitik kiwik-
    hotan.

49. Pakimitzin sakimanep tawa-
    nitip.

42. Well-Praised was chief; he fought at the south.

43. He fought in the land of the Talega and Koweta.

44. White-Otter was chief; a friend of the Talamatans.

45. White-Horn was chief; he went to the Talega,

46. To the Hilini, to the Shawnees, to the Kanawhas.

47. Coming-as-a-Friend was chief; he went to the Great
    Lakes,

48. Visiting all his children, all his friends.

49. Cranberry-Eater was chief, friend of the Ottawas.

50. Lowaponskan   sakimanep ganshowenik.

51. Tashawinso sakimanep shayabing.

52. Nakhagattamen nakhalissin wenchikit,

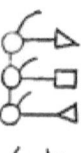

52. *bis*. Unamini minsimini chikimini.

53. Epallahchund   sakimanep mahongwipallat.

54. Langomuwi sakimanep mahongwichamen.

55. Wangomend sakimanep ikalawit,

56. Otaliwi wasiotowi shingalusit.

50. North-Walker was chief; he made festivals.

51. Slow-Gatherer was chief at the shore.

52. As three were desired, three those were who grew forth,

52. *bis.* The Unami, the Minsi, the Chikini.

53. Man-Who-Fails was chief; he fought the Mengwe.

54. He-is-Friendly was chief; he scared the Mengwe.

55. Saluted was chief; thither,

56. Over there, on the Scioto, he had foes.

57. Wapachikis sakimanep shayabinitis.

58. Nenachihat sakimanep peklinkwekin.

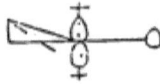

59. Wonwihil lowashawa wapayachik.

60. Langomuwak   kitohatewa
   ewenikiktit?

57. White-Crab was chief; a friend of the shore.

58. Watcher was chief; he looked toward the sea.

59. At this time, from north and south, the whites came.

60. They are peaceful; they have great things; who are
they?

NOTES.

☞ The references to authorities on Algonkin picture-writing are the Appendix to Tanner's *Narrative of Captivity and Adventures*, Copway's *Traditional History of the Ojibway Nation*, and Schoolcraft's *Synopsis of Indian Symbols*, in Vol. I of his *History and Statistics of the Indian Tribes*. I have not pursued an investigation of the symbols beyond the first chant.

I.

1. Rafinesque translates *wemiguna* "all sea-water." The proper form is *weminguna*, "at all times" (Anthony). The symbol is that of the sky and clouds above the earth. Compare Copway, p. 134; Schoolcraft, *Synopsis*, Fig. 17.

2. *Kwelik*, a dialectic form of *quenek*, Z. long, stretched out. *Kitanito*, a compound of *kehtan*, great, and *manito*, mysterious being, is rendered by Raf. as Creator; *wit* is the substantive verb-affix.

Heckewelder (MSS.) distinguishes between the synthetic form, *ketanittowit*, which he translates "Majestic Being," and the analytic form, *kitschi manito*, which he renders "Supreme Wonder-doer." In the latter, the sense of *manito* is brought out. In the Delaware and related dialects it conveys the idea of making or doing (*maniton*, to make, Zeisberger, *Gram.*, p. 222; *maranito taendo*, make a fire, Campanius; Chipeway, *win ma-nitawito*, he himself makes it, or, can make it).

The idea of making or creating is at the bottom of many native titles to supernatural powers, as the Shawnee *We-shellaqua*, "he that made us all." (Rev. David Jones, *Journal of Two Visits*, etc., p. 62.) See notes to line four. The Algonkin root, *etu*, he does, he acts, he makes, would therefore seem to be a radical of the word. (See Howse, *Gram. of the Cree Lang.*, p. 160.)

Dr. Trumbull, on the other hand, believes the only radical to be *an*, = *el* or *al*, in the sense of "to be more than," "to surpass," "to exceed;" and maintains that the syllable *it*, of the theme *manit*, is a formative suffix. (In *Old and New*, March, 1870.)

Heckewelder, in his translation "wonder-doer," recognizes the force of both elements, and from the analogous expressions I have quoted, is probably correct. The element *an* is thus an intensive prefix to the real root *it*, and the compound radical thus formed in the third person, singular, *manito*, means "he or it does or acts in a surpassing or extraordinary manner."

Essop, pl. *essopak*, frequently recurring words, are suppositive (see p. 90) forms of the verb *lissin*, "to be *or* do so, to be so situated, disposed, *or* acting" (Zeisberger, *Gram.* p. 117). The terminal *p* is the sign of the preterite. They are dialectic for *elsitup* and *elsichtitup*.

The symbol of a head with rays represents a manito. Schoolcraft, *Synopsis*, Fig. 10.

3. Squier omits the word *elumamek*. These terms are formal epithets applied to the highest divinity. See page 158.

Squier also adds that Fig. 3 represents the sun, and is the symbol of the Great Spirit. Both these statements are incorrect. The oval is the earth-plain, with its four cardinal points, and the dot in the centre signifies the spirit. See Copway, p. 135.

4. *Sohalawak* is not a Delaware form, but is a true Algonkin word, as seen in the Cree *oosch-ayoo*, animate, *oosch-taw*, inanimate, he, it, makes, produces. (Howse, *Cree Grammar*, p. 166.) It appears in the Shawnee *w'shellaqua*, quoted in notes to verse 2; in the Minsi dialect the corresponding word is *kwishelmawak;* *owak* is a mistake for *woak*, and Rafinesque translates it "much air." *Awasagamak*, heaven, sky, literally, "the land or place beyond," from *awossi*, beyond; but Dr. Trumbull prefers a derivation from a root signifying "light," *Del. waseleu*, it is clear or bright (Trans. Am. Philol. Soc., 1872, p. 164); this latter appears to me overstrained. The symbol is the earth surmounted by the sky.

5. The symbol represents the sun, moon and stars in the sky, which is repeated with change of relative positions in the next verse. In Minsi, the fifth line would read, *Kwishelmawak kischohk nipahenk alankwewak.*

7. On the termination *wagan* see page 101. The prefix *ksh*, properly *k'sch*, is intensive, as it is an abbreviation of *kitschi*, great, large. Thus *sokelan*, it rains, *k'schilan*, it rains very hard.

The symbol seems to indicate the waters flowing off.

8. Mr. Anthony renders this line in Minsi :—

Pilikin	*ameni-menazen*	*epit,*
Grew-clean	groups of islands	where they are;

That is, that the islands rose dry and clean from the water, as they now are found.

Delsin-epit; the first part of this compound, properly *w'dell-sinewo*, is the indicative present, 3d p. pl., of *lissin*, to be thus, or so situated ; *epit* is what Zeisberger (*Gram.* p. 115) calls the "adverbial" form of *achpin*, to be there, in a particular place. This adverbial is really the suppositive form of the verb, after the vowel-change has taken place. (See above, page 107.)

Former renderings of the line are : "It looks bright, and islands stood there" (Rafinesque). "All was made bright, and the islands were brought into being" (Squier).

The symbol is a three-cornered point of land, rising above the water under the sky.

9. *Manito manitoak,* "made the makers'," Raf.; "made the Great Spirits," Squier. Either of these renderings is defensible, as will appear from the senses of *manito*, above given.

This line can be read in Minsi, *Lapi-up Kehtanitowit man'ito mani'towak,* Again-he-spake, Great-Spirit, a spirit, spirits. The symbol represents the communion of the spirits. Compare Tanner, *Narrative,* p. 359, fig. 24.

10. Raf. and Squier absurdly translate *angelatawiwak,* angels. It is from a familiar Del. verb. *angeln,* to die. Compare Abnaki *Sanangmes8ak,* "revenants," Rasles, and *w'tanglowagan,* his death, Zeis. The form in the text, according to Mr. Anthony, has the sense, "things destined to die," mortal, perishable. He gives the line in Minsi as follows :—

Aweniwak	*angelatawawak*	*wtschitschwankwak*	*wemiwak.*
Beings	mortals	souls	and all.

The *wak* of the last word is not the plural but the conjunction "and ;" as in the Latin, *omniaque.*

11. Raf. translates *jinwis* as "man-being," and Squier thinks it the Chipeway *inini,* men ; but it appears to be the adverb *janwi,* ever, always. The symbol is apparently that of birth, or being born. Compare Tanner, *Narr.,* p. 351, fig. 1, with that meaning, an armless figure with wide spread legs.

12. The pictograph is a woman, with breasts, but armless. The "first mother" here represented was an important personage in

the mythology of the Chipeways and neighboring tribes. She was called "the grandmother of mankind" (*Me-suk-kum-me-go-kwa*, in Dr. James' orthography), and it was to her that Nanabush (Manibozho), imparted the secrets of all roots, herbs and plants. Hence, the medicine men direct their songs and addresses to her whenever they take anything from the earth which is to be used as a medicine. Tanner's *Narrative*, p. 355.

13. The figure of a square, the world, with the four varieties of animals named.

14. The bad spirit was, in Algonkin mythology, the water god, and was represented as a serpent-like figure. See Copway, pp. 134, 135. Schoolcraft, *Synopsis*, figs. 93, 100.

Amangamek, plural form of the compound *amangi*, great; *namaes* fish; but *amangi* has the associate idea of terrifying, frightful, hence the reference is to some mythical water monster (Cree, *am*, faire peur, Lacombe).

Raf. translates both *nakowak* in this line, and *nakowa*, in II, 6, as "black snake." They can have no such meaning, black, in Lenape, being *suckeu*, and in none of the Algonkin dialects does *nak* mean black.

16. The figure represents the earth-plain under the form of the area of a lodge, with central fire and the people in it, typifying friendliness. Comp. Tanner, *Narr.*, p. 348, fig. 1.

V. 16 pursues the topic of v. 13, and it looks as if v. 14 and 15 should be transposed to follow v. 20.

17. The former renderings are.—

"Thou being Kiwis, good God Wunand, and the good makers were such."—*Rafinesque*.

"There being a good god, all spirits were good."—*Squier*.

Rafinesque mistook the adverb *kiwis* for a proper name.

18. Raf. translates *nijini*, the Jins, and *nantinewak*, fairies, and Squier follows him in the latter, but could not go as far as the former! As seen in the vocabulary, I attach wholly different notions to these words. The two figures united refer to the sexual relation. Compare Tanner, *Narr.*, pp. 371, figs. 8, 9.

19. *Gattamin* cannot mean "fat fruit," as Raf. translates it. He has evidently mistaken the explanation given by Heckewelder, of Catawissa, *Gattawisu*, becoming fat, and thought that *gatta*, was fat, whereas *wisu* is "fat." (Zeis. *Gram.*, p. 229.)

Wakon is understood by Rafinesque as the proper name of the evil spirit, connecting it with the Dakota *wakan*, divine, supernatural.

20. The dream of "the good old times," the happy epoch of yore, when men dwelt in peace and prosperity, was, as I have shown, page 135, a myth of the Delawares, and George Copway tells us that the Chipeway legends also recalled it with delight. (*Traditional History of the Ojibway Nation*, pp. 98 and 169–175.)

21. The symbol is the same as that of the "bad spirit under the earth," given by Copway, p. 135.

A similar figure is given by Copway to signify "bad," p. 135. I do not understand its allusion.

22. *Mattalogas;* the prefix is the negative *matta*, no, not, and generally conveys a bad sense, as *matteleman*, to despise one, *mattelendam*, to be uneasy. Zeis.

Pallalogasin, to sin, from *palli*, elsewhere, other than, hence *pallhiken*, to shoot amiss, to miss the mark, to go wrong.

Maktaton, unhappiness. There is a relation in Lenape between the negative *matta*, in Minsi, *machta*, and the words for bad, ugly, evil, and the like; *machtisisu*, here it is bad, or ugly. *Zeisb.* It would seem to be an intuitive recognition of the profound philosophical maxim that evil is ever a negation; that Mephistopheles is, as he says in Faust—

"Der Geist der stets verneint."

23. The symbol is apparently trees on hills, bent by a storm, and beneath a death's head.

24. The picture seems to be two countries connected by a bridge.

Atak kitahican, = *attach*, beyond, above; *kitahican*, the ocean, literally "the great tidal sea." It is possible this has reference to the deluge, which is described in the next section; but usually *kitahican* meant the ocean.

II.

1. *Maskanako;* the Lenape words would be *mechek*, great, *achgook*, snake; but *maska* is more allied to the Cree *maskaw*, strong, hard, solid. Raf. translates the close of the line "when men had become bad."

2. *Schingalan*, to hate; from the adjective *schingi*, disliking; unwilling. This is the contrary of *wingi*, liking, willing. Both are from the subjective radical *n* or *ni*, I, *Ego*, the latter with the prefix *wĕl*, signifying pleasurable sensation (see page 104).

Shawelendamep, preterite form, strengthened by the prefix *ksch*, of the verb *acquiwelendam*, Zeis., to disquiet, to trouble; it has not the passive sense given in Rafinesque's translation. All verbs terminating in *elendam* signify a disposition of mind, the root being again the subjective *n*, ego. Raf. translates: "This strong snake had become the foe of the Jins, and they became troubled, hating each other."

3. *Palliton*, from *palli*, elsewhere (from what was intended), hence "to spoil something, to do it wrong," and later "to fall out, to fight."

Lungundowin, from *langan*, easy, light to do, Chipeway, *nin nangan*, I find it light, of no trouble; hence, "*peace*," as being a time free from trouble; and by a third application of the idea, *elangomellan*, friends, those who are at peace with us.

4. Raf. translates this line: "Less men with dead-keeper fighting," which is a total misunderstanding of the words. On the derivation of *nihanlowit* see *ante*, page 102.

6. On *nakowa*, see I, line 14. Here I consider it a derivative from *nacha*, three, and both the sense of the line and the symbol, with three marks to the right of the figure, indicate this meaning. The three antagonists are the monster, the waters, and the Great Snake himself.

7. The repetition of the words is to add force to the phrase.

8. This is an important line, as indicating the origin of the Walam Olum. *Nanaboush* is not the Delaware form of the name of the Algonkin hero-god, so far as known, but the Chipeway *Nanabooshoo*, Tanner, *Nanibajou*, McKinney, properly *Nänäboj*, the Trickster, the Cheater, allied to Chip. *nin nanabanis*, I am cheated. This term, like the Cree *Wisakketjāk*, which has the same meaning (*fourbe, trompeur*, Lacombe), was applied to the hero-god of these nations on account of his exhaustless ingenuity in devising tricks, ruses, disguises and transformations, to overcome the various other divine powers with whom he came in conflict. This seemingly depreciatory term arose from the same admiration of versatility of powers which has imparted such uni-

versal popularity to the story of the wily (πολυτροπος) Ulysses, and the trickery of Master Reynard.

The appearance of this form of the name indicates that the version of the legend here given has been influenced by Chipeway associations, as, indeed, we might expect, since it was obtained in Indiana, where the Delawares were in constant intercourse with their Chipeway neighbors.

Tulapit menapit = tulpe epit, menatey epit, "it was then at the turtle, it was then at the island." The form *Tula* has given rise to the strangest theorizing about this line, as, of course, the antiquaries could not resist the temptation to see in it a reference to the Tula or Tollan of Aztec mythology, the capital city of the Toltecs and the home of Quetzalcoatl.

The similarity of the words is purely fortuitous. The Lenape word *tulpe* means turtle or tortoise, especially, says Zeisberger, a water or sea turtle. In their mythology, as I have already shown (ante, p. 134) the earth was supposed to be floating on a boundless ocean, as a turtle floats on the surface of a pond. Hence, symbolically, the turtle represents the dry land.

Maskaboush = Chip. *mashka*, strong, *wabos*, usually translated hare or rabbit, but really "White One." I have fully explained this mistaken sense of the word in *American Hero Myths*, pp. 41, 42, and elsewhere.

9. The Algonkin myth relates that Michabo or Nanaboj after having formed the earth on the primal ocean, walked round and round it, and by this act increased it constantly in size.

Rafinesque's translation is :—"Being born creeping, he is ready to move and dwell at *Tula*;" and in his note to the line he adds, "*Tula* is the ancient seat of the Toltecas and Mexican nations in Asia; the *Tulan* or *Turan* of Central Tartary."

The entire absence of connected meaning in this and other lines of Rafinesque's translation is strong evidence that he did not fabricate the text; otherwise he would certainly have assigned it some coherent sense.

The turtle is, as usual, the symbol of the land or earth (see page 133).

12. *Manito-dasin,* the Divine Maiden, or the Daughter of the Gods, as it might be freely translated. The reference is to the Virgin who at the beginning of things descended from heaven, and

alighting on the back of the turtle became the mother of Nanaboj and his brothers. She was well known in Eastern Algonkin mythology, as I have already shown. (See above, p. 131.)

13. This and the three following verses form, observes Rafinesque, a rhymed hymn to Nanabush.

14. In this line the men are referred to as *Linapi*, not *lennowak* as before. Here then begins the particular history of the Lenape tribe, whose chief sub-tribe was the Turtle clan.

The meaning of the line is very obscure. It seems to refer to the origin of the Unami, or Turtle sub-tribe of the Delawares.

16. *Kwamipokho*, translated by Raf. "plain and mountain," does not appear to me to bear any such rendering. I take it as a form of *champeecheneu*, Z. "it is still or stagnant water," the appropriateness of which to the context is evident.

Sitwalikho, Raf. renders "path of cave," deriving it obviously from *tsit*, foot, and *woalheu*, a hole. It has no sort of meaning in this rendering, and I assume, therefore, that it is a derivative from *tschitqui*, silent.

Maskan wagan, probably an error for *maskanakon*, as in v. 1.

Palliwi, palliwi, "is elsewhere, is elsewhere," or, "is foiled, is overcome."

III.

1. *Wittank talli:* in the MS. these words are first translated "dwelling town there," but the last two words are erased and "of Talli" substituted. This is one of a number of instances where Rafinesque altered his first translations, which is further evidence that he did not manufacture the text. In this instance, as frequently, he altered it for the worse. *Wittank* is from *witen*, to go with or be with, Zeis., and *talli* is the adverb "there."

3. *Meshautang*, "many deer" (see Vocabulary), translated by Rafinesque, "game."

Siliewak, rendered by Rafinesque *sili*, cattle, *ewak*, they go. The *wak* is the terminal "and" (see notes to I. v. 10). The word *sisile*, in modern Delaware *sizil'ia* (Whipple's Vocabulary), means "buffalo." Its older form is seen in the MS. vocab. of the New Jersey Indians, 1792, where it is *sisiliamuus*. This is a compound of the generic termination *muus*, Cree, *mustus* (whence our word "moose"), meaning any large quadruped, and probably the prefix *tschilusi*, strong, powerful, with an intensive reduplication.

4. *Powalessin*, from the same root as *powwow* (see page 70). The course of thought was that the dreamer (*powwow*) became wise beyond his followers, and hence obtained power and riches, though not of a martial character.

Elowichik, hunters; *allowin*, to hunt, doubtless connected with *alluns*, an arrow.

5, 6. A note in the MS. states that the symbols of these two verses were united together in the original drawings.

7. In this verse the pre-eminence of the Turtle sub-tribe, the Unami, is asserted to have obtained from the most ancient times.

8. The verses 8, 9, 10, are referred in Rafinesque's free translation to the "Snake people." They seem to me to be descriptive of the grief of the Lenape on leaving their ancient home.

12. *Pokhapokhapek*, "Gaping Sea," Raf. Both this and the preceding word are descriptive of the sea, referred to as offering means of subsistence; *namaes*, fish, *pocqueu*, muscles or clams, being the two main food-products of the water for the Indians.

The location of this productive spot I leave for future investigators to determine. The Detroit River and the Thousand Isles in the St. Lawrence are the most appropriate localities, to my mind.

13. The last word of the line is given in the MS. both as *menakinep*, and *akomenep*, the latter a later interlineation. I prefer the former.

Wapasinep, may mean "at the East," as well as "in the light." The latter is a metaphor, common in the native tongues, for prosperity.

Verses 13 to 20 inclusive were printed by Rafinesque in the original, and called by him, "the poem on the passage to America," as he understood this narrative to refer to the period when the ancestors of the Lenape crossed Behring straits from Asia to America on the ice.

17. *Kitahican*. This is the term given by Zeisberger to the Ocean. The prefix *Kit* is "great," and the termination *hican* appears to have been confined to tidal waters (see above, p. 21). Elsewhere this termination signifies an instrument. Probably it was applicable to all large bodies of water.

On *pokhakhopek*, doubtless a carelessness for *pokhapokhapek*, line 12, see note to the latter.

18. Squier does not give the numerals, but says simply "in vast numbers." No doubt this is the intention of the expression.

20. *Shiwaking*, "the place of spruce firs" (see Vocab).

They crossed in mid-winter a broad stream, rich in fish and shell-fish, and arrived at a land covered with forests of spruce. For a long time this appears to have remained their home.

IV.

2. *Sittamaganat*, Raf. translates "Path Leader." The word *tamaganat* appears in other verses, as *w'tamaganat*, IV, 37 ; *tamaganat*, IV, 55 ; *tamaganend*, V, 2. I derive it from the root *tam*, literally to drink, but generally, to smoke tobacco, as in Roger Williams' Key *wut-tammagon*, a pipe (see above, page 49). Hence I take *tamagamat* to be the pipe-bearer, he who had charge of the Sacred Calumet. If it is objected that this puts the use of tobacco by the Lenape too remote, I reply that we do not know when they began to use it, and moreover, this may be an anachronism of tradition.

13, 14. The lands toward the four cardinal points are described from a centre where the tribe was then located. Neither Rafinesque nor Squier understood this, and their renderings do not mention the territories North and West. From the description, I should place the then location of the tribe in Western New York and Northern Ohio.

16. The four names seem to be appellatives of different tribes. One of the extinct tribes remembered in Chipeway tradition was the *Assizunaik*, Stone People (Schoolcraft, *History and Statistics of the Ind. Tribes*, Vol. I, p. 305).

25. The legend here relates that the cultivation of maize began after they had reached a low latitude, presumably Southern Indiana or Ohio. The legend of the New England Indians was that a crow flew down from the great God Kitantowit, bringing in one ear a grain of corn, in the other a bean, and taught them the cultivation of these plants. (Roger Williams, *Key into the Language of America*, p. 114.) See further, ante, p. 48.

34. *Wisawana*, the Yellow River. There is a small river, so-called, in the State of Indiana, a branch of the Kankakee, called

on Hough's "Map of the Indian Names of Indiana" *We-tho-gan*, a corruption of *wisawanna*. (See Hough's map, in *Twelfth Annual Report of the Geology and Natural History of Indiana*, 1883.) When the Minsi made their first migration west, about 1690, they directed their course to this spot, where they were found by Charlevoix in 1721.

36. *Tamenend*, the name of the celebrated chief now better known to us as Tammany, who dealt with William Penn. Heckewelder translates it as "Affable." This is the first of the name. A second is mentioned, V, 32. The friend of Penn was the third.

46. *Towakon pallitonep*, Raf. translates "father snake, he was mad!"

48. Perhaps this line should be translated: "They speak well of the east; many go to the east."

49. *Nemassipi*, Fish River. In the MS. this name was first written *mixtu sipi*. The name "Fish River" was applied to various streams by the Delawares, but never, so far as I know, to the Mississippi. In the present connection it seems to refer either to the St. Lawrence, about the Thousand Isles, or else its upper stream, the Detroit River, both of which were famous fishing spots.

50. *Talligewi*. No name in the Lenape legends has given rise to more extensive discussion than this. It is usually connected with *Alligewi* and this again with *Alleghany*. This seems supported by Loskiel, who, writing on the authority of Zeisberger, says, "Nun nennen die Delawaren die ganze Gegend, so weit die Gewässer reichen, die in dem Ohio fallen, Alligewinengk, welches so viel bedeutet, als das Land, in welches sie sich aus weit entfernten Orten begeben haben." (*Geschichte der Mission*, etc., p. 164.)

The meaning here assigned to Alligewinengk, "land where they arrived from distant places," is evidently based on the resolution of the compound into *talli*, there, *icku*, to that place, *ewak*, they go, with a locative final. The initial *t* is often omitted in adverbial compounds of *talli* (itself a compound of *ta*, locative particle, and *li*, to), as *allamunk*, in there.

Bishop Ettwein gives to the word a different meaning. He writes: "The Delawares call the western country *Alligewenork*, which signifies a War-Path; the river itself they call *Alligewi*

Sipo." (*Legends and Traditions*, etc., in *Bull. of the Pa. Hist. Soc.* p. 34.) Here the derivation would be from *palliton*, to fight, *ewak*, they go, and a locative, "they go there to fight." The omission of the initial *p* was not uncommon, as Campanius gives *ayuta = alliton*, to make war. (*Catechismus*, p. 141.)

Basing his opinion on an expression in the Journal of C. F. Post, to the effect that Alleghany means "fine or fair river," Dr. J. H. Trumbull analyzes it into *wulik, hanné, sipu*, which he translates "best, rapid-stream, long-river (*Connect. Hist. Soc. Colls*, Vol. II).

Rafinesque, in the MS. of the Walum Olum, gives Talligewi the translation "there found," from *talli*, there, and I know not what word for "found."

There have not been wanting those who would derive the name Alleghany from Iroquois roots, as the Seneca *De-o-na-ga-no*, "cold water" (*Amer. Hist. Mag.* Vol. IV, p. 184). But there is no probability that the word is Iroquois,

Whatever its origin, the name was not confined to the Alleghany river, but included the whole of the Upper Ohio, as the interpreter Post distinctly says.

The Rev. Mr. Heckewelder was of opinion that *Talligewi* was a word foreign to the Algonkin, a *nomen gentile* of another tribe, adopted by the Delawares, just as they adopted *Mengwe* for the Iroquois from the Onondaga *Yenkwe*, men (see above, page 14). It is not necessarily connected with Alleghany, which may be pure Algonkin. He says, "Those people called themselves *Talligeu* or *Tallige wi*." (*Indian Nations* p. 48.) The accent, as he gives it, *Tallige'wi*, shows that the word is, *Talliké*, with the substantive verb termination, so that *Talligewi* means, "He is a *Talliké*," or, "It is of (belongs to) the Talliké."

This appears to me the most probable supposition of any I have quoted, and it reduces our quest to that of a nation who called themselves by a name which, to Lenape ears, would sound like *Talliké*. Such a nation presents itself at once in the Cherokees, who call themselves *Tsa'laki*. Moreover, they fill the requirements in other particulars. Their ancient traditions assign them a residence precisely where the Delaware legends locate the Tallike, to wit, on the upper waters of the Ohio (see above, page 17). Fragments of them continued there until within the historic period; and the persistent hostility between them and the Delawares points to some ancient and important contest.

Name, location and legends, therefore, combine to identify the Cherokees or Tsalaki with the Tallike; and this is as much evidence as we can expect to produce in such researches. I can see no reason whatever for Dr. Shea's opinion that the Lenape "in their progress eastward drove out of Ohio the Quappas, called by the Algonkins, Alkanzas or Alligewi, who retreated down the Ohio and Mississippi." (Shea, Notes to Alsop's *Maryland*, p. 118.)

The question remains, whether the Tallike were the "Mound Builders." It is not so stated in the WALAM OLUM. The inference rather is that the "Snake people," *Akowini* or *Akonapi*, dwelt in the river valleys north of the Ohio river, in the area of Western Ohio and Indiana, where the most important earth-works are found—and singularly enough none more remarkable than the immense effigy of the serpent in Adams County, Ohio, which winds its gigantic coils over 700 feet in length on the summit of a bold bluff overlooking Brush Creek.

According to the RED SCORE, the Snake people were conquered by the Algonkins long before the contest with the Tallike began. These latter lay between the position then occupied by the Lenape and the eastern territory where they were found by the whites. In other words, the Tallike were on the Upper Ohio and its tributaries, and they had to be driven south before the path across the mountains was open. For this reason they are called *wapawullaton*, "possessing the East," that is, with reference to the then position of the Lenape in southwestern Ohio.

54. *Talamatan*. This was the Lenape name of the Huron-Iroquois or Wyandots. It is found in the form *Telamatinos* in a "List of 11 Nations living West of Allegheny" present by deputy at a Conference in Philadelphia, 1759 (*Minutes of the Prov. Council of Penna.*, Vol. VIII, p. 418). Heckewelder gives *Delamattenos* (*Ind. Nations*, p. 80).

Rafinesque translates the name in one place by "not Talas," and in another by "not of us," from Len. *matta*, not, Latin *nos*, us. That the Lenape did not speak Latin made no difference in his linguistic theory, as he held all languages to be at core the same! On the Hurons, see above, p. 16.

V.

2. *Wapalaneng*, apparently the White River, Indiana, or else the Wabash.

16. In this line the three tribes are mentioned which were previously named in IV, 44, 45, 46, and the difference in the spelling shows that the chant was written down by one unacquainted with the forms of the language.   The correspondent names are:—

IV.	V.
Akowini,	Sinako.
Towakon,	Towako.
Lowanuski,	Lowako.

The termination *ako*, uniformly rendered by Rafinesque *snake*, appears to be either the animate plural in *ak*, or the locative *aki*, place or land.

The *Towako* are probably the Ot-tawa called by the Delaware *Taway;* or the Twightees, called by them *Tawatawee* (see "List of 11 Nations," etc., in *Minutes of the Prov. Council of Pa.*, Vol. VIII, p. 418).

There is difficulty in reconciling *Akowini* and *Sinako*.   In the former, the prefix *ako* may be from *achgook*, snake, as Rafinesque and Squier rendered it.

The word *Lowanuski* appears again in v. 18, where Raf. inserts the note, " Lowushkis are Esquimaux."   It means simply " winter land," or " Northern people," and is not likely to have any reference to the Eskimo.

22. " Without snakes," *i. e.*, free from enemies.

24. On the derivation of Susquehannah, see page 14.

25. *Winakaking*, Sassafras Land, the native name of eastern Pennsylvania.

29. The Wapings and the Minsi seem to be referred to.

33, 36. The omission of the numbers 34 and 35 is in the original MS.

50. *Ganshowenik;* Raf. translates this " the noisy place, or Niagara."   It is a derivative from the root *kan*.   See Vocab.

60. *Ewenikiktit*, may be translated " whites " or "Europeans." See Vocabulary.

VOCABULARY.

In the following Vocabulary the meaning placed immediately after the word is that assigned to it in Rafinesque's original MS.; the probable composition of it is then added, with its correct rendering. The standard of the language adopted is that of the Moravian missionaries (see above, p. 97). The initials referring to authorities are: Z., for Zeisberger, K., for Kampman, H., for Heckewelder, R. W., Roger Williams, C. or Camp., Campanius, etc.

Aan. I, 6. To move; to go; Z. conjugated, *Gram.*, p. 142. Chip. *ani*, he goes; *aunj-eh*, he moves. Cf. *Payat*.

Agamunk. III, 16. Over water. *Acawenuck*, over the water. R. W. *Acawmenoakit*, land on the other side of the water, *i. e.* England. R. W. The proper names Accomac, Algonkin, etc., are from the same roots.

Agunouken. III, 13. Always our fathers. *Nooch*, my father, Z. in which *n* is the possessive *our* or *my*.

Akhokink. III, 9. Snake land at. Derivatives beginning with *akho*, and some with *ako* appear to be compounds of *achgook*, Mohegan *ukkok*, the generic name for snake.

Akhomenis. IV, 3. Snake Island. *Menatey*, island, and *achgook*, snake.

Akhonapi. IV, 16. Snaking man. *Achgook*, and *ape*, man; a *nomen gentile*.

Akhopayat. IV, 6. Snake coming. *Achgook*, snake; *payat*, he comes.

Akhopokho. IV, 6. Snake hill. *Achgook*, snake. *Pockhcpokink*, a river between hills. Heck.

Akhowemi. IV, 7. Snake all. *Achgook*, snake, and *wemi*, all.

Ako. II, 1, 2. Snake. *Achgook*, snake. See *Akhokink*.

Akolaki. IV, 13, and Akolaking. IV, 18. At beautiful land. *Achgook*, snake; *aki*, land. A form of *Akhokink*, q. v.

Akomen. III, 14, 18. Island snake. *Achgook*, snake; *menatey*, island.

Akomenaki. III, 10. Snake fortified island. *Akomen*, q. v., and *aki*, land.

Akomenep. III, 13. Snake island was. *Akomen*, with the preterit termination.

Akopehella. II, 6. Snake water rushing. *Kschippehellan*, strong stream in a river. Z. See *Pehella*.

P   233

Akowetako. V, 43. Coweta snakes. *Weta*, a house, II., and *aki*, land; the Coweta land.

Akowini. IV, 44. Snake beings *or* like. The Snake people; a *nomen gentile*.

Akpinep. III, 2. Was there. *Achpil*, to stay, abide; *achpiney*, a sleeping place.

Alankwak. I, 5. Stars. *Alank*, star.

Alkosohit. IV, 26. Keeper and preserver. *Allouchsit*, strong and mighty. K.

Allendyachick. IV, 32. Some going. *Alende*, some.

Allendhilla. IV, 52. Some kill. *Alende*, some, and *nihillan*, to kill.

Allendyumek. II, 11. Some of them.

Allowelendam. III, 20. Preferring above all. *Allowelendamen*, to esteem highly. Z.

Allumapi. III, 19. With dogs of man. *Allum*, dog; *ape*, man; men having dogs.

Alokuwi. IV, 46. Lean he. *Alocuwoagan*, leanness. Z.

Amangaki. V, 21. Large land. *Amangi*, great, large. See p. 146, note.

Amangam. II, 6. Monster. *Amangi*. See p. 146, note.

Amangamek. I, 14. Manitos or large reptiles. II, 11. Waters of sea. *Amangemek*, a large fish.

Amokolen. III, 13. Boating. *Amochol*, canoe or boat.

Amigaki. V, 21. Long land. *Amangi*, great; *aki*, land.

Angelotawiwak. I, 10. Angels also. From *angeln*, to die. See note to the passage.

Angomelchik. IV, 4. The friends *or* friendly souls. *Melechitschant*, soul. Z.; *melih*, corruption, Z., and *angeln*, to die; "the souls departed."

Anup. II, 1. When. *Aanup*, when *or* if I went. Zeis. *Gram.*, p. 143. Doubtful.

Apakachik. III, 6. Spreaders. *Apach tschichchton*, to display, to attach oneself to or upon. K.

Apakchikton. IV, 11. Spreading. See *Apakachik*.

Apendawi. IV, 26. Useful he. *Apendamen*, to make use of; *apensuwi*, useful, enjoyable.

Aptelendam. III, 9. Grieving. To grieve to death. Zeis.

Askipalliton. V, 43. Must make war. *Aski*, must, obliged, and *palliton*.

Askiwaal. IV. They must go. *Aski*, must, and *aan* or *aal*, to go.

Assinapi. IV, 16. Stone man. *Assin*, a stone; *ape*, a man; a *nomen gentile*.

Atak. I, 24. Beyond. *Attach*, beyond, above. Zeis.

Atam. III, 8. Let us go. *Atam*, let us go. Z. *Gram.*

Attagatta. IV, 31. Unwilling. *Atta*, or *matta*, negative prefix; *gatta*, to want, or wish.

Attalchinitis. IV, 62. Not always friend. *Atta*, neg. prefix; *nitap*, friend, or our friend.

Attaminin. IV, 28. No corn. *Atta*, neg. prefix; *min*, berry or corn.

Attasokelan. IV, 28. No raining. *Atta*, neg. prefix; *sokelan*, rain.

Awasagamek. I, 4. Much heaven. *Awosegame*, heaven. Z.

Awesik. I, 13. Beasts. *Awessis*, a beast.

Awolagan. V, 12. Heavenly. *Awullakenim*, to praise. K.

Ayamak. IV, 15, 17. The great warrior. *Ajummen*, to buy, purchase. K.; from *aji*, take it! hence "the Buyer," or "the Seizer."

Chanelendam. III, 20. Doubting. *Tschannelendam*, to consider, to be in doubt. K.

Chichankwak. I, 10. Souls also. *Tschitschank*, soul.

Chihillen. III, 11. Separating. *Tschitschpihielen*, to split asunder; cf. *chipen*, it separates.

Chikimini. V, 52. Turkey tribe. See above, p. 37.

Chikonapi. IV, 16. Robbing man. *Cheche*, to rob, R. W., K'y, p. 102.

Chiksit. III, 5. Holy. *Kschiechek*, clean; *kschiechanchsopannik*, holy. Z.

Chilili. IV, 10, 12, 15. Snow-bird. *Chilili*, snow-bird, Heck. *Ind. Names*, p. 363.

Chingalsuwi. IV, 30. Stiffened he. *Tschingalsu*, stiff.

Chintanes. III, 4. Strong. *Tschintamen*, strong. Z.

Chitanesit. III, 5. Strong. *Tschitani*, strong. K.

Chitanitis. IV, 51. Strong friend. *Tschitani*, strong; *nitis*, friend.

Chitanwulit. IV, 45. Strong and good. *Tschitani*, strong; *wulit*, good.

Cholensak. I, 13. Birds. *Tscholens*, bird.

Dasin. II, 12. Daughter. *N'danüss*, my daughter.

Danisapi. III, 19. Daughters of man. *N'danüss*, my daughter; *ape*, man.

Delsin. I, 8. Is there. *W'dellsin*, he is *or* does so. Zeis. *Gram.*, p. 117.

Delsinewo. III, 5. They are. *W'dellsinewo*, they are or do so. Zeis. *Gram.*, p. 117.

Eken. II, 2. Together. Probably an error for *nekama*, those.

Elangomel. V, 38. Friendly to all. *Elangomellan*, my friend. Z.

Elemamik. I, 3. Everywhere. *Elemamek*, everywhere. Z.

Elendamep. I, 20. Thinking. On *elendam*, see above, p. 100.

Eli. I, 21. While. *Eli*, because, then, so, that. K. Also a superlative prefix, as *eli kimi*, very privately.

Elmusichik. IV, 4. The goers. *Elemussit*, he who goes away. Z.

Elowaki. III, 17. Hunting country. *Eluwak*, most powerful. Z. In this word and in *elowapi*, Rafinesque mistook the meaning of the prefix. Compare *elowichik*.

Elowapi. III, 19. Hunting manly. *Eli*, intensive, best or most, and *ape*, man, or perhaps *wapi*, knowing.

Elowichik. III, 4, 5, 6. Hunters. From *allauwin*, to hunt. Z.; *allau-witaa*, let us go hunting. H.

Eluwi. III, 5. Most. The superlative form *eli*, with the substantive verb suffix, *wi*.

Eluwiwulit. IV, 36. The best. From *eluwi*, and *wulit*, good.

Enolowin. IV, 9. Things who. Doubtful, perhaps, *nanne*, those; *owini*, beings, people.

Epallahchund. V, 53. Failer, who fails. *Pallikiken*, to shoot amiss; *palliaan*, to go away.

Epit. I, 8. Being there. I, 24. At. This is a suppositive form from *achpin*, called the "adverbial" by Zeis., *Gram.*, p. 115, who translates it "where he is." It may also be translated by the preposition "at." See Heckewelder, *Correspondence with Duponceau*, Letter XXI.

Eshohok. II, 7. Much penetrate. *Eschoochwen*, to go through. Z.

Essop. I, 2, 3. He was.

Essopak. I, 17. Were. II, 1, 2. Had become. A form from *lissin*, to be *or* do so.

Ewak. III, 3. They go. *Ewak*, they go. Z.; from *aan*, to go.

Ewenikiktit. V, 60. Who are they? *Auwenik*, who are they? Z. *Gram.*, 116. The term *Awanuts* was that applied to the whites in general by the New England Indians. The Abbé Maurault derives it from *aSeni*, who, *uji*, whence; = whence come they? *Histoire des Abéna-kis*, p. 10.

Gahani. II, 10. Shallow water. *Gahan*, shallow. K.

Gaho. I, 12. Mother. See *Nixoha*.

Gandhaton. IV, 7. Concealing or hiding themselves. *Gandhatton*, to hide, to conceal. K.

Ganshowenik. V, 50. Noisy place (Niagara). *Ganschewen*, to roar, to make a great noise, Z.; or from *kanti*. See above, p. 73.

Gattamin. I, 19. Fat fruits. *N'gattamen*, I wish, desire. Z. See note to passage.

Gattawisi. V, 25. Becoming fat. *Gatta*, do you want? Z.; *gattawisi*, becoming fat, proper form of Catawissa. Heck., *Ind. Names*, p. 360. See note.

Gentikalanep. IV, 39. Festivals he made. *Kanti*, to sing and dance. See p. 73.

Gichi. II, 5. Ready. See the root *kich*, p. 102.

Gikenopalat. V, 23. Great warrior. *Gischigin*, to be born; *netopalisak* = warrior. Z.

Gishelendam. IV, 62. Conspiring. *Gischelendam*, to hatch or meditate something good or bad. See p. 103.

Gishikin. II, 9. Being born. *Gischigin*, to be born. See pp. 102-3.

Gishikshawipek. V, 26. Sun salt sea. *Gischihan*, to make; *schejek*, wampum.

Gishuk. I, 5. Sun. See p. 103.

Gotatamen. IV, 51. He desires. *N'gattamen*, I want, *or* wish. Z.

Gunehunga. IV, 33. They tarry. *Guneünga*, they stay long. Heck., *Ind. Names*, p. 365.

Gunehungtit. IV, 61. They settle. *Gunehunga*, they stay.

Guneunga. III, 12, 20. They tarry. See *Gunehunga*.

Gunitakan. IV, 62. Long-and-mild. *Guneu*, long.

Gunokim. IV, 22. Long while fatherly. *Guno*, snow. Z. *Ooch*, father.

Gutikuni. III, 18. Single night. *Gutti*, one; *nuktogunak*, one night. R. W.

Hackung. I, 2. Above. *Hacki*, the earth. Z. *Hackunk*, on or at the earth. Raf. translates it as *hockung*, the place above, the sky, heaven. Camp.

Hakhsinipek. III, 17. On hard, stony sea. *Achsin*, a stone; *pek*, a sea. It may mean "stony sea;" but in the connection I think it is metaphorical " stone-hard," *i. e.*, frozen sea.

Hakik. I, 4. Much land. *Hacki*, the earth. Z.

Hallemiwis. I, 3. Eternal being. *Hallemiwi*, eternally. Z.

Hanaholend. V, 24. River loving. *Amhanne*, river. H. *Ahoala*, to love.

Hattanwulaton. IV, 60. He-has-possession. *Hattan*, to have; *wulaton*, to own, to possess.

Huminiend. IV, 25. Corn eater. *Pach-hamineu*, parched and beaten corn, R. W., whence our word *hominy*.

Ikalawit. V, 55. Yonder between. *Ikali*, thither.

Init'ako. I, 21. Worship snake. *Aan*, to come; *aki*, earth. Raf. derives the suffix from *achgook*, snake.

Italissipek. IV, 28. Far from the sea. *Ikalissi*, further, more; *pek*, standing water, or sea.

Janotowi. IV, 9. True-maker. *W'nutikowi*, he keeps watch. Z. Doubtful.

Jinwis. I, 11. Man-being. See note to passage.

Kamik. I, 24. Age or foretime. "*Kamiz*, at the end of words, alludes to the ground." Baraga, *Otch. Dic. Gamunk*, on the other side of the water. Z.

Kelik. III, 3. Much. Comp. *Kwelik*. An intensive prefix.

Kelitgeman. V, 3. Much planting corn. Comp. *kelik; min*, corn or berry.

Kichipek. V, 26. Big sea. *Kitschi*, great; *pek*, a body of still water. See p. 100.

Kichitamak. V, 11, 36. Big Beaver. *Kitschi*, great; *tamaque*, beaver.

Kicholen. III, 14. Big bird. *Kitchi*, great; *tscholens*, bird.

Kihillalend. IV, 6. Thou killest some. *Nihillan*, to kill, *k'*, thou.

Kimi. I, 21. Secretly. *Kimi*, privately. Z.

Kiminikwi. IV, 32. Secretly far off. *Kimi*, privately.

Kinchepend. IV, 55. Sharp he was. *Kineu*, sharp.

Kipemapekan. V, 47. Big Lake going. *Kitschi*, great; *pek*, lake; *aan*, to go.

Kitahikan. I, 21. Great ocean. III, 17. Of great ocean. *Kitahican*, the sea, ocean. Z.

Kitanitowit. I, 2, 3, 9. God-Creator. See p. 218.

Kitelendam. III, 9. Earnestly. To be in earnest. Z.

Kitohatewa. V, 60. Big ships or birds. *Kito*, great; *haten*, he has.

Kitshinaki. IV, 13. Big firland. *Kitschi*, great, and *shinaki*.

Kiwis. I, 17. Thou being. *Kitschiwi*, truly, verily. Z.

Kiwikhotan. V, 48. Visiting. *Kiwiken*, to visit.

Kolachusien. V, 6. Pretty bluebird. *Kola = wulit*, pretty. Doubtful.

Kolakwaming. IV, 29. Fine plain at. *Wulit*, fine, beautiful. The sense is doubtful.

Kolawil. Beautiful head. IV, 5, 8. *Wulit*, fine; *wil*, head.

Komelendam. III, 11. Having no trouble. To be free from trouble or care. K.

Kowiyey-tulpaking. III, 20. Old turtle land at. *Kikey*, old. K. *Tulpe*, turtle. Doubtful.

Kshakan. I, 7. It blows hard. III, 2. It storms. *Kschachan*, the wind blows hard. K.

Kshipehelen. II, 16. Water running off. *Kschippehellan*, the water flows rapidly, a strong current. Z. Z. also uses *higih hillen*, the waterfalls. *Spelling Book*, p. 122.

Kshipehelep. I, 7. It ran off. *K"schippehellenp*, the water ran off. Zeis. *Gram.*, p. 224.

Ksin. I, 20. Easy. *Ksinachpo*, he is at leisure.

Kundokanup. IV, 3. Searching when. *N'doniken*, I seek, or, *n'donam*. Z.

Kwamipokho. II, 16. Plain and mountain. *Klampeechenen*, it is still or stagnant water. Z.

Kwelik. I, 2, 4. Much water. I, 7. Deep water. *Quenek =kwelek*, long, extended. Z. Compare *kelik*.

Kwitikwond. IV, 31. Reprover. *Quittel*, to reprove. Z.

Lakka welendam. III, 8. Troubled *or* afraid. *Lachan welendam*, to be troubled in mind. K.

Lamatanitis. V, 44. *Lamatan* (Huron), friends. See above, p. 16.

Lanewapi. III, 19. Eagle manly. *Woapalanne*, bald eagle. Z.

Langomuwak. V, 60. Friendly they. *Langamu winaxu*, he looks friendly. Z.

Langomuwi. V, 54. Friendly he. *Langundo*, peaceful. Z. From *langan*, light, easy.

Langundit. V, 32. ·Made peace. *Langundo*, peaceful.

Langundo. V, 1. Peaceful. *Langundo*, peaceful. Z.

Langundowi. IV, 18. Peaceful he. See above.

Lapawin. IV, 40. Whitened. *Lappi*, again; *pawa*, rich.

Lappimahuk. IV, 41. Again there is war. *Lappi*, again; *machtagewak*, they are at war. Z.

Lappinup. I, 9. Again when. Mr. Anthony translates this "again he spoke;" *aptonen*, to speak. Zeis.

Lapihaneng. V, 27. Tide water at. *Lappi*, again; *amhanne*, flowing water. H.

Lekhihitin. V, 5. Writer writing. *Lekhiket*, writer; *lekhiken*, to write. K.

Leksahowen. IV, 23. Writing who. *Lekhasik*, written. K.

Lennowak. I, 11, 18. Men. II, 1, 5. Men also. *Lenno*, man.

Lessin. III, 4. To be. *Lissin*, to be *or* do so.

Linapi-ma. II, 14. Men there. *Lenape*, with suffix *ma*, there.

Linapioken. IV, 1. Men fathers. Qy. "The fathers of the Linapi."

Linkwekinuk. V, 19. Looking well about. *Linquechin*, to look, behold; *linquechineck!* Look here, behold! Z.

Linnapewi. III, 1. True manly. III, 7. True men. "They are Lenape."

Linni wulamen. IV, 63. Man of truth. *Lenno*, man; *wulamen*. See p. 104.

Linowi. II, 10. Men. *Lenno-wi*, he is a man.

Linowimokom. II, 8, 13. Of men grandfather. *Lenno*, man; *mohomus*, grandfather.

Lissilma. IV, 5. Be thou there. *Lissil*, imperative of *lissin*. Zeis. *Gram.*, p. 118.

Lohxin. II, 9. To move and dwell. *Lowin*, to pass by. K. *Lauchsin*, to walk, to live. Zeis. *Gram.*, p. 132.

Lokwelend. V, 15. Walker. *Lauchsin*, to live, to walk.

Lowako. V, 16. North snake. *Lowan*, winter; *aki*, land.

Lowaniwi. III, 6, 11, 16. Northerlings. *Lowan*, winter; *lowaneu*, north. Z.

Lowanaki. III, 7. North country. *Lowan*, winter; *aki*, land.

Lowanapi. III, 19. Northern manly. *Lowan*, winter; *ape*, man; a *nomen gentile*.

Lowanipekis. IV, 61. North of the lakes. *Lowan*, winter; *pek*, lake; or *lowan*, *ape*, man; *aki*, land, "the land of the Northern men."

Lowankwamink. III, 3. In northerly plain. *Lowan*, winter or north; *wemenque*, as we came from. Z.; with the locative suffix *nk*.

Lowanuski. IV, 45. Northern foes. *Lowan*, north or winter.

Lowaponskan. V, 50. North walker. *Lowan*, winter; north; *pomsin*, to walk. Z.

Lowashawa. IV, 41; V, 59. North and south. *Lowan*, north; *shawano*, south.

Lowushkaking. V, 18. North land going. *Lowan*, north; *aki*, land. Doubtful.

Luchundi. III, 14. They saying. *Luehundi*, they say, or, it is said. Z. *Gram.*, p. 175.

Lumowaki. III, 7. White country. *Loamoe*, long ago, ancient; *aki*, land.

Lungundowin. II, 3. Peaceful or keeping peace. *Langundowi*, peaceful.

Lusasaki. III, 10. Burned land. *Lussin*, to burn; *lusasu*, burnt. Z.

Machelinik. IV, 58. Many places or towns. *Macheli*, much. K.

Machigoklos. IV, 38. Big owl. *Macheu*, great; *goklos*, owl.

Machiton. II, 3. Spoiling. *Matschihilleu*, spoiled. K. *Matschiton*, to spoil something, to make mischief. Z. *Gram.*, p. 222.

Machitonanep. IV, 17. Much warfare then. Made mischief. See *Ante*.

Madawasim. IV, 34. Great meadow. *Matta*, no, not; *assin*, stone.

Mahiliniki. V, 46. There was Hilinis. Perhaps "Illini," the Chipeways or Illinois.

Mahongwi. V, 31. There Hong (Mengui) *or* lickings. Mengwe? See p. 14.

Mahongwipallat. V, 53. Mengwi was. See last word.

Mahongwichamen. V, 54. Mengwi frightened.

Makatapi. IV, 16. Blacking man. *Machit*, bad, evil; *ape*, man.

Makdopannik, V, 4, and Makdupannek, II, 11. They were many. *Macheli*, many.

Makeleyachick. V, 9. Many going. See above.

Makelohok. IV, 48. They are many. See above.

Makeliming. V, 6. Much fruits at. *Machelemuwi*, honorable, precious. K. Or *macheli*, much; *min*, fruits.

Makelining. V, 8. Much river at. *Machelensin*, to be proud or high-minded. K. Or, *macheli*, much or many; *amhanne*, rivers, "the place of many streams."

Makelima. IV, 56. Much there is. *Macheli*, much or many.

Makelinik. V, 7. Many towns. *Macheli*, many; *wik*, houses.

Makeliwulit. V, 38. Much good done. *Macheli*, much; *wulit*, good.

Makelomush. V, 41. Much honored. *Machelemuxit*, he that is honored. Z.

Makhiawip. V, 27. ˙ Red arrow. *Machke*, red.

Makimani. I, 14. Bad spirit. *Machi manito*, the bad manito.

Makonowiki. V, 46. There was Konowis. Qy. *Achgunnan*, he is clothed. Z. *Mach*, = red; *mecaneu*, dog.

Makowini. I, 14; II, 1. Bad beings. *Mach*, from *machtit*, bad; *owini*, q. v.

Makpalliton. V, 15. Much warfare. *Macheli*, much, and *palliton*, q. v.

Maktapan. I, 23. Bad weather. *Machtapan*, stormy weather. K.

Maktaton. I, 22. Unhappiness. *Machtatemamoagan*, unhappiness. K.

Mangipitak. IV, 22. Big teeth. *Amangi*, big, great; *wipit*, his teeth.

Mani. I, 8. Made. *Maniton*, to make.

Manito. I, 9, 10. He made. II, 12. Spirit. See notes.

Manitoak. I, 9, 17. The spirits or makers.

Manup. IV, 1. There were then. Doubtful. Comp. *anup*.

Mapawaki. V, 22. There is rich land. *Pawa*, rich; *aki*, land. Doubtful.

Mashawoniki. V, 46. There was Shawonis. *Meshe*, great, in comp.

Mashkipokhing. IV, 7. Bear hills at. *Machk*, bear; but probably from *maskick*, Chip. *mashkig*, swamp or marsh, and *pachhink*, the division or valley between the mountains.

Maskaboush. II, 8. Strong hare. *Maskan* and *wabos*, hare. See anté, p. 130.

Maskan. II, 1, 2, 5, 16. Powerful or dire. *Mechek*, great, large; *mangain*, Nant. *mashka*, Chip. strong. *Máskane*, strong, rapid. Heck., *Ind. Names*, p. 355.

Maskanako. II, 1, 2, 5. Strong snake. *Maskan*, large or strong; *achgook*, snake.

Maskansisil. IV, 37. Strong buffalo. *Maskan*, and *sisil*.

Maskansini. IV, 43. Strong stone. *Maskan*, and *assin*, a stone.

Maskekitong. V, 28. Strong falls at (Trenton). *Maskan*, and *kithanne*, main stream. See Heck., *Ind. Names*, p. 355, where this word is given and analyzed.

Matemik. IV, 20. Builder of towns. *Matta*, not; *mequik*, blood. Z.

Matta. II, 3. Not. *Matta*, no, not.

Mattakohaki. V, 22. Without snake land. *Matta*, not; *achgook*, snake; *aki*, land.

Mattalogas. I, 22. Wickedness. *Machtit*, bad, evil; *mattalogaso-wagon*, a sinful act. Zeis. *Gram.*, p. 103.

Mattapewi. II, 4. Less man. *Mattapeu*, he is not at home. Z.

Matemenend. IV, 36. There *or* now Tamenend. .

Mawulitenal. V, 22. There is good thing. *Wulit*, good.

Mayoksuwi. IV, 53. Of one mind. *Mawat*, one, only one. K.

Mboagan. I, 23. Death. *M'boagan*, death. Z.

Mekenikink. I, 21. On earth. *Mach*, prefix indicating evil or misfortune, from *machtit*.

Mekwazoan. II, 4. Fighting. *Mechtagan*, to fight. K.

Menak. I, 8. Islands. *Menatey*, an island.

Menalting. IV, 4, 42. In assembly met. *Menachtin*, to drink together. K. *Menáltink*, the place where we drank. II. *Ind. Names*, p. 371.

Menapit. II, 8. At that island. *Menatey*, island; *epit*, at.

Meshautang. III, 3. Game. *Mechtit*, much; *achtu*, deer. Z. In the N. J. dialect, deer is *aatu;* hence the meaning is "many deer."

Messisuwi. IV, 44. Whole he. *Metschi-schawi*, very, ready. Z.

Metzipannek. II, 11. They did eat. *Mitzopannik*, they have eaten. Zeis. *Gram.*, p. 124.

Michihaki. IV, 3. Big land. *Mechti*, much; *aki*, land.

Michimini. IV, 34. Much corn. *Mechtil*, much; *min*, edible fruit.

Milap. I, 12, 13. He gave him. *Mil* or *miltin*, to give. The terminal *p* marks the preterit.

Minigeman. IV, 25. Corn planting. *Min*, edible fruit; for corn, see p. 48.

Minihaking. IV, 24. Corn land at. *Min*, edible fruit; *aki*, land.

Minsimini. V, 52. Wolf tribe. See p. 36.

Mitzi. I, 19. Food. *Mitzin*, to eat.

Mokol. II, 12. Boat. *Amochol*, a boat. Zeis. *Gram.*, p. 101.

Mokolakolin. V, 17. In boats he snaking. See above. *Aki*, land.

Mokom. V, 17. Grandfather. *Muchomsena*, our grandfather. Z.

Mokolmokom. V, 17. Boats grandfather. *Amochol*, boat; *muchom*, ancestor.

Moshakwat. I, 7. It clears up. *Moschhakquat*, clear weather. K.

Mukum. I, 11. Ancestor. *Muchomes*, grandfather. K.

Nahiwi. II, 10. Above water or afloat. *Nahiwi*, down the water, down stream. K.

Nakhagattamen. V, 52. 3 desiring. *Nacha*, three; *gattamen*, to wish.

Nakkalisin. V, 52. 3 to be. *Nacha*, three; *lissin*, to be *or* do so.

Nakopowa. III, 8. The snake priest. *Pawa*, priest. See above, p. 70. The prefix doubtful.

Nakowa. II, 6. Black snake. *Nachoak*, three persons. Z.

Nakowak. I, 14. Black snakes. *Nachohaneu*, he is alone. Z. *Sukachgook*, black snake. Z. Doubtful.

Nallahemen. III, 13. Navigating. *Nallahemen*, to boat up the stream. K.

Nallimetzin. IV, 29. At last to eat. *Nall*, that, at last; *mitzin*, to eat.

Namenep. I, 20. Pleased. *Namen*, to know, understand.

Namesaki. IV, 14. Fish land; *Namaes*, fish; *aki*, land.

Namesik. I, 13. Fishes. *Namessall*, fishes. Zeis. *Gram.*, p. 101.

Namesuagipek. III, 12. Fish resort sea. *Namaes*, fish; *pek*, lake.

Nanaboush. II, 8, 13. Nana-hare. See p. 130.

Nantiné. I, 19. The fairies. *Naten*, to fetch. Z.

Nantinewak. I, 18. Fairies also. Pl. form from *naten*, to fetch.

Nekama. IV, 9, 10, 19. Him. Him, them.

Nekohatami. IV, 35. Alone the first. *Netami*, the first.

Nemassipi. IV, 49. Fish river. *Namaes*, fish; *sipi*, river.

Nenachihat. V, 58. Watcher. *Nenachgistawachtin*, to listen to one another, to hear one. K. Hence *hearer*.

Nentegowi. V, 16. The Nentegos. *Nentégo* is the proper name of the Nanticokes, who inhabited the eastern shore of Maryland. See p. 22.

Netamaki. I, 24. First land. *Netami*, first; *aki*, land.

Netami. I, 12, 18, 19. The first. *Netami*, the first. Z. *Gram.*, p. 108.

Nguttichin. III, 16. All agreed. '*Nguttitchen*, to be of one heart and mind. Z.

Nigoha. I, 18. Mother. *Ngahomes*, my mother. See Zeis. *Gram.*, p. 100.

Nihantowit. II, 4. Dead keeper. '*Nihillowet*, murderer (*nihillanowet*). See p. 102.

Nihillanep. IV, 43. He killed. See p. 102.

Nihillapewin. III, 11. Being free. *Nihillapewi*, free. Z. See p. 101.

Nihillen. III, 15. To kill *or* annihilate. *Nihilla*, I kill. Z. See p. 101.

Nijini. I, 10, 19; II, 2. The Jins. *Nik*, these, those. K. *Nigani*, the first, the foremost. Z. See notes.

Nillawi. III, 18. By night or in the dark. *Nipahwi*, by night. Z.

Nipahum. I, 5. Moon. *Nipahump*, moon, *Min*.

Nishawi. II, 3. Both. *Nischa*, two.

Nitaton. IV, 11. To be able. To know how to do it. Z.

Nitatonep. IV, 43. He was able. See above. Preterit.

Nitisak. I, 16. Friends. *Nitis*, confidential friend. (Heck, p. 438.)

Nitilowan. IV, 54. Friends of north. *Nitis*, and *lowan*, north.

Nolandowak. IV, 49. Lazy they. *Nolhand*, lazy. K.

Nolemiwi. I, 3. Invisible. Invisible. Z.

Nungihillan. III, 10. By trembling. *Nungihillan*, to tremble. K.

Nungiwi. IV, 64. Trembling he. See above.

Okwewi. I, 18. Wives. *Ochquewak*, women. Z.

Okwisapi. III, 19. With wives or women of man. *Ochque*, woman ; *ape*, man.

Oligonunk. IV, 29. Hollow mountain over. *Wahlo*, a cavern *or* a hollow between hills. *Oley*, in Berks county, Pa., the name of a Moravian settlement, is from this root.

Olini. III, 18. The men *or* people. From root *ni*, p. 101.

Olumapi. IV, 23. Bundler of written sticks. See p. 161.

Onowutok. V, 12. Prophet. *Owoatan*, to know. K.

Opannek. III, 16. They went. From *aan*, to go, and perhaps with prefix *wab* or *op*, east.

Opekasit. IV, 47. Easterly looking. *Waopink* or *oplünk*, opossum. From the root *wab*, white. See p. 43.

Opeleken. I, 8. It looks bright. Root *wab* or *op*. See last word.

Otaliwako. V, 43. There snake *or* Otalis (Cherokis).

Otaliwi. V, 56. Cherokees of Mts.

Ouken. III, 12. Fathers. *Ochwall*, his father. Zeis. *Gram.*, p. 100.

Owagan, I, 22, or **Owagon,** I, 7. Deeds, action. A verbal suffix. See p. 101.

Owak. I, 4. Much air or clouds. An error for *woak*, and. Comp. Zeis. *Spelling Book*, p. 122.

Owanaku. I, 2. Foggy. *Awonn.* Z. *Auan*, N. J., fog.

Owini. I, 12. First beings. I, 16; II, 5, 9. Beings. Rafinesque says of this word, that it " may be analyzed *o-wi-ni*, 'such they men' or beings." It would seem to be a form of the substantive verb termination *wi*.

Owinkwak. I, 10. First beings also. *Owini*, and *wak*, and.

Paganchihilla. IV, 59. Great fulfiller. *Pachgihillan*, to break, break asunder. K.

Pakimitzin. V, 49. Cranberry eating. *Pakihm*, cranberries ; *mitzin*, to eat.

Pallalogas. I, 22. Crime. *Pallalogosawagan*, crime, evil deed. Zeis. *Gram.*, p. 103.

Palliaal. III, 9. Go away. The same. Zeis. *Gram.*, p. 243. An imperative ; but not so used in the text.

Pallihilla. IV, 56. Spoil and killing. From *pallilissin*, to do wrong. Zeis. *Gram.*, p. 243.

Palliton. II, 3. Fighting. II, 5. To destroy or spoil. II, 7. Much spoiling or destroying. *Palliton*, to do ill, to spoil. Zeis. *Gram.*, p. 222.

Pallitonep. IV, 44, 46. He war made. It is the imperfect of *palliton*, to despoil, fight.

Pallitonepit. IV, 47. At the warfare. Preterit of the above.

Palliwi. II, 16. Elsewhere. Ibid. Z.

Palpal. II, 12. Come, come. *Palite,* when he comes. Z.

Paniton. II, 15. Let it be. *Paliton*, to spoil, injure. Z.

Pataman. II, 15. Praying. *Pataman*, to pray. K.

Pawanami. V, 14. Rich water turtle. *Pawalessin*, to be rich.

Pawasinep. III, 13. Rich was. *Pawa*, rich.

Payat. I, 23. Coming. *Paan*, to come. Conjugated in Zeis. *Gram.*, p. 148. *Payat*, he who comes *or* is coming. From the root *an*, to move. Cf. *Aan*.

Payat-chik. I, 22. Coming them. See above.

Payaking. III, 20. Coming at. See above.

Payat payat. II, 12. Coming, coming. See above.

Pechimin. III, 10. Thus escaping. *Pach-*, to separate, divide, to split asunder.

Pehella. II, 7. Much water rushing. II, 10. Flood. See *K'schippe-hellen.*

Peklinkwekin. V, 59. Sea looking. *Pek*, still water, lake, sea.

Pekochilowan. V, 23. Near north. *Lowan*, north.

Pemaholend. IV, 20. Constantly beloved. *Ahoala*, to love.

Pemapaki. IV, 14. Lake land. Apparently for *menuppekink*, at the lake.

Pematalli. V, 17. Constant those. *Talli*, there.

Penauwelendamep. II, 5. Resolved. *Penauwelendam*, to consider about something. Z.

Penkwihilen. II, 16. It is drying. *Penquihillen*, dried. K.

Pepomahemen. V, 8. Navigator up. Doubtful.

Petonep. II, 6. He brought. *Peton*, to bring. Z.

Peyachik. III, 4. Comers. See *Payat.*

Pikihil. III, 10. Is torn. *Pikihillen*, torn, rent in pieces. K.

Pilwhalin. IV, 21. Holy goer. *Pilhik*, clean, pure.

Pimikhasuwi. IV, 57. Stirring about he.

Piskwilowan. V, 31. Against north. *Tipisqui,* against. Z. *Lowan*, north.

Pitenumen. V, 39. Mistaken. *Pitenummen*, to make a mistake. Z.

Pohoka. II, 7. Much go to hills. *Pokawachne*, creek between two hills. The word does not refer to hills, but to the division, cleft or valley between hills.

Pokhapokhapek. III, 12. Gaping sea. *Poequeu*, a muscle, clam. Z. An important article of food to the natives; *pek*, a lake or sea.

Pokhakhopak. III, 17. At gap snake sea. See above.

Pokwihil. III, 4. Divided or broken. III, 10. Is broken. *Poquihillen* or *poquiecheu*, broken. K. The root is *pach*, to split, divide.

Pomisinep. IV, 52. Went *or* passed. *Pomsin*, to walk. K.

Pommixin. II, 9, 10. Creeping. *Pommisgen*, to begin to walk; *pom-'mixin*, to creep. K.

Ponskan. III, 18. Much walking. *Pommauchsin*, to walk.

Powa. III, 4. Rich, for *Pawa*, rich, etc. See p. 70. See words under *pawa*.

Powako. I, 21. Priest snake. See above.

Powatanep. IV, 39. Pontiff was. See above.

Powatapi. III, 19. Priest manly. See above.

Psakwiken. III, 1. Close together. *Psakquiecehen*, close together. K.

Pungelika. V, 31. Lynx well like (Eries). *Pongus*, sand fly. K. Doubtful.

Pungusak. I, 15. Gnats. *Pongus*, sand fly, K.

Sakelendam. IV, 47. Being sad. *Sakquelendam*, to be sad. K.

Sakima. IV, 5. King. See p. 46.

Sakimachik. IV, 26. See above.

Sakimak. IV, 17. Kings. See above.

Sakimakichwon. V, 33. With this great king. See above.

Sakimalanop. IV, 33. King was made. See above.

Sakimanep. IV, 8, 9, 15, 18. King was. See above. Preterite form.

Saskwihanang. V, 24. Susquehanah (branchy R.) at. See p. 14.

Sayewis. I, 3. First being. *Schawi*, immediately, directly. Z.

Shabigaki. IV, 13. Shore land. This seems a more correct form than Heckewelder's *scheyichbi*. See p. 40.

Shak. I, 14. But. *Schuk*, but.

Shakagapewi. IV, 64. Just and upright he. *Schachachgapewi*, he is honest, righteous. K.

Shakagapip. IV, 19. A just man he was. *Schachach*, straight; here used in a metaphorical sense for just.

Shawaniwaen. IV, 12, 24. South he goes. *Shawano*, south

Shawanaki. IV, 13. South land. *Shawano*, south; *aki*, land. Zeis. gives *schawenneu* for south.

Shawanaking. V, 10. South land at. See above.

Shawanapi. III, 19. Southern manly. *Shawano*, and *ape*, man.

Shawaniluen. IV, 10. South he saying. *Shawano*, and *luen*, to say.

Shawaniwak. IV, 59. South they go. *Shawano*, and *ewak*.

Shawanipalat. V, 42. South warrior. *Shawano*, and *itapalat*.

Shawanipekis. IV, 60. South of the lakes. *Shawano*, and *pek*, lake.

Shawaniwi. III, 6. Southerlings. *Shawano*, with suffix *wi*.

Shawanowi. V, 10. The Shawani. See above.

Shawapama. IV, 17. South and east there. *Shawano, wapan*, east, and *ma*, there.

Shawelendamep. II, 2. Become troubled. *Acquiwelendam*, to disquiet. Z. With intensive prefix *ksch*.

Shawoken. III, 10. So far going. *Schewak*, weak?

Shayabinitis. V, 57. Shore friend. See next words. *Nitis*, friend.

Shayabian. V, 37. Shore (or Jersey) going. *Schejck*, a string of wampum. Z.

Sheyabing. V, 51. At New Jersey *or* shore. *Scheyichbi*, Indian name of New Jersey. (Heck., p. 51.) See p. 40.

Shinaking. III, 20; IV, 1, 5. At fir-land. Chip. *jin-goh*, spruce fir. Bar. *Schind*, spruce. Z. *Aki*, land; *nk*, locative termination, "the place of spruce firs."

Shingalan. II, 2. Hating. *Schingalan*, to hate somebody. K.

Shingalusit. II, 2; V, 56. Foe, foes. *Schingalusit*, enemy, adversary. K.

Shiwapi. IV, 27. Salt man. *Schwewak*, salt meat; *sikey*, salt.

Showihilla. IV, 7. Weak. *Schawek*, weak.

Shukand. I, 20. But then. *Schukund*, only, but then.

Sili. III, 3. Cattle. *Sisili*, a buffalo. See note to verse.

Sin. III, 4. To be. *Lissin*, to be *or* do so.

Sinako. V, 16. Strong snake. *Assin*, stone; *aki*, land.

Sipakgamen. IV, 55. River over against. *Sipi*, river. See *Agamunk*.

Sisilaki. IV, 14. Cattle land. *Sisiliamuus*, a buffalo, N. J.

Sisilaking. IV, 29. Cattle land at. *Sisili*, buffalo; *aki*, land.

Sittamaganat. V, 2. Path leader. Pipe-bearer. See note to IV, 2.

Sitwahikho. II, 16. Path of cave. *Tschitqui*, silent; *tschitquihillewak*, they are silent. Z.

Slangelendam. IV, 31. Disliking. *Skattelendam*, to loathe, to hate.

Sohalawak. I, 4, 5, 6, 14, 15; IV, 23. He causes them. See note.

Sohalgol. IV, 25. He causes it. See last word.

Taquachi. IV, 24. Shiverer with cold. *Tachquatten*, frozen. K.

Takauwesit. III, 5. The best. *Tach*, together, to tie, etc. Hence united, harmonious.

Talamatan. IV, 54, 61, 63, 64. Hurons. See p. 16.

Talamatanitis. IV, 61. Huron friends. See *Lamatanitis.*

Talegachukang. V, 19. Allegheny Mts. going. Doubtful.

Talegaking, V, 1. Talega land at. See p. 230.

Taleganah. V, 14. Talega R, at. See p. 230.

Talegawik. IV, 56. Talega they. See p. 230.

Talegawil. IV, 52. Talega head *or* emperor. See p. 230. *Wil,* head.

Talegawunkik. V, 45. Talegas west visitor. See p. 230. *Wunken,* west; *kiwiken,* to visit.

Talligewi. IV, 50. Talegas *or* there found. See p. 229.

Tamaganat. IV, 55. Leader. *Gelelemend* = the leader. Heck. *Ind. Names,* p. 392. See note to IV, 2.

Tamaganena. V, 2. Chieftain such *or* Beaver leader. Pipe-bearer. See note to IV, 2.

Tamakwapi. III, 19. Beaver manly. *Tamaque.* Camp. *Ktemaque.* Zeis. A beaver. Mohegan, *amuchke,* Schmick.

Tamakwi. IV, 12. Beaver he. See last word.

Tamenend, IV, 35; **Tamanend,** V, 32. Affable (beaver like). *Temenend,* affable. Heck.

Tankawun. V, 9. Little cloud. *Tangelensuwi,* modest, humble; *tangitti,* small.

Tapitawi. II, 14. Altogether. *Tachguiwi,* together. Z.

Tashawinso. V, 51. At leisure gatherer.

Tasukamend. IV, 19. Never black *or* bad. *Ta,* not, *suckeu,* black. Z.

Tatalli. II, 10. Which way *or* shall there. *Tatalli,* whitherwards. K.

Tawanitip. V, 49. Ottawas made friends; *nitis,* friend.

Tellen. IV, 17. Ten.

Tellenchen kittapakki. III, 18. 10,000.

Tenche kentit. IV, 58. Opening path. *Tenk, titit,* little. K. Doubtful.

Tendki. III, 8. Being there. *Tindey,* fire. Z. *Tenden, Min.; yawagan tendki,* the cabin-fires.

Tenk wonwi. IV, 27, 30. Dry-he. *Teng-* or *tenk-* = little. K.

Thupin. III, 2. It is cold. *Teu,* it is cold. K.

Tihill. III, 3. Coolness. *Tillihan,* it is cool. K.

Topan. III, 2. It freezes. *Tepan,* white frost.

Topanpek. III, 16. Frozen sea. *Tepan,* and; *pek,* lake.

Towakon. IV, 46. **Towako.** V, 16. Father snake. *Tawa* and *aki,* the Ottawas or Twightees. See note to V, 16.

Tsehepicken. IV, 49. Separated. *Tschetschpicchen,* to separate. K.

Tulagishatten. II, 9. At Tula he is ready. *Tulpe,* turtle; *gischatten,* it is ready, done, finished.

Tulamokom. II, 13. A turtle's grandfather. *Tulpe*, turtle. See *Mokom*.

Tulapewi. II, 14. Turtle there. *Tulpe*, a water turtle. K.

Tulapewini. III, 1. Turtle being. See above.

Tulapima. II, 14. Turtle there. *Tulpe*, and *ma*, there.

Tulapin. II, 10. Turtle-back. *Tulpe*, turtle.

Tulapit. II, 8. At Tula or turtle land. *Tulpe*, and *epit*, q. v.

Tulapiwi. III, 7. The turtling. *Tulpe*, and suffix *wi*.

Tulpenaki. III, 7. Turtle country. *Tulpe*, and *aki*, land.

Tulpewi. II, 15. Turtle he. See above. *Tulapewi*.

Tulpewik. I, 13. Turtles. See above.

Tumaskan. IV, 42. Wolf strong. *Temmeu*, wolf, Z.

Tumewand. V, 29. The wolfers (mohican). *Temmeu*, wolf, *anit* = the wolf god, or magician.

Tumewapi. III, 19. Wolf manly. *Temmeu*, and *ape* man; a *nomen gentile*.

Uchewak. I, 15. Flies. *Utschewak*, flies. Z.

Unamini. V, 52. Turtle tribe. See p. 36.

Unchihillen. V, 39. Coming from somewhere. *Untschihilleu* it come s from somewhere rapidly, to flow out.

Wagan. II, 16. Action. See *Owagan*.

Wak. I, 2. And. Id.

Wakaholend. IV, 33. Loving, beloved. *Ahoalan*, to love. *Woaka-holend*. Heck. *Ind. Names*, p. 395.

Wakon. I, 21. Snake god. *Wachunk*, high (Min.) Perhaps a form of *akiuk*, earthward.

Wallama. IV, 40. Painted. See p. 161.

Wallamolumin. V, 5. Painted-booking. See p. 161.

Wangomend. V, 55. Saluted. Id. Heck. *Ind. Names*, p. 395.

Wapachikis. V. 57. White crab. *Woapeu*, white. Z. The root *wab*, *wap*, or *op*, white, light, the east, etc., occurs in numerous words.

Wapagumoshki. V, 44. White otter. See above.

Wapagishik. IV, 48. East sun *or* sunrise. *Wap*, and *gischuch*.

Wapagokhos. IV, 8. White owl. *Wap*, and *gokhos*, owl. Z.

Wapahacki. V, 37. White body. *Wap*, and *hackey*, body.

Wapahoning. V, 11. White Lick at. *Wap*, and *mahoning*. Z. A the deer lick.

Wapakisinep. V, 21. East land was. *Wap*, and *aki*, land, with pre-terit suffix.

Wapalaneng. V, 2. White river at. *Wap*, and *amhannink* at the river.

Q

Wapala wikwan. V, 20. East settling place. *Wap*, and *wikwam*, house.

Wapallanewa. IV, 2. White eagle. *Woaplanne*, the bald eagle. Z.

Wapallendi. IV, 52. East some. *Wap*, east; *allende*, some.

Wapanaki. III, 18. Eastern land. *Wap*, east; *aki*, land.

Wapanapi. III, 19. Eastern manly. *Wap*, east or white; *ape*, man.

Wapaneken. IV, 48. East going together. *Wap*, east; see *Eken*.

Wapanen. III, 9. Easterly. *Wap*, east.

Wapanand. V, 29. The easters. *Wap*, east.

Wapanichan. IV, 32. East moving. *Wap*, east.

Wapaniwaen. IV, 12, 28. East he goes. *Wap*, east; *aan*, to go.

Wapaniwi. III, 6, 16. Easterlings. *Wap*, east; *wi*, substantive verb suffix.

Wapashum. V, 45. White big horn. *Wap*, white; *wschummo*, horn. Z.

Wapasinep. III, 13. East was *or* bright. *Wap*, east; preterit termination.

Wapawaki. IV, 51. East rich land.

Wapawullaton. IV, 50. East possessing. *Wap*, east; *wullaton*, to possess.

Wapayachik. V, 59. White or east coming. *Wap*, east; *payat*, q. v.

Wapekunchi, V, 40. East sea from. *Wap*, east; doubtful.

Wapkicholan. IV, 38. White crane *or* big bird. *Wap*, white; *tscholen*, bird.

Waplanowa. III, 12. White eagle. *Woaplanne*, a bald eagle. Z.

Waplowaan. V, 29. East, north, do go. *Wap*, east; *lowan*, north, *aan*, to go.

Wapsipayat. V, 40. Whites coming. *Wap*, white; *payat*, q. v.

Waptalegawing. V, 20. East of Talega at. *Wap*, east; *talega*, q. v.

Waptipatit. IV, 41. White chicken. *Wap*, white; *tipatit*, chicken.

Waptumewi. III, 12. White wolf. *Wap*, white; *temmeu*, wolf.

Wapushuwi. V, 3. White lynx he. *Wap*, white.

Wasiotowi. V. 56. Wasioto. Doubtful.

W'delsinewap. I, 16. Were there. Preterit of *lissin*, to be so.

Wekwochella. IV, 30. Much fatigued. *Wiquehilla*, to be tired. Z.

Wellaki. IV, 3. Fine land. *Wulit*, fine; *aki*, land.

Wemaken. III, 15. All snaking. *Wemi*, all; *aki*, land, earth; the whole land.

Wematan. III, 14. All let us go. *Wemi*, and *atam*, q. v.

Wemelowichik. V, 26. All hunters. *Wemi*, all; *elauwitschik*, hunters.

Wemi. I, 7, 6, 16, 20. All. Id.

Wemiako. III, 8. All the snakes. *Wemi*, all; *achgook*, snake; or, *aki*, land.

Wemiamik. V, 48. All children (Miamis). Doubtful.

Wemichemap. II, 12. All helped. *Wemi*, all; *mitschemuk*, he helps me. Z.

Wemiguma. I, 1. *Wemi*, all; *guma*, sea water. See note to passage.

Wemiluen. III, 15. All saying. *Wemi*, all; *luen*, to say.

Wemimokom. II, 13. Of all grandfather. *Wemi*, and *mokom*, q. v.

Wemilowi. IV, 53. All say. *Wemi*, all; *luen*, to say.

Weminitis. IV, 35. All being friends. V, 33. All friendly. *Wemi*, all; *nitis*, friends.

Wemipalliton. IV, 43. To war on all. *Wemi*, and *palliton*, q. v.

Wemima. IV, 2. All there. *Wemi*, åll; *ma*, there.

Wemilat. IV, 58. All given to him. *Wemi*, and *miltin*, q. v.

Wemilo. IV, 5. All say to him. *Wemi*, and *luen*, to say.

Weminilluk. IV, 15. All warred. *Wemi*, and *nihillan*, q. v.

Weminitik. V, 48. All friends *or* allies. *Wemi*, and *nitis*.

Weminungwi. V, 31. All trembling. *Wemi* and *nungihillan*, to tremble.

Wemi owenluen. III, 8. To all saying. *Wemi*, and *luen*, to say.

Wemi tackwicken. V, 33. All united. *Tachquiwi*, together.

Wemiten. III, 11. All go out. IV, 54. To go all united. *Wemiten* (infin), to go all forth or abroad. Z. *Gr.* 244.

Wemoltin. II, 10. All go forth. III, 9, 18. They go forth. They are all going forth. Z. *Gr.* p. 244.

Wemopannek. III, 17. All went. *Wemi*, with past preterit suffix.

Wenchikit. V, 52. Offspring. *Wentschiken*, to descend, to grow out of. Z.

Wetamalowi. IV, 33. The wise they. *Wewoatamamine*, wise man. Z.

Wewoattan. IV, 42. To be wise *or* by wise. *Woaton*, to know. Z.

Wich. I, 7. With. *Witschi*, with.

Wichemap. II, 12. Helped. *Witscheman*, to help somebody.

Wihillan. I, 23. Destroying or distemper. *Nihillan*, to destroy.

Wihlamok. III, 14. Head beaver. *Wil*, head; *amuchke*, beaver. Moh.

Wikhichik. III, 4. Tillers. *Wikhetschik*, cultivators of the earth. Z.

Wiki. II, 4. With. *Witschi*, with.

Wikwan. V, 20. *Wikwam*, house.

Wilawapi. III, 19. Rich manly. *Wil*, head; *ape*, man.

Winakicking. V, 25, 27. Sassafras land at or Penna. *Winak*, sassafras. Z.

Winakununda. V, 36. Sassafras tarry. *Winak*, sassafras, *guneunga*, q. v.

Winelowich. V, 18. Snow hunter. *Wineu*, snow; *elauwitsch*, hunter.

Wineu. III, 2. It snows. *Wineu*, it snows.

Wingelendam. IV, 60. *Wingelendam*, to approve, to like. Z.

Wingenund. IV, 39. Mindful.

Wingi. I, 20. Willingly. *Wingi*, fain, gladly, willing.

Winiaken. III, 11. At the land of snow. *Wineu*, it snows; *aki*, land.

Winimokom. II, 13. Of beings grandfather. *Owini* and *Mokom*, q. v.

Wisawana. IV, 34. Yellow River. *Wisaweu*, yellow; *amhanne*, river.

Wishanem. II, 15. 'Frightened. *Wischaleu*, he is frightened. Z.

Wishi. I, 17. Good. Probably for *mesitche* = Chip, *mitcha*, *etc.*, great.

Witchen. III, 15. Going with. *Witen*, to go with. K.

Wittank. IV, 34. Town. *Witen*, to go or dwell with.

Wittanktalli. III, 1. Dwelling of Talli. *Witen*, to go with. Z. *talli*, there. Z.

Wiwunch. I, 24. Very long. *Wiwuntschi*, before now, of old. K.

Wokenapi. IV, 11. Fathers men. *Woaklappi* repeatedly, again. K.

Wokgetaki. I, 1. *Wokget*, on the top; *aki*, land. *Wochgitschi*, above, on top; *aki*, land, earth.

Woliwikgun. III, 1. Cane house. *Walak*, hole; *walkeu*, he is digging a hole. Z.

Wolomenap. V, 28. Hollow men. *Wahhillemato*, wide, far. K.

Won. I, 24. This. *Won*, this, this one. K.

Wonwihil. V, 40, 59. At this time. *Won*, this, *wil*, head.

Wsamimaskan. IV, 57. Too much strong. *Maskan*, great.

W'shakuppek. III, 17. Smooth deep water. *Wschacheu*, it is slippery, smooth, glossy; *pek*, lake, sea.

Wtakan. III, 3. Mild. *Wtakeu*, soft, tender. Z.

W'tamaganat. IV, 37. And chieftain. The smoker or pipe bearer. See note to IV, 2.

Wtenk. I, 11. After. Ibid.

Wulakeningus. V, 42. Well praised. *Wulakenimgussin*, to be praised. K.

Wulamo. II, 1; IV, 1; V, 1. Long ago. *Wulamoe*, long ago.

Wulaton. III, 3; IV, 11. To possess.

Wulliton. III, 16. *Wulaton*, to save, to put up. K. *Wuliton*, to make well. K.

Wulatenamen. V, 41. To be happy. Ibid.

Wulelemil. III, 17. Wonderful. *Wulelemi*, wonderful.

Wuliton. II, 15. To make well, to do well. Z. *Gr.* p. 222.

Wulitowin. IV, 20. Good who (did). See last word.

Wulitshinik. V, 4. Good stony *or* well, hardy. *Wulit*, good; *assin*, stone.

Wulitpallat. V, 30. Good warrior. *Wulit*, good; *itopallat*, warrior.

Wunand. I, 17. A good god. Root *Wun*. See p. 104.

Wundanuksin. IV, 32. Being angry. *Wundanuxin*, to be angry at or for. K.

Wunkenahep. V, 12. West he went. *Wundcheneu*, it is west.

Wunkenapi. III, 20. Western man. *Wundchen*, west; *ape*, man.

Wunkeniwi. III, 6. Westerlings. See above.

Wunkiwikwotank. V, 13. West he visited. See above. *K'wichen*, to visit.

Wunpakitonis. V, 13. West abandoned. *Pakiton*, to throw away.

Wunshawononis. V, 13. West southerners. *Shawano*, south.

Yagawan. III, 8. (In the) huts. Ibid.

Yagawanend. IV, 50. Hut maker. See last word.

Yuch. I, 6. Well. *Yuh*. H. *Yuch*. K. *Yuk*, these. K.

Yukepechi. IV, 1. Till there. *Yukepetschi*, till now, hitherto. K.

Yuknohokluen. IV, 48. Let us go saying. Doubtful.

Yulik. I, 6. These. *Yukik*, these. K.

Yutali. I, 2, 22. There. *Jutalli*, just here. K.

APPENDIX.

AGOZHAGÀUTA. *(page 14, Note.)*

With reference to this word I have been favored with the opinions of Gen. Clark, Mr. Horatio Hale, and the Rev. J. A. Cuoq, all able Iroquois scholars.

Gen. Clark and Mr. Hale believe that it is a dialectic or corrupt form for *agotsaganha*, which is a derivature from *atsagannen* (Bruyas, *Radices Verborum Iroquæorum*, p. 42). This verbal means, in one conjugation, "to speak a foreign language," and in another, "to be of a different language, to be a foreigner." The prefix *ago* or *ako* is an indefinite pronoun, having the same form in both singular and plural, and is used with national or tribal appellations, as in *akononsionni*, "People of the Long House," the general name of the Five Nations. Gen. Clark notes that the term *agotsaganens*, or *agotsaganes*, was the term applied by the Iroquois to the Mohegans, = "People who speak a foreign tongue." (Jogues, *Novum Belgium* (1646), and *Pa. Colonial Records*, vol. vi, p. 183.)

The Rev. Mr. Cuoq believes that the proper form is *akotsakannha*, which in his alphabet is the same as *agotsaganha*, but he limits its meaning to "on est Abnaquis," from *aktsakann*, "être Abnaquis." (See his *Lexique de la Langue Iroquoise*, pp. 1, 155.) The general name applied by the Iroquois to the Algonkins he gives as *Ratirontaks*, from *karonta*, tree, and *ikeks*, to eat, "Tree-eaters" (*Lexique*, p. 88); probably they were so called from their love of the product of the sugar maple.

DIALECT OF THE NEW JERSEY LENAPE. *(p. 46)*

An interesting specimen of the South Jersey dialect of the Lenape is preserved in the office of the Secretary of State, Trenton, N. J. It is a list of 237 words and phrases obtained in 1684, at Salem, N. J. It was published in the *American Historical Record*, vol. I, pp. 308-311, 1872. The orthography is English, and it is evidently the same trader's jargon which Gabriel Thomas gives. (See p. 76.) The *r* is frequent; man is *renus leno;* devil is *manitto;* God is *hockung tappin* (literally, "he who is above"). There are several typographical errors in the printed vocabulary.

REV. ADAM GRUBE. (*p. 84.*)

His full name was Bernhard Adam Grube. Between 1760–63 he was missionary in charge of the Moravian mission at Wechquetank, Monroe County, Pa., and there translated into Delaware, with the aid of a native named Anton, a "Harmony of the Gospels," and prepared an "Essay of a Delaware Hymn Book." Both these were printed by J. Brandmüller, at Friedensthal, Pa., and issued in 1763; but no copy of either is known to exist.

EASTERN ORIGIN OF THE ALGONKINS. (*pp. 12 and 145.*)

Quite recently M. Emile Petitot, in an article entitled, *De la pretendue Origine Orientale des Algonquins*" (*Bulletin de la Société d'Anthropologie*, 1884, p. 248), has attacked the theory that the Algonkin migrations were from the northeasterly portions of the American continent, toward the west and south. His arguments are based on two Cree legends which he relates, one of which is certainly and the other probably of modern date, as the incidents show; and on his criticism of the derivation of the name " Abnaki." Of this he says: "*Wabang* signifie plutôt detroit que orient; et quant au mot *askiy* ou *ahkiy*, il vent dire *terre*, et non pas *peuple*."

Now, no one ever claimed that *abnaki* meant eastern people. The Abbé Maurault translates the form *Abanki* by "terre au Levant." (*Histoire des Abénakis*, Introd. p. ii, Quebec, 1866.) In Cree *wapaw*, in Chipeway *wabi*, mean narrows or strait; but they are derivatives from the root *wab*, and mean a light or open place between two approaching shores, as Chip, *wabigama*, or *wabimagad*, " there is a strait between the two shores." (Baraga, *Otchipwe Dictionary*.) The name Abnaki is, moreover, no argument either for or against the eastern origin of the Algonkin stock, as it was merely a local term applied to a very small branch of it by the French. Hence M. Petitot's criticisms on the theory under consideration are misplaced and of no weight.

To what has been said in the text I may add that the Algonkins who visited Montreal early in the 17th century retained distinct traditions that they had once possessed the land to the east of that city, and had been driven south and west by the Huron-Iroquois. See the Abbé Maurault, *Histoire des Abénakis*, p. 111, and Wm. W. Warren, *Hist. of the Ojibways*, Chap. IV (Minnesota, Hist. Colls., 1885).

INDEX OF AUTHORS.

(The principal references are in full-faced type.)

Abbott, C. C., 44, 52, 57, 69.
Adair, J., 61.
Alsop, G., 14.
Anthony, A., 156, 161, 219.
Aupaumut, H., 18, 20, 23, 45, 113.

Baraga, J., 35, 59, 62.
Barton, B. S., 146.
Beach, W. W., 115, 125.
Beatty, C., 23, 47, 69, 138.
Bozman, J., 15, 23, 29.
Brainerd, D., 46, 62, 65, 127, 137.
Brickell, J., 64.
Brunner, D. F., 52, 57.

Campanius, T., 66, **75**, 96, 116, 126, 131.
Clark, W. P., 152.
Copway, G., 61, 160, 219.
Cummings, A., 87.
Cuoq, F. H., 71, 105.

Darlington, W., 50.
Darwin, C., 140.
De Laet, 31, 44.
Dencke, C. F., 84.
Denny, E., 86, 94.
Donkers, J., 132.
Drake, S. G., 163.
Duponceau, P. S., 77, 102, 121, 155.
Durant, M., 122.

Eager, 36.
Ettwein, J., 14, 18, 47, 51, **83**, 132, 229, etc.
Evelin, R., 41.

Fast, C., 125.
Fleet, H., 27.
Force, M. J., 29, 31.
Foulke, W. P., 116.

Gallatin, A., 31, 112, 120.
Gray, A., 149, 155.
Grube, B. A., 83, 256.
Guss, N. L., 14.

Haldeman, S. S., 150, 162.
Hale, H., 12, 17, 18, 36, 95, 112, 156.
Hammond, W. A., 110.
Harrison, W. H., 64, 112.
Haven, S. F., 150.
Haywood, J., 17.
Heckewelder, J., 15, 16, 18, 20, 21, 22, 23, 30, 35, 43, 78, 92, 128, 136, 140, 146, 219, etc.
Hendricks, Capt., 21.
Henry, M. J., 37, 45, **86**.
Hoffman, W. J., 152,
Holland, F. R., 85.
Hough, 125, 229.
Howse, J., 13, 94, 98, 103, 105.

James, E., 61, 152.
Jogues, I., 255.
Jones, D., 60.
Jones, P., 16.
Johnston, J., 26, 30, 125, 145.

Kalm, P., 46, 50, 52.
Kampman, Rev., 28, 84.

Lacombe, A., 12, 26, 43, 103, etc.
Lawson, J., 61.
Lindstrom, 131.
Long, J., 20.
Loskiel, G. H., 18, 29, 47, 70, 91, 137, 229, etc.
Luckenbach, A., 85.

McCoy, I., 125,
McKenney, T. L., 224.

Mallery, G., 152.
Martin, H., 54.
Maurault, J. A., 256.
Mayer, B., 162.
Meeker, J., 87.
Mezzofanti, Cardinal, 108.
Morgan, L. H., 12, 19, 21, 34, 40, 47, 93.
Morse, J., 31, 113, 145.
Murray, W. V., 24.

Neill, E. D., 27.

Occum, S., 67, 70.

Peale, F., 51.
Peet, S. D., 124.
Penn, Wm., 58, 75, 122.
Petitot, E., 256.
Pickering, J., 94.
Porter, T. C., 57.
Proud, R., 20, 37, 45.

Rafinesque, C. S., **148**, etc.
Rasles, S., 60, 94, etc.
Reichel, W. C., 22.
Richardson, J., 58.
Roth, J., **78**.
Ruttenber, E. M., 20, 21, 36, 42, 55, 116, 119.

Schmick, J. J., 22.
Schoolcraft, H. R., 20, 58, 62, 87, 109, 133, 160, 219, etc.
Schweinitz, E. de, 25, 62, 129, etc.
Scull, N., 36.

Shea, J. G., 14, 231.
Silliman, B., 155.
Sluyter, Peter, 132.
Smith, G., 38.
Smith, J., 23, 26, 114.
Smith, S., 37.
Squier, E. G., 163, 167, 219, etc.
Stiles, Pres., 35.
Strachey, W., 67.

Tanner, J., 152, 160, 219.
Thomas, C., 17.
Thomas, G., 54, **75**, 91, 96.
Thompson, C., 48, 115, 121.
Tobias, G., 87, 88.
Trumbull, J. H., 20, 30, 33, 46, 49, 71, 74, 90, 97, 105, 219, etc.
Tryon, G. W., 150.

Van der Donck, 44, 51, 136.
Vincent, F., 60.

Ward, Dr., 153–4.
Wassenaer, 55, 72.
Watson, J.,
Weiser, Conrad, 60, 123.
Whipple, Lt., 87, 96.
White, A., 27, 28.
Wied, Prince of, 55.
Williams, R., 30, 55, 61, 94.

Young, T., 38, 63.

Zeisberger, 35, 55, 62, 69, **78**, 105, 113, 129, 134, etc.

INDEX OF SUBJECTS.

(The principal references are in full-faced type.)

Abnaki, 11, 19.
 derivation of name, 256.
Age of Gold, 135, 222.
Agozhagauta, 14, 255.
 derivation of, 255.
Algonkins, location, 9.
 dialects, 11, 89, 93.
 dialects, traits of, 89.
 myths, 67, 130, 164, 167.
 legends, 145.
 eastern origin of, 14, 145, 256.
Allemœbi, chief, 123.
Alligewi, 141–2, 229–31.
Alleghany, derivation, 229–31.
Alternating consonants, 94.
Andastes, 14.
Arms, native, 53.
Assigunaik, 228.
Assiwikales, 32.
Auquitsaukon, 35.

Bear, Naked, legend of, 146,
Blackfeet, 9, 49, 130.
Bones, preservation of, 25, 54.
Book, Lenape word for, 59.
Brandywine creek, Indians on, 48.
Brant, Joseph, 122.
Brush nets, 53.
Buffalo, the, 226.

Cachnawayes, 26.
Canai. See *Conoys*.
Canassatego, 15, 114, 121.
Canaways. See *Conoys*.
Cantico, derivation, 73.
Cape May, tribes at, 41.
Cardinal Points, the, 67.
Carolina, tribes from, 25, 31, 32.
Catawbas, 31.
Cherokees, 13, **16**, 166, 230.
Chesapeake Bay, Indians on, 15, 23, 24, 25.

Chicomoztoc, 139.
Chihohockies, 37.
Chiholacki, the, 20, 37.
Chilicothe, 30.
Chipeways, 9, 56, 62, 113, 130, 131, 151–2, 222.
Christina Creek, 15.
Civility, chief, 48.
Cohongorontas, 15.
Condolence, custom of, 18.
Conestoga Creek, 15.
Conestogas, 14.
Confederacy, Algonkin, 19.
Conoys, **25.**
Conoy town, 29.
Copper, use of, 50, 52.
Cree dialect, 10, 12, 98.
Crees, 9.
Crosweeksung, *or* Crosswicks, 45.

Dance, sacred, 73.
Deed, First Indian, 120.
Delamattenos, 16. See *Talamatans*
 and *Hurons*.
Delawares. See *Lenape*.
Deluge, Myth of, 134, 167.
Dialects of the Lenni Lenape, 91.
Dogs, 54.
Dreams, belief in, 70.
Dyes, use of, 53.

Eastlanders, 19.
Eries, 13.
Ermomex, 42.
Eskimos, 70, 232.

Fairfield, founding of, 124.
Fire worship, 65, 73.
Fish River, 229.
Five Nations. See *Iroquois*.
"Four Sticks," the, 152.
Four winds as deities, 65, 67.

Foxes, tribe, 11, 113.
Friends, their relations to the Indians, 63, 126.
Frog Indians, 44.

Ganawese. See *Conoys*.
Gekelemukpechunk, town, 123.
Gesture-speech, native, 152.
Glus-kap, Micmac god, 130.
Gnadenhütten, 124, 125, 128.
Gollitchy, chief, 118.
Gookin, Governor, 118.
Gordon, Governor, 119.
Grave Creek Mounds, 17.
Grandfathers, Delawares as, 23, 113.
Grandfathers, Fire as, 65, 73.
Guaranis, the, 70.

Hare, the Great, 66.
Head, idols of, 68.
Heart, symbolic meaning of, 71.
Hieroglyphics, native, 57.
Hithquoquean, chief, 117.
Hurons, 13, **16**, 144, 165, 168, 231.

Idols, 68.
Indian corn. See *Maize*.
Indian paths, the, 45.
Inscribed stones, 57.
Interments, 54.
Iroquois, location, 13.
    history, 110, 114, 120.

Kanawha, derivation, 26.
Kauawhas. See *Conoys*.
Kansas, Delawares in, 126.
Kikeron, 132, 133.
Kittawa-Cherokees, 16.
Koquethagachton, chief. See *White Eyes*.
Kuscarawocks, 23.

Lenape, the, **33**.
    myths of, 130.
Lenape dialects, 91, sqq.
    prefixes, 99.
    grammatical structure, 105.
    derivation, 33.
Light, worship of, 65, 130, 132.

Long Island, Indians of, 67, 70.
Long Walk, the, 115, 128.

Machtoga, a festival, 73.
Macocks, 38.
Mahicanni. See *Mohegans*.
Maize, native name of, 48.
    origin of, 228.
Manabozho, 167. See *Michabo*.
Manito, derivation of, 219.
Mantes, 42, **44**.
Manufactures, 51.
Marcus Hook, derivation, 39.
Masco, chief, 145.
Meday worship, 71.
Medicine men, 71, 135.
    rattle, 135.
    lodge, 71.
Mengwe, derivation, 14, 116, 141.
Mesukkummegokwa, 222.
Miamis, 9, 144, 146.
Michabo, 130, 167.
Micmacs, 10, 48. 130.
Milky Way, myth of, 70.
Mingo, 15, 116, 118.
Mingo Creek, 15.
Minisink. See *Minsi*.
Minquas, 14.
Minsi, 19, 36, 114, 116, 117, 122.
    dialect, 92.
Mission Delaware dialect, 97.
Mohegan dialect, 22, 93.
Mohegans, 19, **20**, 165.
    myths of, 136, 139.
Monsey. See *Minsi*.
Montauk Indians, 67.
Mounds, building of, 17, 51.
    builders, 231.
Munsees. See *Minsi*.
Myths of Lenapes, 130.

Namaes sipu, 141, 143.
Nanabozho, 130, 131, 166, 224.
Nanticoke dialect, 24.
Nanticokes, **22**, 145.
    traditions of, 139.
Narraticons, 42.
Neobagun, the, 151, 152.
Neutral Nation, 13.
New Albion, 41.
New Jersey Lenape, **40**, 127, 256.

New Jersey Lenape, their dialect, 46, 93, 95.
Ninniwas, 151.
Nottoways, 13.

Obviative, in Lenape, 107.
Ohio, Delawares in, 124, 125.
Okahokis, 38.
Old Sack, 25.
OLUM, derivation of, 153.
Onas, name of Penn, derivation, 95.
Onondagas, 117.
Opings, 21, 42.
Opossum, the, 43.
Opuhnarke, the, 19.
Osages, 151, 161.
Ossuaries, 23, 54.
Otayachgo, tribe, 22.
Ottawas, 113, 122, 140, 145, 232.

Paint, word for, 60.
Paints, use of, 53.
Paint Creek, 60.
Palisades, 51.
Pascatoway, derivation, 26.
Pascatoways, 15, 25, 47.
Passive voice, in American languages, 108.
Peace-belt, the, 47, 114.
Peace chiefs, 47.
Penn, Wm., 75, 116, 122, 127.
    his Indian name, 95.
    his treaties, 120.
Pequods, 30.
Pictographs, 56.
Pipes, 50, 118.
Piquas, 29.
Piscatoways. See Pascatoways.
Playwickey, derivation, 39.
Pohhegan, the, 35.
Pomptons, 42, 43.
Potomac, Indians near, 25, 67.
    Iroquois name of, 15.
Pottawatomies, 11, 113.
Pottery, native, 51.
Powwow, derivation, 70, 227.
Priests, native, 70.
Pueblo Indians, 110.

Record Sticks, 59.
RED SCORE, the, 161.

Sachem, derivation, 46.
Sacs or Sauks, 11, 113.
Safe Harbor, inscription, 57.
Sanhicans, 43.
Sapoonies, the, 31.
Scheyichbi, 40, 143.
Scythians, disease of, 110.
Senecas, 117, 121.
Serpent worship, 71-2, 167, 222, 231.
Seven, as a sacred number, 139.
Shamokin, 29, 115, 123.
Shawnees, 29, 39, 113, 119, 145, 219.
    sacred song of, 145, note.
Shekomeko, 128.
Sign-language, native, 152.
Snake, the Great, 71, 167.
Snake people, the, 165, 227, 231.
    land, the, 167, 231.
    water, 136.
Soap-stone, use of, 52.
Soul, doctrine of, 69.
Spears, use of, 53.
Stars, knowledge of, 55.
Stockbridge Indians, 45, 113.
Sun worship, 65.
Susquehanna, derivation of, 14.
    lands, 120.
Susquehannocks, 13, 53, 116, 121.

Tadirighrones, 31.
Talamatans, 165, 168, 231.
Talega, the, 165-6.
Talligewi, 141-2, 229, 231.
Tamany, 41, 117, 229.
Tatemy, Moses, 128.
Taurus, constellation of, 55.
Tawatawas, 146.
Taway or Tawas, 232.
Tedpachxit, chief, 124-5.
Tedyuscung, 33, 40.
Thahutoolent, chief, 125.
Thousand Isles, the, 165.
Tiawco, the, 22.
Time, computation of, 55.
Tobacco, name and culture, 49, 228.
Tockwhoghs, 23.
Tollan, 225.
Totemic animals, the, 39, 68.
    marks, 39, 57.

Towanda, derivation, 23.
Tsalaki, 166, 230.
Tula, 225.
Turkey River = Ohio, 39.
Turkey sub-tribe.   See *Unalacht-gos.*
Turtle, symbol of, 132–35.
Turtle sub-tribe.   See *Unamis.*
Twelve, a sacred number, 73.
Twightees, 146, 232.

Unalachtgo, derivation, 36.
Unalachtgos, 37.
Unami, derivation, 36.
    dialect, 79, 80, 91.
Unamis, 37.

Virgin-mother, myth of, 131.
Vowel change in Lenape, 107.

WALAM, derivation, 60, 104, 161.
WALAM OLUM.
    evidences of its authenticity,
        67, 89, 136, 155–158, 225.
    history of, 151.
    phonetic system, 159.
    metrical form, 159.

WALAM OLUM.
    pictographic system, 160.
    MS. of, 162.
    synopsis of, 164.
Wallamünk, 53, 60.
Wampanos, 21, 128.
Wampum belts, 47, 138.
Wapanachki, the, 19.
Wapeminskink, town, 124.
Wapings, 21, 42, 128.
Wappingers, the, 20.
War captains, 47.
Water god, the, 222.
Wendats.   See *Hurons.*
We-shellaqua, 219, 220.
White Eyes, chief, 58, 121, 123.
White River, the, 124, 144, 153.
Winicaco, 24.
Wingenund, chief, 58.
Wiwash, the, 25.
Women, the Lenape as, 109.
Wonameys, 36.
Wolf sub-tribe.   See *Minsis.*
Wyandots, 13, 16, 231.

Year, the native, 55.

Zinzendorf, Count, 128.

LIBRARY
—OF—
ABORIGINAL AMERICAN LITERATURE,

GENERAL EDITOR AND PUBLISHER:

D. G. BRINTON, M.D.

The aim of this series of publications is to put within the reach of scholars authentic materials for the study of the languages and culture of the native races of America. Each work is the production of the native mind, and is printed in the original tongue, with a translation and notes, and only such are selected as have some intrinsic historical or ethnological importance. The volumes of the series are sold separately, at the prices named.

NOW READY.

No. I. THE CHRONICLES OF THE MAYAS.

Edited by DANIEL G. BRINTON, M.D. 279 pages. Cloth, uncut, $5.00. ($3.00 when a complete set is ordered.)

This volume contains five brief chronicles in the Maya language of Yucatan, written shortly after the Conquest, and carrying the history of that people back many centuries. To these is added a history of the Conquest, written in his native tongue, by a Maya Chief, in 1562. The texts are preceded by an introduction on the history of the Mayas; their language, calendar, numeral system, etc.; and a vocabulary is added at the close.

No. II. THE IROQUOIS BOOK OF RITES.

Edited by HORATIO HALE. 222 pages. Cloth, uncut, $3.00.

This work contains, in the Mohawk and Onondaga languages, the speeches, songs and rituals with which a deceased chief was lamented and his successor installed in office. It may be said to throw a distinct light on the authentic history of Northern America to a period fifty years earlier than the era of Columbus. The Introduction treats of the ethnology and history of the Huron-Iroquois. A map, notes and a glossary complete the work.

No. III. THE COMEDY-BALLET OF GÜEGÜENCE.

Edited by DANIEL G. BRINTON, M.D. 146 pages. Cloth, uncut, $2.50.

A curious and unique specimen of the native comic dances, with dialogues, called *bailes*, formerly common in Central America. It is in the mixed Nahuatl-Spanish jargon of Nicaragua, and shows distinctive features of native authorship. The Introduction treats of the ethnology of Nicaragua, and the local dialects, musical instruments, and dramatic representations. A map and a number of illustrations are added.

No. IV. A MIGRATION LEGEND OF THE CREEK INDIANS.

By A. S. GATSCHET. 251 pages. Cloth, uncut, $3.00.

This learned work offers a complete survey of the ethnology of the native tribes of the Gulf States. The strange myth or legend told to Gov. Oglethorpe, in 1732, by the Creeks, is given in the original, with an Introduction and Commentary.

No. V. THE LENÂPÉ AND THEIR LEGENDS.

By Dr. DANIEL G. BRINTON. Cloth, uncut, $3.00.

Contains the complete text and symbols, 184 in number, of the WALAM OLUM or RED SCORE of the Delaware Indians, with the full original text, and a new translation, notes and vocabulary. A lengthy introduction treats of the Lenâpé or Delawares, their history, customs, myths, language, etc., with numerous references to other tribes of the great Algonkin stock.

IN PREPARATION:

THE ANNALS OF THE CAKCHIQUELS. By Francisco Arana Ernantez Xahila. With a translation and notes by Dr. D. G. Brinton.

ABORIGINAL AMERICAN ANTHOLOGY. Chiefly original material, furnished by various collaborators.